Counter

David Lipsey is a Labour peer and racing fanatic. He is a director of the Starting Price Regulatory Commission, a former director of the Tote and chair of the Shadow Racing Trust. He is President of the British Harness Racing Club (and drives pacers) and ex-Chairman of the British Greyhound Racing Board. In between racing engagements he is chair of the Trinity Laban Conservatoire of Music and Dance. He has been a political adviser to the Foreign Secretary and to James Callaghan as Prime Minister, a senior journalist on *The Times* and *Sunday Times*, 'Bagehot' of *The Economist* and a member of the government commissions on long-term care of the elderly, the voting system, and the funding of the BBC. He lives on the Welsh borders with two point-to-pointers.

Counter Coup

DAVID LIPSEY

HAY
PRESS

First published 2008 by Hay Press,
a division of Present Arts Ltd

www.haypress.co.uk

Copyright © David Lipsey 2014

All rights reserved. No part of this publication may be reproduced, stored in or introduced into a retrieval system, or transmitted, in any form, or by any means (electronic, mechanical photocopying, recording or otherwise) without the prior written permission of the publisher. Any person who does any unauthorized act in relation to this publication may be liable to criminal prosecution and civil claims for damages.

A CIP catalogue record for this book is available from the British Library.

ISBN: 978-0-9550050-9-1

Typeset by Wendy Smith, Llandrindod Wells
Cover Design by C & C Design Ltd, London
www.candc-design.com
Printed and bound in the UK by Berforts Information Press, Stevenage and King's Lynn.

This book is sold subject to the condition that it shall not by way of trade or otherwise, be lent, re-sold, hired out, or otherwise circulated without the publisher's prior consent in any form of binding or cover other than that in which it is published and without a similar condition including this condition being imposed on the subsequent purchaser.

Counter Coup

Chapter 1

As steeplechase fences go, the last at Bangor-on-Dee is not the most formidable of obstacles. At 4'6" high, the birch is not packed tight like Cheltenham or Newbury. The apron at the bottom invites a horse to stand off but the flat approach to the fence inhibits the over-flamboyant leap. Except on a dodgy jumper or tired horse, a top jockey would reckon to clear it ninety nine times out of a hundred.

On Robber Earl, Brendan Donoughue had nothing to worry about. The horse had been safe as houses over fences for the whole of his career. Today, he had jumped particularly fluently. As for tiredness, Brendan could feel him swinging along beneath him, full of zest. He could go another circuit without feeling the strain. Which was more than could be said of his rivals. Behind, Brendan could hear only the crack of the whips and the curses of the jockeys as they vainly pursued him at a distance that grew by the second.

David Lipsey

But Donoughue did not have time to savour the moment. For one decision stood between him and the winner's enclosure, a decision every top jockey has faced hundreds of times. Should he drive his horse into the last - nothing stupid, mind, but a kick behind the saddle and a shake of the reins, to get the adrenalin up and the body over? Or should he take it nice and easy, a pull on the reins, just pop it in his own time and up, up, up and away?

Both techniques have their aficionados. Probably, season through season, each is as good as the other. Each attracts the same proportion of relieved cheers from those who backed the leader as they start to move towards the bookmakers to collect their winnings. Each leads to the same number of moments, rare but terrible, when the horse disobeys his jockey's instructions and the air is full of the gasps of disappointed punters. But what every jockey knows (at least, every jockey who survives in the game knows) is that you must decide. Half going for it, half not, is the recipe for disaster.

Earlier in the race everything had seemed clear and good. Brendan had jumped off handy, flown the early fences, and taken it up three out, no problems. But afterwards, Brendan couldn't remember how far he was from the last fence when he realised that he couldn't make up his mind.

Everything had gone fuzzy. All he could remember – and that distantly - was the looming fence and a horse with him as a passenger on top. 'Kick, pop, kick, pop,' seemed to have gone round and round in his fuzzed-up head, like a cracked record. He had a final memory. One of his booted legs kicked. The

Counter Coup

other seemed paralysed. One hand pulled the reins. The other gave the horse a sharp backhander with the whip.

His body resembled one of those weird marionettes, apparently shorn of all co-ordination. Champion jockey five times he may have been, but at that moment, he would have made the average eight year-old in the Pony Club gymkhana look tidy.

Twenty, a dozen, six strides out and it was obvious to the world and his aunt that the horse was all wrong. He wasn't going to make it. For the spectators it was like the moment that drives people to watch motor racing: the hope and fear that they would see someone horribly injured, perhaps killed.

Even from the hill which served at Bangor for a grandstand, they could hear the sickening crunch as Robber Earl tried to take off, then dived drunkenly into the heart of the fence. They could see the shove from behind as the horse's back legs tumbled over its front legs and its rump hit Brendan's rump, catapulting him from the saddle as surely as if he was in an ejector seat of a jet fighter.

To all this the stricken jockey was mercifully oblivious. Oblivious, that is, until a horrible moment when he was briefly returned to reality by a loud crack. His right shoulder had ploughed into the solid turf, shattering the battered bone and steel plates that did duty, for him, as clavicle.

There was a moment of relief as he saw Robber Earl scamper away, terrified but miraculously unharmed, followed by a moment of mental agony as the favourite and second favourite jumped past, missing him narrowly in a head-to-head duel to the line. Then came the unique, unalloyed pain that a broken collarbone delivers.

He must have passed out. The next thing he heard was the passionless voice of the course announcer. 'First, number one, Guilder; second, number 11, Firstpastthepost; third number 9; Referendum. The distances: a head and ten lengths.'

And after hearing that, he saw something even less palatable. For among the paramedics, bustling towards him with their stretchers and their neck collars, was an all-too-familiar sight. Dave Futtnam.

Futtnam was Robber Earl's trainer and he didn't look sorry for Brendan. He looked like a man who was not planning to forgive and forget.

As the paramedics turned to the ambulance, Futtnam saw his opportunity. He deliberately drew back his leg, took careful aim, and kicked Brendan's stricken shoulder, not hard but hard enough, just where a fragment of bone had punctured the skin. 'Who paid you to fall off?' Futtnam hissed over Brendan's groan. 'How much?'

If it was possible for the jockey to go an even greyer shade of pale, he did.

'Let me tell you, however much it was,' the trainer continued, 'it wasn't worth it. Because when I've finished with you in that press room, you won't just never ride for me again, you'll never ride for anybody. And that's not a threat: that's a promise.'

Through the pain, Brendan heard the public address system crackle into life. 'The stewards are holding an inquiry

Counter Coup

into the riding of Number 12, Robber Earl.'

*****

Dave Futtnam was not the kind of trainer who was born with a silver spoon in his mouth. Not for him Eton and the Guards and riding out each morning while the regimental grooms stood by to look after the horses. Not for him the string of expensive horses wintered in the Gulf and then jetted over by their Arab owners, seduced into thinking British racing the best in the world and British toffs the epitome of it. When his 10% of prize money arrived there was no holiday break in the Caribbean where he and his posh totty were waited on by grinning, obsequious natives. Not for him the Pimms-soaked days and champagne-fuelled nights of the upper class twits who, being useless for anything else, took naturally to training.

No, the hard way Dave Futtnam had come up really was the hard way. The runt of a miner's family from Durham, without an O-level to his name, he'd been sent off to the local stables because he was too weak to pick coal and too stupid to push a pen. Up at five am for early stables, a horsehair mattress in a shared dormitory, thirteen days a fortnight, fifty weeks a year, with no breaks for Christmas and extra duties for Easter - all for a wage less than the price of a bottle of a toff trainer's Bollinger. That was where Futtnam had started.

There was the odd ride he'd been promised - always at some godforsaken gaffe track, hundreds of miles away, on a knob-kneed hack in the seller - all-out seventeenth of twenty-three on the days he did get round; bruised, battered and broken on the days he didn't. Then the hundreds of miles back, through the racing traffic, down the motorway, up the narrow lanes in a saloon that would have been put out of its misery years before if it had been a horse.

To keep his weight down he had coffee for breakfast, soda water for lunch and two boiled eggs, if he was lucky, for supper. Dave Futtnam had come up the hard way, and he let everybody know it.

And the way was still hard for Futtnam. He was a third-division trainer, a name known only to those fascinated by the lower reaches of the trainers' table in the *Racing Post*.

He soon learned the brutal secret of being a third division trainer: you lied for a living. You lied to potential owners about your fees. Only when their horse was installed in the yard did they realise that you were going to charge them for vets' fees and gallop fees and shoes, and grazing and hay. They had no way of checking that their prides-and-joys had actually consumed what appeared on the monthly account.

Then you lied about their horses. Never mind that the horse was as slow as a snail, as sickly as a parrot and as genuine as a Monopoly note, the owner had to believe that the next Arkle was in their hands. When they were young, you talked about how promising they were but, like all young horses, 'weak'. As they got older, you had more and more elaborate theories. About their preferences for going. 'A bit soft for him', 'jockey says he didn't act on the firm bits', 'doesn't like the mud'.

Counter Coup

After the going came the distance, 'too far', 'not far enough', and then elaborate combinations of the two. 'Didn't stay the trip on this ground but would get it when it hardens up', 'went too quick for him at two miles on the firm.' Then he would only act left-handed or right-handed, or under this jockey or that jockey, or in the spring or the autumn, or when the wind was in the West.

An artist like Futtnam, thirty years in the game, could keep this stuff going for years before the owner despaired and dispatched his beast to the cat food cannery.

Bullshit got you so far. But bullshit didn't make for a good living, for bad horses generally came with bad owners. Too mean to pay a proper price for a horse in the first place, they were too mean to pay their bills too. Arrears mounted. The trainer had an unenviable choice - send the horse away, and with it the chance of an income if the owner finally consented to pay up, or keep it and risk paying for it yourself. Somehow the bottom line had to be made to add up.

Of course, there were the usual tricks of the trade. Someone a bit worse for wear bumped into you at the races, asked you to look out for a horse for them, and was surprised to find a bill for a few thousand pounds for something plausible you had picked up for a few hundred at the sales. Someone else was persuaded to start a syndicate, where you hoped each member's share of the bill was so small that they could not be bothered to argue the toss. When things got really desperate, you could get into arrears yourself, with the wages, with the fodder bills, with the vet, though you had to be careful not to go too far and get yourself warned off by the authorities.

But at the end of the day there was only one way to make it pay – to bet. And there was only one sure way to make betting pay – to cheat.

Though there is but a single way to race a horse straight, there are a thousand ways to race a horse crooked. He could be left short of a gallop before one race, then got fit as a fiddle for the next. Plenty of jockeys would pull a horse if you wanted them to, so long as it was out in the country, behind other horses, anywhere where the stewards (fortunately, with the eyesight of bats) could not see. Some, for an extra fee, would fall off. The only rule was that you didn't dope, because if you doped, in the end, you'd be caught.

Dave Futtnam may not have been a very good trainer but he was a very good cheat. As he arrived at the racecourse, the bookies could be seen scanning his face to see if he was up to anything, and, if so, whether 'anything' was pulling a horse, or backing it until they screamed for mercy. Dave, naturally, was inscrutable. The bookies looked out for Dave's other 'faces', the little team he employed to put the money down when one was ready to win. Naturally, Dave changed the team. The bookies had an informer in his stables. Naturally, Dave knew and fed him with enough information to keep his employers happy and enough misinformation to aid him in his big coups. Year after year, Dave lost a few hundred pounds from training, made a few thousand pounds from horse-trading, but lived well enough from the proceeds of perhaps half a dozen £10,000 coups. That day at Bangor-on-Dee was supposed to

Counter Coup

provide the coup of coups.

Trainers like Dave did not often get horses like Robber Earl. Robber Earl had been top-notch in his day. When he won his first, a bumper at Huntingdon by six lengths, his trainer described him as having 'all the gears', 'the best I've had since Mate's Best.'

So he seemed for a race or two after that, winning the big novice hurdle at Sandown and being fancied for the two-and-a-half mile novices chase at the Cheltenham Festival. But then there were corns; and a splint in his off-fore; and a mystery virus that struck the stable low. His trainer, Hattie Parsons, as honest as she was competent, told his owners to retire him, especially as she had another horse from the same stock, Robber Baron, which she thought had just as much potential. Instead the owners sent Robber Earl to the sales where Dave grabbed his chance to get something flashy for his yard.

Strangely, the gamble paid. Whether it was the switch to Doncaster's grimy air, or the gritty realism of Futtnam's rundown yard, or the hard Midland riders who did not spare the whip, it was hard to tell. But the corns got better, the splint disappeared and the virus went. Robber Earl was no worldbeater anymore, no Festival prospect. Anything with a touch of class would beat him in a hack canter. But on the right day with the right weight on the right ground with the right jockey, the Earl was just the sort of conveyance on which a betting man might choose to rely.

Futtnam's preparations for Bangor had been painstaking. A jockey had been induced to fall off at Leicester. He had pulled up in palpably unsuitable ground at Nottingham. He failed to get into the race after an unfortunate slow start at Southwell and he uncharacteristically failed to give his true running under a callow apprentice at Market Rasen.

For a year, his record continued to unimpress. In particular it unimpressed the handicapper, whose job it is to decide how much a horse should carry on its back so in theory to give them all the same chance. Robber Earl slid down the weights: from 12 stone to lump round on his back to 10 stone 4lb on that day at Bangor. His form figures ahead of the race read "U09P68"(unseated rider, unplaced, 9th, pulled up, 6th, 8th) - about as bad a record as you can have with four legs. He was 20/1 in the tissue, the bookies' guide to likely odds.

Of course, there was a risk in putting Donoughue up. Robber Earl, on his recent record, was not the sort of horse that champions, even ex-champions, are normally seen riding. Ergo, the bookmakers might smell a rat and cut the horse's price. But for this coup, Futtnam did not want to risk having anything but the best on board. It was a race that he could not afford to lose.

In any case, he figured that this was a risk worth running. For one thing, the ploy was so transparent that the bookies would more likely conclude it was double-bluff, and knock Robber Earl's price out rather than shortening it up. For another, Futtnam had worked out his way to fix the price.

The plan was simple enough. The odds at which bookmakers pay out on a winner are decided only by the odds that are available on the racecourse. Bets placed in betting

Counter Coup

shops do not directly affect those odds.

So Robber Earl was not to be backed on the racecourse. Futtnam's agents, indeed, were not even to visit the racecourse: not his old familiar team, not the new ones, brought in for the day. Instead, they were sent out to betting shops up and down the country, mostly small ones, often independent ones not run by the big, canny bookmakers. And the bets were small: a score (£20) here, a pony (£50) there; the bets of enthusiastic amateurs, not professionals.

On the course, nobody wanted to back Robber Earl. He opened at 20/1 with no takers. 25/1 attracted only a few fivers and tenners from mug punters who remembered him from his glory days. Even the 33/1 was barely sniffed at.

Five minutes before the off, Futtnam produced his master stroke. Drawing from his pocket a huge wedge of £20 notes, he strolled about the ring, examining the prices.

He sidled up to Alf Richardson, Dee's biggest and shrewdest bookmaker. Futtnam managed at once to appear to be avoiding attention while attracting it. The bookies shouting the odds feel silent. So they all heard his low but somehow audible voice. '£2,000 to win Firstpastthepost.'

Now, on some tracks £2000 to win a 2/1 shot would be a perfectly normal bet. Bangor-on-Dee, however, was not one of those tracks. This was farmers' country, labourers' country, a land of small men and small gambles. You didn't see a dozen two grand bets at Dee in a decade.

Besides, the source of the £2,000 mattered. Had it been some Flash Harry with more money than sense, the effect would have been very different. But when Futtnam was splashing out the cash, you could be sure as eggs are eggs that he knew something.

Firstpastthepost was cut to evens. As the odds against him shortened, the others got longer and longer, among them, Robber Earl's. 40/1 was everywhere, 50/1 with one bookmaker. Robber Earl was unconsidered as other punters noticed Firstpastthepost's odds tumble. With all that smart money pouring on Firstpastthepost, they figured, someone knew something. They rushed to join in, and the gamble caught fire.

As Futtnam sauntered back into the members' enclosure, he looked like a man without a care in the world. As indeed any man would have looked who knew he had struck £12,000 of bets at an average price of 40/1 on a horse that was home and hosed before the race had even started. Nearly £500,000, not bad for a day, or even a year's work.

Violence is never justified. But considering all that, Futtnam's kick to Brendan's shoulder seemed just a mite less surprising.

Counter Coup

Chapter 2

Once upon a time, you would not have found a girl like Tanya Smyth-Robinson dead in bed with a jockey. All right, she was not quite out of the top drawer. In truth, she owed her epithet, 'Honourable' not to some ancient barony but to her dad, an obscure Conservative backbencher who had been given the title for vacating his seat to provide a Labour defector with a Commons seat for life. And she had had a positively modern upbringing by comparison with the true pearls-and-twin set brigade.

Her mother, poor dear, had made do with day nannies until she was five because her husband would not pay for live-ins. Even after that, a rather minor independent day school was made to suffice until she was nine. Only then did her mother, citing Tanya's need for more concentrated study rather than her and her husband's demanding programme of overseas visits as guests of the British Council, send her to board at Cheltenham Ladies. She made up for her academic shortcomings with her spirit; smoking cigarettes at twelve, cannabis at fourteen, and taking to ecstasy soon after. Not all her talcum containers contained cosmetics. Drugged or not, she was a party girl. Every red-blooded Hooray Henry in Britain wanted inside her knickers, and not a few got lucky.

Tanya at twenty-six had all the attributes of the perfect Sloane Ranger. She could not be accused of being a slave to diets. Her bottom looked better in jodhpurs than jeans and her chest seemed to carry all before it. Everything was in perfect proportion, however, so the generosity of her figure never shaded into bigness. Tanya was an ample girl but it was an amplitude to savour. She was, indeed, the very opposite of a jockey, which was why so many looked up to her (literally), and adored her.

Besides, she had her connections. At first, her mother had made Prince James laugh and then (which was even more impressive) she had made him come in the back of his Daimler on the long drive back from his Norfolk duchy. The Prince just happened to have a free apartment near Windsor, conveniently equipped with stables and grooms. This was made available to the Smyth-Robinsons at an appropriately accommodating rent. After all, one didn't want anyone blabbing to those ghastly red-tops, did one? One day, Her Majesty herself, seeing Tanya ride by, complemented her on her seat.

So did Brendan, though that was not what he called it. The day in 1995 when they met, Brendan had ridden a brilliant

Counter Coup

treble at Cheltenham, one of the three for Her Majesty's mother. That night after the ball, with Tanya in a magnificent four-poster at the Logon Arms, he managed another.

There had been a time when a jockey would have as much chance of cadging an invite to the legendary Grassington ball as he would, mounted, of passing through the eye of a needle. Jockeys were a form of specialised servant, somewhere below a decent valet, and neither to be seen or heard more than was necessary. But in this age of celebrity all that had changed. A jockey who could ride was worth a bob or two these days. And, these days too, how many bobs you had was becoming as important to your place in life as the school your parents sent you to.

Being invited to the Grassington was one thing, however. Getting off with Tanya was something else. For by then, Tanya was officially spoken for.

Tanya was not, of course, the heir to the family fortune. Her four lusty younger brothers would have to meet some unimaginable fate before that happened to her. But within four brothers was close: close enough that the family, never knowing for sure if her mother and the Prince might not turn into something permanent, was making its usual attempts to turn her into a pastiche of what girls from posh families used to be like.

Cornelius Suffolk was part of their plot. Though they put it about that he had sowed his wild oats before going into the army, evidence was thin on the ground. Indeed, what hints there were suggested that Cornelius preferred chaps. Still, that was not the point. He came from an old family. His parents were the nearest thing that the Queen had to personal friends. He did not have enough intelligence to rebel against the future others planned for him, while having just enough not to be an embarrassment. And the Suffolks were religious for generations - no danger whatsoever, so they calculated, of divorce if he and Tanya could be spliced. The Suffolks also spawned large families. The notion that the man's sexual preferences could stop him doing his duty in that regard would have seemed to them simply absurd. And the cure for Tanya's excesses was obvious. She must give them up.

At first, this did not seem an enticing prospect to Tanya. A moral sense is something the upper classes prescribe for other people, while managing perfectly well without it themselves. She enjoyed her wicked life, and she was in no hurry to relinquish it prematurely.

On the other hand, Cornelius wasn't a bad sort, really. He looked well enough on his hunter. The army had taught him to produce a fair verisimilitude of authority over his inferiors. And she caught in him a certain vulnerability which brought out in her the woman's instinct to save. As she began to think that one day her adventures might begin to bore her, the artificial domesticity of Cornelius Suffolk and his title started to hold out unexpected charms.

Had she not bumped into Brendan that evening, if she had not been at Cheltenham to witness his valour that afternoon, had they not found out swiftly that they liked the same music (Garage) and the same television (*Blind Date*) and the same

Counter Coup

champagne (Krug) and the same cars (Lotus), if they had not found - at a speed that shocked them both - that they fancied each other with a ferocity that would not be denied, life might have been very different.

Afterwards, Brendan did regret that he had found it necessary to adjust the setting of Cornelius's nose.

There must surely be more sophisticated ways of conveying to someone that their girl has just ceased to be their girl, and it was lucky that a convenient marble pillar stopped anyone observing the punch. But by then, the affection that Tanya had managed to summon up for Cornelius had gone for ever. As for her family, they could lump it or like it and that English touch of pragmatism that had kept such families in business for so many centuries led them rapidly to conclude that they might as well like it. After all, a popular jockey, a household icon: well, in this new democratic era, why not?

There was nothing out-of-the-way in such an affair for Brendan, or come to that, for most of his colleagues. Jockeys were bad boys and they had glamour. The perils of the profession made them indifferent to the perils of sex, whether VD, AIDS or emotional complications. Tomorrow would bring another course, miles away, another bed, another girl. The day after tomorrow could see to itself. However, the up-market groupies of the weighing-room fraternity fell some way short of Tanya's class.

It was not only her bum Brendan liked. He liked her soft mouth and her bouncy hair and her willowy legs. Above all, he liked the air of innocence which was so tantalisingly juxtaposed with her record of naughtiness. It helped, too, that she knew exactly what to do in bed.

'Ouch!' Brendan yelped.

'Lie still, you silly boy. We'll never get that bone of yours together if you squeak every time I touch your neck.'

It was not simply the pain of his shattered collar bone, though, that caused Brendan to cry out. Physical pain was as much a part of his profession as early mornings, tiny meals and long drives. He simply learned to ignore it. This time the pain in the mind was as bad as the pain in his body and it was so sharp that not even Tanya's magic helped.

'What's the point of getting it together when I'll never ride another good horse again?' he moaned.

*****

Dave Futtnam had been true to his word. Once he'd collected the racing journalists together, they could see from his puce face that it was going to be a good story. On the record he confined himself to a few uttered bromides, no less deadly for being familiar.

'No comment,' he began with but then elaborated enough to comment very effectively. 'It's between Brendan and me. You saw the race; you draw your own conclusions. We'll have to consider who rides Robber Earl in future.'

Off the record, however, he swiped about him with a bludgeon. It was pretty obvious wasn't it? Brendan hadn't lost his bottle. Five winners in the previous three days proved

Counter Coup

that. So there could only be one other explanation for what had happened. Someone had made it worth Brendan's while to fall off. Since the champion was not a poor man, very, very worthwhile.

Yes, Futtnam admitted, he had gone for a touch that day. Normally his security was as good as any man's, but with ill-paid stable lads and big walleted bookmakers, who could be sure? Someone must have got wind of what he was planning. Someone must have tipped the bookies off in advance. And, given the size of what he planned, any bookie that had been tipped off might have made the appropriate arrangements to make sure that Robber Earl got beat and he did his dough.

No wonder Robber Earl had been so easy to back. No wonder Donoughue could not get him over the last.

Racing journalists are not fools. They know that it's libelous to accuse a jockey of throwing a race. They know juries, and their partiality to sportsmen. They could have had Donoughue on film, collecting his readies in a package from the bookmakers, and still the women on the jury who fancied him and the men on the jury who had done well out of him would have given him the benefit of the doubt.

The racing press knew what was evidence and what was not, and the mouthings of a disappointed trainer did not constitute evidence. So the papers next day contained not a hint of Futtnam's private poison. Instead, they dwelt lovingly on every detail of Robber Earl's fall. They rehearsed their memory of the event, and, laced with adjectives, dusted down and polished every dreadful second of the human incompetence that precipitated it. They pointed out that even the local stewards had noticed that something was up and had referred the matter to the Jockey Club. They interleaved their own observations with Futtnam's public comment in a lethal cocktail.

Some dared to question why the Dee stewards had merely interviewed Brendan, instead of punishing him. He owed them - press, punters and the rest of the racing world alike - an explanation. The editor of the *Racing Post* saw his chance to gain a bit of publicity and besides, he had had a fiver each way on the Earl himself. He demanded a full Jockey Club inquiry.

Within twenty-four hours, a message on Brendan's answering machine ordered him to report to the Jockey Club's Head of Security, Jim Dodgson, on Monday, 8:00 AM sharp. Within forty-eight there was another, saying that Superintendent John Noakes of Dee County Police would appreciate a word.

'Ride again?' Brendan reflected bitterly to Tanya. 'I'll be lucky if I get the chance to ride a rocking horse.'

Tanya listened to the self-pity.

'You'll soon be more than riding, you'll be winning.'

'What makes you think that?'

'Would blind faith do?'

Brendan was in too much pain to shake his head. He grunted instead.

'Well then,' Tanya tried to look confident, 'it'll just have to be love.'

Counter Coup

*****

To the modern jockey, the mobile phone is an essential tool of the trade, as important as whip and colours and saddle. There had been times when successful jockeys rode only for the stable that retained them. No more. They were no longer the servants of patron trainers, who were themselves bound to their jockeys by an umbilical cord of mutual loyalty and confidence. Gone were the days when the trainer could treat a jockey as if he was a competent but ultimately disposable parlour maid, grateful for such crumbs as fell from his table.

Now if you wanted to get to the top, you went about it a different way. You hired an agent. He kept your book of rides. More importantly, he had a pretty shrewd grasp of other jockeys' books of rides. And if one of them was injured, or out of form, or out of fashion, it was his job to grab their rides for you.

Even now, Brendan reflected bitterly, his rivals' agents were ringing round his owners and trainers, offering their men's services. And not just for the three weeks that his collarbone was likely to keep him out of the saddle. Already that day in the *Racing Post*, the name of Sean Fitzpatrick, his greatest rival, who had taken the jockey's championship off him, had been associated with Brendan's pride and joy, the Gold Cup favourite Grey Finch.

Brendan glanced at the display on his mobile and picked up the call warily. Jack Gressop, his agent, was sharp as a razor and rather more cutting.

David Lipsey

'How are you feeling?' Gressop didn't sound as if he cared a great deal.

'It hurts.' Brendan admitted.

'I don't mean your bloody shoulder. I mean the rest of you.'

'That hurts too.'

Gressop grunted. 'I should bloody think so.' There was an awkward pause, as though Brendan was going to offer an explanation without asking.

When it became obvious he was not, Gressop launched in.

'What am I going to tell them Brendan? It was a mistake? Forgive and forget? Just because he goes and falls off one which the stable fancies it doesn't mean he's going to fall off yours?' Gressop waited for Brendan's answer. There was none. The agent tried a different line. 'There are lots of other jockeys, you know, and some are damn near as good as you are. By the way, the Tote's just been on. They don't want your tipsters' act at their client lunch at Newbury on Saturday. In fact, they are not at all sure they want you at all.'

That was another £50,000 a year down the drain Brendan thought bitterly. The Lotus. The house. Perhaps even Tanya. Finally Brendan stood up for himself. 'Look, Jack, let's get one thing straight. I wasn't bribed. I didn't take a dive. I wanted to win that race just as much as the other 2,509 I have won. And I want to win another 2,509 too.'

There was a pause on the line that was less than reassuring. 'Brendan, thousands wouldn't, but I believe you. But I have to deal in the real world. Racing's a hard game. There are hard

Counter Coup

men out there, and even the men who are not hard have to pretend to be. Otherwise, they'd be eaten alive.'

'I've met them, thank you,' Brendan pointed out, 'just as often as you have.'

Gressop ignored him. 'What am I to say to them? What's your story? Don't say it was just a mistake. Because those men don't like being lied to. They don't like being crossed.'

Brendan swallowed. His shoulder sent a red-hot needle down his back, through his scrotum, into his legs. He was aware of Tanya in the background, silent, listening.

'I don't know Jack. I don't know what happened. I don't know what went wrong, why I didn't kick him in or why I didn't take a pull. I don't know why I ended up in the ground with my shoulder shattered and my life apparently over. But I do know that I intend to find out.' Brendan pushed the 'end call' button.

Tanya stood up slowly. She walked over and put her long arm around his neat waist, being careful not to brush against his shoulder. She looked at him, gave a little shake of her head, and let herself out quietly. The buzz of her GTi took a little time to fade while Brendan wondered if he would ever see her again.

With the pain, and the shock, and the thought of the interviews; with Tanya gone – who knew if she'd come back? – the talk with Dodgson yet to happen, sleep did not come easily to Brendan that night. One Famous Grouse yes. Another - why not? A third, well, he would not be riding again so he could stop worrying about the weight. Before he knew where he was he was alone in his lounge, lying precariously on the edge of his leather sofa, the near-empty bottle lying tantalisingly just

David Lipsey

beyond his reach.

He knew he had laying into the sauce a bit too readily. As often as not, when Tanya joined him in bed, she found him out like a light. Morning was no longer the pleasure it used to be. The scales told the story too. It now took him two hours in the sauna if he had to ride one around the 10st 7lb mark.

He was not sure whether it was because he had ceased to be champion jockey that he had started to drink more, or because he drank more that he had ceased to be champion jockey. He kept saying he would give it up. But then there would be something to celebrate, or something to forget about, and another bottle would be open and emptied. Tonight he really did have an excuse, but there had been many nights when any excuse would do.

The ancient medicine began to work. The throb in his shoulder seemed more distant. The ache in his heart seemed duller. Merciful release, his eyelids gradually grew heavier and heavier. Yet his brain would not stop.

He tried to remember what exactly had happened. But between the moment at which he perceived a moment of dizziness and the moment at which he had woken in agony his brain was empty. Nothing. Void. Zilch.

The obvious explanation was simply that he had made a mistake. Top golfers occasionally miss tiny putts, top cricketers occasionally deck dollies, and top jockeys occasionally make a bog of races they should have won. That, Brendan's rational mind conceded, was by far the most likely thing to have happened. But its consequences were so

Counter Coup

calamitous, and the blow to his pride so heavy, he was reluctant to believe it could be so.

Drifting between drunken sleep and semi-consciousness, a famous image came into Brendan's mind. It was of Devon Loch, the Queen Mother's great steeplechaser, crossing the last in the Grand National with his race won. The television archive pictures made up in drama what they lacked in sharpness.

Fifty yards off the line, Devon Loch had simply done the splits. Dick Francis, his jockey, had not come off, but by the time the horse had recovered it was too late. Devon Loch finished perfectly sound, but not the winner. Whole books had been written about the affair. Had the crowd spooked him? Had he thought he was crossing a path and tried somehow to jump it? Were his muscles simply giving up after four-and-a-half stamina-crushing miles? Or was there something more sinister? Perhaps even dope?

No-one will ever know, thought Brendan. Just as in his case, they would never know. Except that Devon Loch was the royal horse in the world's greatest race, and the story therefore one that everyone longed to crack. One jockey's career end at Bangor would be forgotten in months.

At last, he fell into the deep sleep of the drunk.

David Lipsey

Counter Coup

Chapter 3

Brendan woke, after one of those booze-laden nights when you cannot be sure if you feel you have slept badly or well. He forced open his eyes, glanced at the alarm. It was a little after eight: a world-class lie-in by jockey standards, even on a Sunday. But then he didn't have anything to do but lie in now in the mornings.

'Or ever again,' he mused sourly, as he remembered the full horror of his predicament.

Now two-thirds awake, he glanced to his side. The bed was a mess all right, but it was a one-person mess of tangled clothes, crunched-up pillows, and a stale alcohol smell.

'Tanya,' he called, then called again. 'Tanya?' There was no reply, not a sound. By degrees, he stood, first conquering the nausea, then the pain in his head, then the bloody collarbone. 'Tanya?' She wasn't there and that hurt more than anything.

David Lipsey

His Californian ranch house on the outskirts of Lambourn was big, all of 4,500 square feet of the local architect's best modern. He had commissioned it the year after his first championship, when the living was easy. Young jockeys on the cusp of deciding whether to pursue their ambitions or settle for a quieter life would drool as soon as they got through the front door, and decide to stick at it. But for such a large house it had few rooms: an enormous lounge, a kitchen-diner and their bedroom suite with just one small spare bedroom. Brendan liked open space; hated pokey rooms. The architect had suggested provision for children. He'd been told to forget it.

It was not a place where you could easily lose someone. 'Tanya,' he kept calling. Whether his voice concealed a hint of panic he could not say. It made no difference. He was alone.

Slowly, he hauled on his dressing gown, letting it hang loose over what remained of his shoulder. He manoeuvred himself from bedroom to bathroom to relieve his immediate needs. He swigged from a bottle of mouthwash. Then he dragged himself towards the kitchen: microwave, bread maker, six-burner hob and the oven you could turn on remotely so supper was ready when you got back from the races, together with the Aga that Tanya insisted made the place homely.

He needed a cup of tea.

He found a mug, put it on the farmhouse table. Only then did he notice the little yellow post-it note.

'Gone to the village for milk. Didn't want to wake you. You looked like a baby, you naughty boy. T.' That fleeting thought

Counter Coup

of her kindness was about as good as today looked likely to get.

As he grabbed the tea bags, he remembered Dodgson. He took the drop of milk which Tanya had thoughtfully left in the cardboard carton and remembered Futtnam.

Then, as he lifted the bag out of the cup he remembered Gressop's words. 'Tell me Brendan, I want to know. What am I to say to them? What's your story?'

Brendan's problem was that he didn't have a story. He couldn't have a story because he still couldn't remember a thing about what happened. He could imagine the stories that were being at that moment cooked up and embroidered upon by others. A mistake might be the obvious explanation but racing is not a world that naturally accepts obvious explanations. Where the heady mix of horseflesh and money come together, conspiracy theories abound.

He could hear now one set of voices. 'Poor old Brendan,' they would be saying. 'Like all drunks he thinks he can knock it back and still cut the mustard. But it's catching up with him. Before his whisky days, he wouldn't have made a mistake like that in a million years.'

Those were the charitable voices.

There would be others, more cynical, less forgiving. Lots of people knew that money was not as plentiful for Brendan as it had been in his heyday. He rode plenty of winners. Sure, it was a good living, but the booze cost and so did his high-maintenance girl-friend.

Losing races can be even more profitable than winning

them. For the bookmakers, the knowledge that Robber Earl would not win was gold dust. Every bet laid on Robber Earl would be certain profit. The more of Futtnam's cash they could extract, the better for them. There was no doubt that it would be worth a lot of their cash to bribe Brendan to fall off.

The worst of the bookies would have another motive too. If they knew that Brendan had been bribed, they would have him set up for blackmail. Today, it might be money that persuaded him to fall off a horse in an unimportant race at Bangor. Tomorrow, it would be the threat of shopping him to the authorities that persuaded him to fall off the favourite in a big race at Cheltenham. That could earn the bookmakers hundreds of thousands, even millions of pounds.

Brendan would have to be a fool to have fallen for such a trick. But there were plenty of foolish jockeys, more concerned with today than tomorrow. The lure of lucre was never to be underestimated, especially when you didn't have as much of it as you used to. So many people - including, thought Brendan bitterly, many of my one-time friends - would be walking around that day thinking he had been bribed.

The bookies of course were not the only ones to have a motive to get Brendan to fall off. Other jockeys might too. For example - the inescapable example - there was Sean Fitzpatrick.

Fitzpatrick was the new champion already, but he wanted more. He wanted all the best horses too. He had made no secret of the fact that he thought he, not Brendan, was the right rider for Grey Finch. Fitzpatrick was not a man much troubled by

Counter Coup

scruples.

If he saw a chance to get Brendan, there was little doubt he would take it. Damage to Brendan's reputation was music to his ears. The racing world would understand that. But it was not clear how that fact was going to help Brendan. For even Fitzpatrick would have a bit of a job persuading Brendan to fall off a horse.

The same went for the other usual suspects. The owners of the winner would have been glad to have a danger to their horse out of the way. Other owners looking to future big races would be delighted if they could be sure that Brendan would not be aboard a rival. Then there were the punters who, in the course of a long career, Brendan had disappointed. Who was to say that one of them was not harbouring a desire for revenge?

But all these theories knocked up against a single seemingly insuperable obstacle. The motive was clear. But what could be the method? How could Brendan be forced to fall off without he or anyone else knowing how?

All such speculation was probably a waste of time, thought Brendan. Even so, he had to check. And if he was to check, he had somehow to find out what had happened that afternoon, in the brief spell between the moment his memory went blank and the moment it came back again.

Another thought came to Brendan, a thought which, though blighted and bitter, was still potent enough to have him striding towards his back door. He opened it, took a lungful of fresh air, and then lifted the dustbin lid. An unmistakable stink of days-old human excrement assailed his nostrils and assaulted his already nauseous stomach.

He retched but he did not put the lid down. Instead, he gingerly reached in and withdrew a padded envelope from which the smell leaked. There was no need to reread the letter inside. Red ink underlinings and all, it was imprinted on his skull. I read:

'You bastard! You double-dyed bastard. I've backed you for years. I thought you tried. I backed you on Robber Earl. I was looking forward to collecting. Look what you've done to me!! It's all right for you with your house and your car.'

'And that posh piece with her big arse.'

'You greedy bastard, I suppose a few extra quid for cheating is just the icing on the cake for you,'

'You should try my place. You try watching the last of your dole money go down. You try watching a dirty shitty cheat. You try watching you.'

Occasionally Brendan hung onto such letters. He was self-critical, but he did not lack self-confidence. For every one like that there were fifty admirers, and the odd dissenter made life more interesting. This time, though, the writer had a point. He wouldn't keep this one in his fat box of fan mail. He wouldn't have done even if it was not oozing brown.

'Watching you,' meant there must be something with it: pictures perhaps.

There was a reason for the padded envelope. Now he saw what he had missed in his disgust the day before. A videotape.

Counter Coup

A handwritten label gave the title which the sender had given to the contents: *Robber Brendan at Bangor*.

Very funny. Brendan's sides hurt with laughing.

Brendan pulled out the video, went to the kitchen and wiped off the crap with some kitchen roll. Remembering Tanya's fastidiousness, he took a box of matches and the paper outside the back door and burnt it. He inserted the video in his machine, and pressed play.

At first, there was simply a fuzz. Then some film Brendan did not want to watch. He liked sex as much as the next man, and he was not entirely immune to the lure of porn - but *this*. It was surely illegal to have it in the house and, besides, if Tanya caught a glimpse, that would be her out, this time for good. Brendan pressed fast forward.

The bodies humped and lurched at high speed so it was not possible to be sure if they were man, woman or child. Sometimes, even at that speed, Brendan noticed items which he would rather not have done. He wanted to get to the real point as quickly as possible, or at least, he would have liked to get to the real point as quickly as possible if he did not have a shrewd suspicion what that it was going to be.

Finally, there it was. Bangor-on-Dee and John Secker appeared in a trilby, morning coat and a pink waistcoat with a carnation in each buttonhole. Secker was not noted for underselling his own presentations but even by his standards, he was clearly excited by the action in the betting ring.

'There's a huge gamble on Firstpastthepost...the punters who know can't get enough of it...and Robber Earl and the champion jockey are friendless in the ring. Even the Booby would know that there's something up. What do these bookies know that we don't?'

The camera panned round the bookmakers. They managed a faint cheer at Secker's tired old jeer at his lovely wife Jenny before returning to shouting the odds and stuffing their satchels.

Fast forward again. 'And at the fifth fence, it's Firstpastthepost disputing it with Referendum. Guilder going well on the far side in the blinkers. Leaping Lady, pushed along, and Donoughue is giving Robber Earl a peach of a ride on the rails....'

Forward. 'And with three fences to jump, it's Robber Earl coming to dispute it with Firstpastthepost. Robber Earl going much the better there.'

Forward. 'Coming to two out, Robber Earl is going clear from Firstpastthepost, whose jockey is hard at work.'

Forward. 'And, as they jump the fence....'

Brendan's finger jabbed the freeze frame button. This was the bit, painful though it was, he really wanted to see. Robber Earl's mighty leap was interrupted in mid-flight before, frame by frame, he went on.

The video was old VHS where you couldn't see clearly what was happening. It did not help that it seemed to have been recorded on long play. Whereas to the ordinary viewer trying to follow the race it would have been fine, Brendan was not an ordinary viewer. Indeed, viewing the race again was the last thing Brendan ever wanted to do for fun. But if he

Counter Coup

wanted ever to know what had happened, there was no alternative.

He had eyes only for his performance. It did not make a pretty picture. At first, as the horse landed after the fence, all seemed well. But then he seemed to lose all co-ordination. A drunk on a fairground roundabout would ride a horse better than he was riding Robber Earl. Indeed, the miracle was less that the horse came down at the last fence than that Brendan did not fall off before it.

After four or five playings of this charade, Brendan decided to turn his attention elsewhere. Who was around?

Brendan stared intently at the right hand side of the screen, in the narrow gap between the rail and Bangor's picturesque cornfield. There was, as usual, quite a little crowd by the second-last fence.

He couldn't see them clearly. Most were pictures of innocence. There was a woman in her thirties holding an excited small child. There was an ambulance man, and a man with a big, flat beater used for smoothing down the birch after the horses had disturbed it.

There were others. A small man, no more than five foot six - ex-jockey size, thought Brendan, and Flat at that. He could have been anyone but he could also be one of the bookmakers' representatives, some of them respectable, some of them not, who haunted every racecourse snuffling out trifles to pass onto their masters.

Another, younger man was also jockey-sized, though not a jockey Brendan recognised.

David Lipsey

Then there was a man whom it was hard to ignore because of his sheer ugliness. He might have been forty-five or fifty-five. He looked bad for either, with a potbelly like a pregnant gorilla's and a face that looked crimson even on video. His cheeks seemed puffed out. In his mouth was what Brendan took to be a cigarette.

For a moment, Brendan felt hope. Wild theories swept through his mind. The bookies' representative - could he somehow be trying to interfere with the horse? The jockey look-alike: Fitzpatrick's brother?

He tried moving the picture forwards and back, painstakingly, a frame at a time. He tried turning the contrast up and down, more colour and less, brighter and darker. He even lay on the floor and looked at it through binoculars turned inside out. He tried everything, but to no avail. The disappointment hit Brendan like a kick in the guts. On the day his career had come to a humiliating end at Bangor-on-Dee there had been a little knot of people by the second-last fence, none of whom Brendan properly recognised. So what? So bloody what? Dodgson, the policeman Noakes, Gressop; what would be the use of that with them?

They would be predictably direct. 'You fall off a horse, half Britain wants to lynch you, you will probably be warned off, you may be arrested and you expect us to listen to you blathering on about who might or might not have been in the crowd by the second last fence? Are you taking the Mickey?'

Brendan heard the gentle purr of the GTi coming up the drive. Watching dirty videos of fat men: this would never do.

Counter Coup

He pressed the eject button and stuffed the tape into his dressing gown pocket.

The key turned softly in the lock, carefully the latch was opened, then closed. Brendan was back in bed, the tape under the mattress, before Tanya was through the door.

Thank God – she really had only popped out on an errand. And she'd clearly left with the minimum of fuss, clad only in a short skirt and blouse that showed no sign of pants or bra. She crept into the kitchen on tiptoe, clutching only the bottle of skimmed milk. She had bought no newspapers, not even the *Racing Post*. She knew there would be nothing in the pages to make them enjoy their Sunday. Once she had set them down Brendan heard her rustling as she made a pot of tea.

He made a good pretence of just waking as she carried a pair of mugs through to the bedroom.

'Been up long?' he asked drowsily.

She set down the tea, leaned over to kiss him and slipped into bed.

'Only an hour or so. Just been down to the village to pick up the breakfast. How are you feeling?

'I don't know yet. I think things hurt less.'

Tanya wriggled out of her blouse, leaving the skirt to ride up as it wanted.

'Let's see how much.' She began to play with him. 'It's time you stopped feeling sorry for yourself and remembered some of the things you can do with humans, not horses.'

Soon after the culmination of their reconciliation they were both asleep again. His was fitful even so. Faces and names flashed across his brain. Futtnam contorted with rage, laughing bookmakers, even Robber Earl neighing at him in puzzled reproach.

As he tossed and turned, something in his subconscious nagged him that the clue was there, in that little crowd. But there, his subconscious ceased to assist him. Who? Why? He had not got the faintest clue.

Counter Coup

Chapter 4

From the imposing Georgian frontage of 42 Portman Square, you would not believe its old servant quarters could be so cramped and dark. Brendan knew the receptionist well. A tall, pretty girl, she had not inherited the Senior Steward's brains. But racing is a kind-hearted industry that looks after its own, particularly the daughter of a member of the Jockey Club. And she had repaid racing's generosity by looking after not a few of the more dashing jockeys in the backs of their cars. Brendan blushed at the memory.

'How are you, Sarah?' he asked as cheerfully as he could. But he soon saw this was a new Sarah he hadn't come across before.

The girl's features darkened and her voice took on a noticeably harsh tinge. 'Mr. Donoughue. You'll find Mr. Dodgson on the fourth floor, the room at the back on the right. Please don't use the lift,' she added spitefully. 'We're expecting

David Lipsey

the Marquess any moment.'

Brendan had not previously had cause to meet Dodgson. But he knew plenty about him by reputation. After the doping scandals of the early 1990s, the cry had gone up to clean up British racing. The Jockey Club thought Dodgson just the man for that. His conviction rate at Stoke Trent police station had been the best in the land. When you walked the streets round about it, you could smell the fear.

Of course, the Club knew about the tragic episode that had ended Dodgson's time there. A local man - vocal but harmless, spliffs only, no crack - had been found dead in his cell by his wife. She swore that she had seen bruise marks around his face. But, as Dodgson pointed out, she must be lying. How could anyone see bruises on a black man? It wasn't the best choice of words at a sensitive time.

By an unfortunate oversight, the body had been cremated swiftly when he had asked for burial. The campaign that followed was backed by the Commission for Racial Equality, naturally, but also by all the usual hangers-on and those with a grievance against Dodgson and all his kind - the Legalise Dope Brigade, the Soldiers of the Twelfth Reincarnation, the Socialist Workers.

They had not a shred of evidence. Every policeman in Stoke Trent that night swore the dead man had come in drunk. They had left him in his cell to cool off, checking every half hour out of concern for his welfare. He must have choked on his own vomit which, naturally, they had cleared up so as not to distress his wife when she arrived. Dodgson, the

Counter Coup

superintendent in charge, contended that nothing untoward had happened that night.

An investigation by an outside force was well briefed on the sensitivities. It concluded sternly that procedures should be tightened, prisoners should be inspected every fifteen minutes, and training in resuscitation improved. Above all, the Stoke Trent police force – indeed the whole police force – needed increased resources to do their job. No blame lay, however, with any individual officer, all of whom had acted in the best traditions of the service. Accordingly, the Crown Prosecution Service declined to bring charges. A private prosecution was brought, and collapsed.

A few months after that, Dodgson was granted early retirement, his health, so the police briefed the press, permanently destroyed by the stress of liberal persecution. He was appointed Head of Security by the Jockey Club without the sort of gap that suggested permanent stress. They did not care whether he was racist or not. They cared only that he should get results.

His deputy, Don Simmonds, was already there. The days of 'hard man, soft man' had gone for the Jockey Club. Even jockeys were intelligent enough not to fall for that old trick any more. The new regime was to fight fire with fire and iron with iron. For this, Simmonds was brilliantly qualified. He was feared even in Arabia.

An outbreak of betting in the Gulf Kingdom of Abdul Khalef had scandalised the Middle Eastern racing world. It was bad enough that their people could see their extraordinarily extended royal families blowing their country's oil money on strings of thoroughbreds worldwide. It was worse when those thoroughbreds brought with them betting, an affront to the teachings of the Prophet and a threat to the moral order of their state.

Simmonds' past record commended him for the job in Abdul Khalef. The security forces in Northern Ireland had been his playmates. They had a splendid record as long as you did not have too many scruples as to how it was earned. Simmonds deserved much of the credit. Veteran IRA men had been known to jibber when they heard that he was to be their interrogator. A devotee of *Lawrence of Arabia*, he differed from his master by preferring to apply the lighted cigarette to tender parts of other people's anatomy. It was, after all, well-known that tobacco harms your health.

With the Easter Friday peace deal in Ireland signed, Simmonds' skills were less in demand. Hence, he leapt at the opportunity of a stint in Abdul Khalef and the bonus he was promised if he succeeded. Within a few months, a Chinese bookmaker had died after receiving a hundred lashes delivered by a policeman specially selected by Simmonds for his strength. A jockey's whip hand was amputated in public. Six immigrants from Taiwan, found placing bets, were sentenced to five years in Shiah-el-Sheikh, a prison in which few survived more than five months.

Betting in Abdul Khalef came to an abrupt halt. So when two of the ruling family's horses were unexpectedly beaten in big Ascot handicaps by horses that had shown little recent

Counter Coup

form, they knew what to do. A word was had with their friends at the Jockey Club. There was talk of the Sheiks' insistence that that their horses should run only where the racing was a straight as the word of Allah. France was mentioned, even Germany. No more had to be said. The decent ex-plods who had staffed Jockey Club security and the racecourse bars for years were shown the door. Simmonds took their places.

The new regime did not have it entirely easy. There was a fuss in the papers when Britain's most popular jockey, Bill Cowes, was first suspended, then prosecuted, for doping horses. The judge, whose own horses had been touched off not a few times over the past year in suspicious circumstances, did his best to persuade the jury to find him guilty. It did not matter to him whether Cowes had done it or not so long as an example was set. The jury was more scrupulous. Twelve good men and true declined to convict.

The Jockey Club, however, was an organisation which regarded itself as above normal criteria of justice. It thought it had survived, and fervently believed that it would survive, only by being impervious to public opinion. If the courts could not be trusted to help them with the job of keeping racing straight, they would get on with it themselves.

They didn't want to know too much about the methods Dodgson and Simmonds employed. They wanted results, and they felt assured that they were getting them. As for the public... well, why did the Jockey Club have a highly-paid press spokesman, if not to lie for racing?

David Lipsey

*****

The tiny room in which the two investigators sat was lit only by a single, unshaded 150-watt bulb. Their desk was clear, except for a few papers, a rather old-fashioned tape recorder and a sharp-looking paper knife. They, Brendan could not help but notice, were sitting in comfortable adjustable chairs, which compared favourably with the battered bentwood he was offered.

Dodgson was a large man with the kind of trim moustache now seen only on policemen. You could tell he had been fit, before too many years of too many free drinks had created his paunch. Simmonds had given up the booze during his Middle Eastern years. The indignity of being flogged if he was caught outweighed even his thirst. Even so, his hair was now greying at the front, and a certain seediness was creeping across him as if caught from too many years in the company of petty criminals.

'Sit down, Donoughue,' said Dodgson. 'Make the best of it. We can do this the easy way or we can do it the hard way. And if you choose the hard way, you're going to be standing for a good few hours later. I hope you don't have anything planned for the day?'

The ends of his little moustache seemed to twitch, perhaps with pride at this sally. He poured himself a cup of inky-black coffee. Then he poured one for Simmonds. For fully thirty seconds, no-one spoke. It seemed like thirty minutes. Eventually Brendan took the initiative.

Counter Coup

'Look,' Brendan said, trying to remain calmer than he felt. 'I know what you think, but it wasn't like that. I made a mistake. I had a fall, it still hurts, if you want to know.'

'It could happen to anyone,' observed Simmonds with the ghost of a smile, 'even a little crook like you.'

'A crook? Me? Why?' Brendan went on. 'You don't want to believe what they say about money. I've got enough. I've got a nice house, fast car, lovely girl. Owners are already begging me to start training for them. I've had a great past and I have a great future. Why would I risk all that?'

Brendan sensed that his words were not having quite the impact they were meant to. His intuition told him that Dodgson and Simmonds were jealous of his money, his house, his car and above all his woman. If he was to persuade Dodgson and Simmonds, he was going to have to do a great deal better than that.

There was another seemingly endless silence. Then Simmonds leaned forward to the tape recorder which sat on the table between them and pressed 'play'. A few hisses and crackles, and then he could hear a voice. Brendan's voice.

'Hi, Tanya love, I'm on the motorway.'

'Hi darling. How far to Bangor then?'

'Another hour. For what? Two camels which couldn't raise a gallop if they were ridden by the Four Horsemen of the Apocalypse. And then the Robber.'

'But the Robber's got a chance, surely?'

'That's what Futtnam thinks. He's laid him out especially for the race for months. Hence the hiring of yours truly to ride. He thinks this is his day to get into the big time, financially. But between you and me,' Brendan heard himself saying, 'and I'm only telling you this because you don't bet – I've got this feeling that the Robber isn't going to be winning anything today. It's just a feeling and I know he's usually a great jumper. But to tell you the truth, if I get round at all on him, I'll be more than a mite surprised.'

'Oh, shame,' said Tanya, 'all that way for nothing.'

'Have the calendula cream ready for when I get home.'

Brendan's blood ran cold. He knew how innocent his words were. They were typical of a jockey before a race he hoped to win, hiding the excitement behind a protective banter of pessimism. He had a dozen such conversations every week, mostly with Tanya, who knew to take them with half a handful of salt.

That was the reality. But the perception was something else. For he also knew how they would look, in typescript, shorn of his emphasis. He knew how they would sound in the tones of a barrister, heavy with irony.

He could hear the quotes neatly taken out of context.

'Isn't winning anything today.'

'If I get round.'

'I'm only telling you this because you don't bet.' And he knew that it was typescript, not the recording, sworn as authentic by all, that would be produced in any subsequent proceedings. Recording people's mobile phone conversations was illegal. But he already had a feeling that the Jockey Club's discipline committee would not care about that. Brendan's

Counter Coup

face drained of all colour.

Dodgson didn't seem to notice. Instead he held out a crumpled photograph of a middle-aged man in cloth cap and sports jacket. 'Know him?'

'Never seen him in my life,' replied Brendan, suppressing a faint feeling that he might be wrong.

'Sure?'

Dodgson showed him some more photos. The same man talking into a mobile, its mouthpiece masked with a handkerchief, then chatting with one of Britain's leading, though not most reputable, bookmakers and then collecting a very large wad of notes from another of the bookmaking fraternity.

'Quite sure? Dodgson persisted.

Brendan looked him straight in the eye, 'Quite sure.'

The last photograph was of the same man on the edge of the winners' enclosure at Cheltenham. Brendan, walking to weigh in with his saddle, appeared to be looking directly into his face, smiling, nodding, apparently chatting.

'Quite, quite sure?' Dodgson let the impact of the photo sink in. 'Now Donoughue. We're not telling you this to get you to confess. Quite frankly, we don't need you to confess. We've enough evidence here to make sure that you are warned off from tomorrow morning to the day you die. You and racing are over. But we don't just want you. We want your chummy there. We've been trying to nail him for years. And from this photo we think you might just be the one to help us. He seems to be very pally with crooked bookmakers. And so, it appears after Bangor, are you. You should have a lot in common. And our informant has told us that you do.'

Brendan noticed a handwritten letter with the photograph. It was not signed. He didn't recognise the writing but that didn't mean much. Jockeys rarely sent personal letters to each other. The pokey banality of the room began to feel claustrophobic. The schoolroom chairs, the battered utilitarian desk, the chipped mugs in front of the investigators all began to fray Brendan's confidence.

Dodgson went on, as though he was merely briefing the jockey. 'We want to get him. Our informant suggests that what happened at Bangor gives us our chance. But we don't know much about him. We don't know where he is. We have nothing we can pin on him for sure.'

'Then why are you gunning for me?'

'Because we think you do know who he is and where he is and what he's done.'

Dodgson paused and looked intently at Brendan, waiting for a reaction. Brendan just stared at the pictures and frowned.

'Of course you don't have to tell us who he is. You don't have to help us find him.' Dodgson was compellingly reasonable. 'I don't suppose you want to. We know that men like that can be, let's say, a touch unfriendly towards people who have led us towards them. And we wouldn't like you to break any more bones on our account. On the other hand, I believe the police have already been in touch. And Superintendent Noakes and his crew might not see it that way.'

Brendan listened but still said nothing. Simmonds seemed

Counter Coup

to be more interested in the state of his nails than their conversation.

Dodgson sounded almost apologetic. 'They don't get so much crime up their way as we do down ours, you see. They tend to treat things a wee bit more seriously. If they had these photos and the transcript of these tapes, they might think that a warning-off was not enough. They might think it was time men like you went to jail as you deserved.' He gazed at Brendan with chilly blandness. 'Of course, we don't want to give the evidence to Noakes,' he explained. 'It's a technicality, but some people might think that we ought not to be going round bugging other people's telephone conversations. In this namby-pamby crooks'-paradise of a country, the recordings aren't even admissible in court. Anyway, on the whole, we'd rather the world did not know that we have every word said by every jockey on every mobile on tape. But then, that mightn't be too much of a problem. Noakes would just have to find something else to use in court - when you know someone's guilty, that can usually be managed. No, we don't want to give the tape to Noakes. But then you probably don't want to tell us about chummy either. So it seems like one of us is going to have to do something they don't want to do.'

Finally Simmonds spoke. 'You or us, Brendan?'

Brendan found it bad enough facing up to the end of his career. Racing had been his life. Racing was still his life. With it went everything: home, living, friends, and recreation. Many people did manage to exist outside racing, though. He even knew a few ex-professionals who had moved on to be perfectly normal members of society after their racing obsession had ended.

Life without racing was one thing. Life behind bars was another. What might be the sentence for what he had done? Conspiracy to defraud? A first offence, maybe, but a bad one, involving breach of trust and a loss to perfectly innocent members of the public. He thought a fine and community service.

And then he seemed to hear a judge's voice, 'grave offence...appalling greed...unforgivable breach of faith...all the more heinous in one who has been a model for so many young people.' Three years? Four?

Generally, Brendan had been blessed from birth with good psychological health. He was tough as leather and hard as steel. But even strong men tend to have one weakness. From the moment at the age of three when his mother had accidentally locked him in the coal house, Brendan had a fear as deep as the ages of confined spaces. His claustrophobia had resisted every treatment.

He had learned to live with it, so much so that he was rather sorry when he blurted it out to a sympathetic lady journalist profiling him for the Sunday Times. He could see the now-curling cutting on the pile of papers which Dodgson had in front of him.

The very thought of being in prison sent waves of nausea through him. Only a will determined not to weaken in the face of the two bullies in front of him prevented his puking over the table.

Counter Coup

The pair of Jockey Club men sat silent as he brooded some more. There were the months of torment, locked away for an offence he and only he knew he had not committed. Even if he survived that, there would be no house when he came out. Almost certainly no Tanya. No money, no future, a criminal record. No nothing. He'd rather top himself.

Had Brendan known anything about the man in the pictures, a canary would have been a Trappist monk by comparison. He would have told them everything he knew and a bit more besides. Brendan's problem was that he didn't know the man. Leastwise he was pretty sure he didn't know him.

Dodgson and Simmonds did not know him either. They guessed at the source of the anonymous letter that came with the photos and the suggestion that his links with Brendan over the Robber Earl. That was the sort of letter they had a collection of. Often they came from rival jockeys. Despite this, they frequently turned out to be true.

Brendan's throat was dry as the desert. He tried to swallow and failed. His brain, flooded with fear and adrenalin, raced like a top two-year-old in a five-furlong sprint.

Eventually, he found enough strength to speak. 'I don't know anything about the man you are showing me. Nothing, not now, nothing at all.'

Dodgson sighed. Brendan wasn't finished, though.

'But I'm willing to try to find out. I'm not asking you to trust me. I'm not even asking you to suspend the warning-off process. But before you talk to any policemen, I'm asking for

David Lipsey

time.'

Dodgson looked puzzled, then shook his head. 'Oh, come off it.'

'A fortnight, that's all,' Brendan pleaded. 'After that you can do what you like.'

Then he added, 'and by the way Dodgson. I seem to remember a spot of bother at Stoke Trent. After that, are you absolutely sure you want a dead ex-champion jockey on your hands?'

It's funny how quickly you realise that you are talking to someone in language they understand.

Simmonds wouldn't have listened to reason but it wasn't reason that Dodgson was listening to. The interview was completed sullenly and suddenly. Brendan left with time granted.

As he walked past Sarah, he heard her sigh and saw her shake her head.

Counter Coup

Chapter 5

Terrible though it had been, Brendan's interview had been a lot shorter than he'd expected, and he didn't spare his engine on the drive down the motorway. He was sorry, but not entirely surprised, when he got home to find that Tanya was not yet back from her mother's.

Idly, he leafed through the post on the table. Adverts for tipping services, form books for sale, a few bills. Three letters from journalists. Two, wheedling ones, were from racing writers whom he had thought, until that day in Bangor, to be his friends. They asked for interviews 'so he could put his side of the story'. Ha! So they could string him up with his own words, more likely. One, which at least had the merit of being frank, was from the *News of the World*, offering him £5,000 for the same thing. They very much hoped that he would say yes, only he was not to tell anyone, since the Press Council did not allow anyone to profit from selling the story of their crime.

David Lipsey

He turned on his PC to get his emails. Jockeys were early into the email revolution. It suited their itinerant way of life since they could be sent in the odd intervals of a long day. He hoped for a few comforting words from friends. He was disappointed. Their famous camaraderie seemed to have been suspended rather suddenly after he'd fallen off at Bangor.

Just two notes came from jockeys. One was from his best friend, Peter Marston. Peter was not the most articulate of men in conversation, let alone on paper. But he had a good heart, and that counted. 'Looking forward to having you back...so long as you don't pinch my best rides!'

The other was from Sean Fitzpatrick. 'Got you at last, haven't they? Just deserts eh, Brendan boy.' Charming.

As he was staring at the screen, it told him a new email had just arrived. His heart leapt when he saw it was from his Aunt Doris.

Doris was a funny old thing. Bright from an early age, but brought up in the days before working class kids reached for the stars, it was no surprise that she became a teacher, and a dedicated one. No hint of a romantic life had ever been heard round Doris. But it *was* a surprise when she left Gillsford Grammar for one of Britain's poshest public schools. Even more surprising that she was a hit. They loved her northern lilt, but they also sensed she was a touchy old bird, and it wouldn't be wise to take the piss. They became the children she never had. Even after she retired, her home in Berkshire was a place of pilgrimage for hundreds of young men who wanted wise counsel or a shoulder to cry on. She loved them

Counter Coup

all, but none so much as she loved Brendan.

It was because of Brendan that Aunt Doris had become a racing fan in the first place. Because of him she had taken up riding, even on one unforgettable occasion boarding a point-to-pointer in the local hunt race at the age of fifty-four. Sometimes she would drive him to the races. Even when she didn't, she would watch on the telly. Taking to email in her sixties, it was a rare day when Brendan got home to find no message of congratulation or commiseration from Aunt Doris. He loved her as much as she loved him.

He could feel the anguish in her words. 'I don't understand it, Brendan. What happened? It can't be what they are all saying. Are you eating properly? Laying off the whisky? Tanya looking after you? You need help,' it ended decisively, in the no nonsense way of the best teachers.

Aunt Doris was a practical woman. Brendan had hardly closed her email while he thought of a reply when the phone rang.

'Brecon here,' said a clipped, upper-class voice. 'Friend of your aunt. Taught me all I know. Seen the tape and it looks terrible. But D says you wouldn't and if D says you wouldn't, that's good enough for me.'

'Oh, well, thank you...' began Brendan but was cut short.

'I think we should meet before you appear before the disciplinary committee. Let's say four tomorrow, Peers' entrance, House of Lords. If you're free.'

'I'm free.'

'Good. Glad to hear it. See you then.' The line cut.

David Lipsey

Lord Brecon's was a name Brendan knew well, though they had never spoken before. The Tregwynns were one of England's oldest racing families. Their Starcliff had won the Derby in 1795 and only a fall at the last ditch had stopped King of the Winds taking the 1907 Grand National. Their stud, which had survived without public subsidy, had turned out a stream of winners ever since.

Like his father and his grandfather, Henry Tregwynn was elected to the Jockey Club pretty well as soon as he left school and joined the Bank. His knowledge of racing, combined with his professional ability to secure an overdraft, made him a natural candidate to become the Queen Mother's racing manager for the happily fruitful last years of her life.

There was only one odd thing about Henry Tregwynn. From the day he succeeded his father and came into the House of Lords as Lord Brecon, he took the Labour whip.

The family had tried to talk him out of it, naturally. They were all Tories to the core. Still shocked by her husband's death, his mother had implored him. When that didn't work, she threatened him with disinheritance. For a week she really did disown him, before she missed him too much and begged him to forgive her.

The Jockey Club made it clear, through gritted teeth, that Labour chaps were not barred from membership. Not nowadays; indeed there were several members who were rumoured to have voted for Tony Blair in 1997 even though they denied it.

The Club members themselves were broadminded. What

Counter Coup

Henry did with his spare time was no concern of theirs. However, in view of the sensitivities of some of the older members, he would surely agree a little oil should be poured on troubled water. Being Labour would debar him from certain positions in the Club which he was otherwise well qualified to fill. Might it not be better if he sat with the Tories for appearances sake, they asked him? Then he could vote how he liked.

The captain of his golf club reminded him that it was not permitted to talk politics in the bar, not his kind of politics anyway. His boys were bullied at school. The Tory chief whip, in his cups, cut him dead.

Only the Queen Mother herself took his political declaration with equanimity. She regarded all politicians as come-and-go creatures. They were all the same to her, Labour, Liberal, Conservative (if you could call the party of John Major that). They were too far beneath her to merit distinction by party, and she blithely carried on in her usual way as if Henry Brecon had no politics. As long as he could still share a gin and a joke at the expense of his 'comrades', there was nothing to object to. He was in turn oblivious to royal taunts and adored her.

With time, Henry's funny politics were forgotten. It was muttered that, if Labour did get rid of the hereditaries, Henry was odds-on for a Tony Crony life peerage, and so would keep a seat in the Lords.

*****

David Lipsey

Brendan's taxi drew up outside the Peer's Entrance to the House of Lords. An attendant, in top hat and frock cloak greeted him as he walked in. If he recognised him as Britain's currently most notorious race-fixer, he managed to hide the fact.

'Good afternoon, sir. Lord Brecon will be down in a minute.'

Brendan hadn't realised how much it would matter to him, just once to be addressed by someone who did not appear to think he had been dragged in by the cat. Now he understood why members of the House of Lords always put the House attendants at the head of their list of the glories of that otherwise bizarre institution.

Lord Brecon was down punctually as Big Ben struck four. He shook hands, warmly rather than formally. They strolled through the hall where every peer had his personal coat hanger (about the only private facility the House offered most of them), up the stairs past the coats of arms of military heroes gone by, across Prince's Chamber, heeding Henry's warning not to pause or talk as his fellow peers went about what passed for business - and eventually turned left, past the long communal table where peers of all parties and of advanced years mixed promiscuously, into the guest room.

'Ah, Maria, can you find us a table?' Brecon asked one of the attentive waitresses. They were led to one in the corner, obviously Brecon's habitual resort.

The portrait of Thomas, first Baron Coventry four centuries previously, looked down on them. *Bet he's seen a few dramas in his time*, thought Brendan, though it didn't make

Counter Coup

his own any easier to bear.

It had been many years since Brendan had enjoyed a meal called tea, though on days when he did not have to ride at too light a weight he occasionally took a cup, without milk or sugar, before racing. But the House of Lords provided tea as tea used to be - scones, crumpets, anchovy toast, and trays of iced cakes, each with a little chocolate sticker on top saying House of Lords.

At first, Brendan thought of his weight, and the little voice that lives in every jockey's stomach said 'No'. But he remembered his predicament, and the fact that he hadn't been able to keep down any solid food since his meeting with Dodgson and Simmonds.

'A tea cake and a scone please,' he ordered, with all the relish of a monk buying lingerie.

Brendan was against the wall, naturally facing away from the body of the dining room. But he noticed his host cast an eye towards the door; and then he noticed that every peer in the room and most of the baronesses was doing the same thing. He glanced over his shoulder and saw who they were looking at.

Looking at women, of course, is all that most members of the Lords are up to, though they do love talking about it: no debates attracted more of them to the chamber than those about sex. The Lords is nothing but adaptable, so most had now got used to hiding their homophobia beneath a veneer of tolerance when they spoke, though what they said in the bars was a different matter altogether.

David Lipsey

Even so, you could not question their taste, those that way inclined, in the opposite sex. The woman who appeared among them now was no longer a young girl. But if anything the maturity of a woman approaching thirty had improved her looks. She was wearing a black business suit, plain but clearly expensive, its only concession to fashion being the long slashes in the skirt. Her long blonde hair was simply but carefully done. Even by modern magazine standards she was svelte and elegant. There was no spare weight anywhere. She carried her slightness with style, though and did not seem thin, just perfectly understated, as though her body needed only a suggestion of shape to make its point effortlessly. You could tell at once that her mind had the same quality of inherent agility and classical grace.

She walked over to their table. Henry Brecon tried to look as men used to do when a woman came in on business. But he made a bad fist of it. From the look on Henry's face, Brendan instantly deduced that the girl was the apple of his eye. She kissed his Lordship tenderly on the forehead, then offered her hand to Brendan.

'I don't think you've met Brendan, Becky,' said Henry. 'He's a jockey. My daughter, Becky Tregwynn. She's a lawyer.'

Brendan and his fellows did not generally have much need for lawyers except when they bought a house or fell out with their agent. But the racing pages were always writing about her dad, and they rarely avoided the chance to bring Becky into the stories. After all, the page looked a good deal more enticing with a picture of her than it did with one of him.

Counter Coup

In an act of bravery or folly, her father and mother had insisted on sending her to a South London comprehensive (to less fuss from the family than might have been expected, since they still reckoned that educating girls was pretty much a waste of time). She had shone, even managing the only state school GCSE in Latin of her year. Oxford wanted her, being desperate for the kind of comprehensive school child who might nevertheless be expected to fit in with the university and its public school ways. But she chose Liverpool instead. Having avoided those public school types thus far, she told her father, she didn't want to spend the next three years punting the Isis with them. The Mersey suited her far better.

The law was growing so fast that even the fact that her first was not from a blue-bloodied institution did not stop a leading London chambers from taking her on. She earned a rich living from commercial briefs on Monday to Thursday, but then she worked free for poor defendants in Brixton magistrates' court on Friday.

Every few months she rated a profile in one of the glossies. A sure-fire QC, some said. Others thought she would one day lead the Labour party, if it ever got its principles back. Others tipped her as the first female Lord Chancellor, if her principles quietened down a bit. Others again just hoped that it might be them she decided to love. Unfortunately for most of them, she set the same high standards of her lovers as she set for herself. Becky ordered herself an Earl Grey, lemon not milk. She stirred it idly, then turned to Brendan. 'I see from the papers you are in a spot of bother. In fact, to tell you the truth, I'm a bit

David Lipsey

surprised that Dad's prepared to have you in here. You know what they can be like round here but then Dad always was a bit of a softy. Especially where Doris is concerned.'

'I wouldn't call it a spot of bother,' Brendan replied bitterly. 'I'm in a cartload of the brown and smelly.'

Brecon might be a softie. His daughter was not. She had spent many hours in police cells with clients who were guilty as sin but not prepared to admit it. What was different about this jockey she was not sure.

Still, she was a professional. 'You'd better tell me all about it.'

With any good lawyer, it's hard to tell what is part of the act and what is real. Whether or not Brendan's plight really interested her, she knew it interested her dad, and that was enough. For the next fifteen minutes, Brendan told all, every detail, as it had occurred, just as it seemed to him. Whether or not she believed him he didn't know. But Brendan, who had not until then had a high opinion of lawyers, began now to see the point of them.

'When's your hearing at the Jockey Club?' Becky asked when he'd finished.

'Tomorrow at ten.'

'That's a little early for that lot of establishment layabouts isn't it?' Henry Brecon mused. 'Still, I wouldn't like anyone to appear before them alone. It's being bullied at school that gives them a burning desire to get their own back.'

Becky took her father's cue. 'As it happens, you're in luck. The judge in the trial I'm in fainted in court today. Not

Counter Coup

surprising given the temperature and that wig. So we get a day off. Pity the poor client: that's £10,000 in fees and refreshers they won't get anything for. Not that this lot mind. They're city accountants so the profits grow on trees. Especially since that party of Dad's got in and cut their taxes.'

'But New Labour is the party of enterprise, dear', Henry expostulated, 'as it is the party of fairness. Equity and prosperity are not in conflict. We believe that the trees must grow tall so the ferns of the forest also flourish. As our leader himself said put it so eloquently last week...'

Henry Brecon faltered and ground to a halt. It was a speech that would have gone down a treat in the Chamber, with the Labour benches at least. From his daughter in the tea room it evinced only a withering look, especially since, if she had any loyalties, she was a signed-up member of the Brown faction. She was not taking any of that Blairite crap, not even from her sainted dad.

Brendan didn't notice this political passage of arms, which in any case was way above his head. He had however noticed the mention of £10,000. He was used to attracting the attention of top totty, but so far there was very little sign that this girl fancied him. And unless they fancied him, strangers rarely came up to him to offer to do him a favour unless there was something in it for them.

'I'm not sure I can afford you, I'm afraid. I'm a jockey and not quite as successful as I was. I don't get £10,000 for a winner more than twice a year.'

Becky brushed his concerns aside. 'Forget it. Dad wouldn't

David Lipsey

be having tea with you if he didn't think that there must be something to be done. You made his day when you won the Hennessy for the old lady in '94. So tomorrow's a freebie. Besides, nothing would give me greater pleasure than to give that gang of arrogant prats a run for their money. After that, well, let's see how we get on.' She turned to her father. 'Now, Dad, whom exactly will we be appearing before in the morning? What's their form?'

Counter Coup

Chapter 6

The ideal tribunal is one solely concerned with establishing truth. Under England's adversarial system, the prosecution puts its case and the defence rebuts it. Presenting both versions in this way is a procedural tool designed to maximise the chance of truth emerging. By any such criterion, the disciplinary committee of the Jockey Club was far from being an ideal tribunal.

Take for example the main source of its business; appeals from jockeys who reckoned they had been unfairly suspended or fined for riding misdemeanors by local stewards, and by owners and trainers, who felt their horses had been unfairly disqualified as a result. It often happened that the jockeys had indeed been unfairly suspended or fined, and the trainers and owners unfairly deprived of their triumph.

The local stewards were amateurs – at least, they were amateurs in the limited sense that they were unpaid. But they were also amateurs in the wider sense of being minimally equipped (recent improvements in their training notwithstanding) for the demanding task before them.

The job brought with it a certain social cachet which few with an interest in racing would have refused. Once appointed, even fewer readily resigned for reasons of age or infirmity. It was performed in the environment of a place of entertainment, a racecourse. This makes it natural that those who did it should fortify themselves for the task ahead by lunching well. Besides all this, qualifications for the job (in addition to the right quarterings) seemed to include poor eyesight, deafness, and a lack of common sense.

The members of the disciplinary committee of the Jockey Club perceived all this. Its members were not fools. But, not being fools, they also perceived that they must not let on.

For the local stewards, buffoons though they were, had a job to do. They had to make difficult decisions on inadequate evidence, and, what is more, make them quickly so bets could be settled and the show go on. If the Jockey Club had simply undone all their mistakes, confidence in the local stewards would have exploded, and that would never have done. So it did nothing of the kind.

Occasionally, an injustice of such magnitude would be perpetrated that a public scandal was created. Too much scandal would threaten the whole organisational pyramid of racing administration of which the Jockey Club was the apex, and must thus not be permitted. In such cases, the Jockey Club cheerfully recognised necessity, and made a show of doing

Counter Coup

the right thing. But, short of palpable necessity, the job of the disciplinary committee was to defend the indefensible and justify the unjustifiable. 'Sentence first, verdict afterwards', in the words of *Alice in Wonderland*.

Had there been no shred of evidence against Brendan, therefore, the disciplinary committee would have been disposed to warn him off. The local stewards had referred the matter to them. The Club's officers had brought the case against him. Stewards, officers, these were people who had to be backed against jockeys.

In this case, though, there was a pile of evidence against Brendan, even if most of it was circumstantial.

There were the unusual betting patterns on the race and the apparent willingness of the bookmakers to accept huge bets on Robber Earl while all the time lengthening his price. It seemed inconceivable that so many bets in so many betting shops did not lead to bookmakers ordering their course representatives to back the horse on the race course to shorten the odds: 'laying off' as it is known in the trade. The least that could be concluded was that the bookies knew something was up. The most? Well, that they had bribed Brendan to fall off.

There were the tapes of his telephone conversations with Tanya. Most compelling of all, there was the video of the race, and the unforgettable picture of a top jockey looking as if he'd fallen off a child's rocking horse. It was, on the face of it, an open and shut case.

*****

David Lipsey

Brendan had felt less nervous at the start of the Grand National. The room the disciplinary committee sat in was designed to achieve that. Short of a dock and a warder, it could not have been more intimidating. As were the faces, set, hard, of the products of a lot of expensive schooling and a lot of expensive living. The oak paneling emphasised the pedigree of the room as well as its users. On the walls horses from the 18th century, immortalised by Stubbs and pupils, glared down as though adding their own judgment on jockeys who were careless of their successors' reputations.

A fine and highly polished table, that might have graced the dining room of any passing earl, dominated the middle of the room. The middle leaves had been removed so that it fitted across the chamber. Brendan was invited to take a solitary chair on the side that left him with his back to the door. The committee had clearly not expected him to arrive with a representative, although it was common enough practice, and there was some disgruntled huffing before another chair was produced for Becky.

Across the table the three man committee shuffled their paper evidence and arranged their pens. At the end nearest the fireplace a woman who could have fitted into the least conspicuous role in the meanest Whitehall department sat ready to minute the proceedings. Dodgson and Simmonds had taken chairs at the opposite end of the table with their backs to the window.

The formalities were neither lengthy nor reassuring.

'Donoughue,' announced the man in the middle, a small

Counter Coup

weasel-faced man with prim glasses in an immaculate parliamentary grey suit who looked as if he might once have had jockeying ambitions himself. 'And the Honourable Miss Tregwynn, if I am not mistaken. Charming too, if I may say so as one who first saw you in your cradle.'

'Thank you, Sir Clive,' grinned Becky, who, in contrast to Brendan, was perfectly at home in the surroundings. 'Of course I am aware of who you and your colleagues are but perhaps you'd like to introduce them to my client.'

'Oh, yes, quite. Mind you I'd have thought Mr. Donoughue might have deduced that by now.'

'Given the stress of the situation,' began Becky.

'Yes, I see what you mean. Well Donoughue, I'm Sir Clive Cottington and on my left is the Vice-chairman of the Discipline Committee,' Cottington indicated a white-haired but trim man with a luxuriant moustache, 'Colonel Martin Osbourne. And this,' he waved to his right at a tweed-suited bald man in his late sixties, 'is Rutherford Haynes, who as you know has long experience of these matters.'

'Thank you,' purred Becky and smiled sweetly at each of them in turn, 'and these two gentlemen?'

'Donoughue knows perfectly well who they are.'

'But I don't, do I?' murmured Becky.

'Really! They are our security team, Mr Dodgson and Mr Simmonds.' Cottington was starting to look desperate.

Becky was not ready to let him off the hook yet, though. 'And this lady?'

'Ah,' muttered Cottington, embarrassed, 'I'm afraid I'm

not entirely...'

Haynes leaned towards him and scribbled hastily on the chairman's notepad.

'Yes, of course, thank you, Rutherford. Kathy Brown, Miss Tregwynn - here to make sure we're properly recorded.

Becky made a point of beaming especially kindly at Kathy Brown, who looked grateful for recognition of her existence.

'Now back to you, Donoughue,' started Cottington, keen to regain the slipping initiative. 'You have heard the evidence against you from Mr Dodgson and Mr Simmonds. At least, you've heard such of it as it is right for us to lay out in open hearing, though you will understand that there are some matters which we decided to study in private. They remain and will remain for our ears and eyes only.'

Becky jumped in. 'As my client's legal representative I trust there will be full disclosure to me of any evidence you may have, Sir Clive?'

'This is a disciplinary committee, not a court of law, Miss Tregwynn.'

'I think you'll find the rules of evidence need to be the same if any sanction you impose is to stand scrutiny,' Becky persisted.

'We'll see.' Cottington turned to Brendan, 'So, what have you to say for yourself?'

Brendan had thought hard about how to play this moment. Should he seem truculent? Aggressive? Aggrieved? Or, at the other end of the spectrum, should he simply submit to the inevitable, plead guilty or even remain silent? But Brendan

Counter Coup

was a straight man, and he chose the straight approach.

Seeking to control a tremor he looked Cottington straight in the eye. 'Only this, Sir Clive. I know it looks bad. But I can assure you - I had only one wish in the Bangor race, and that was to win it, if I could, by every fair method I know. I don't know why I came off. It's as mysterious to me as it is to anyone. But I no more sought to fiddle that race than I would seek to mislead you and your colleagues today. I ask you to take my word for it.'

He swallowed hard, barely daring to look up at the chairman. But when he did, his examiner's eye seemed momentarily to soften. Evidently Brendan's choice of approach at any rate had been the right one. But the Cottington's next words fell short of being cheering.

'Tell me, Donoughue. If we settled for leniency – for, let us say, a five-year ban not life - might you then not tell us a little more? I believe that Mr Dodgson here may have put some suggestions to you. You'd feel better and maybe those who deserve worse than you would get their come-uppance too.'

Brendan wondered what he would have done had he known more. Would he appease the committee and risk having his legs broken by his paymasters? But since he knew nothing, it was an irrelevance.

He shook his head. 'Sir, I have told you what happened. If I could help with anything else, believe me, I would. But I can't.'

All softness had left the Cottington. Indeed he looked furious – and vengeful. But he did not forget his manners. 'Miss

David Lipsey

Tregwynn?'

She stood, and for a moment fixed him with a steely eye which would have struck fear into a less arrogant, more sensitive soul. 'I must protest on behalf of my client against these proceedings. As you know, this country is a party to the European Convention on Human Rights. I submit to you, sir, that these proceedings palpably fall foul of that convention.' She paused, just long enough to let the idea settle. 'This cannot be regarded as an independent tribunal. You are determined to convict, whether my client is guilty or not. You will do that for what you regard as the good of racing – that is to say, the industry which provides you with your pleasures and from which you seek to profit. All the evidence has not been openly available.'

Cottington opened his mouth to protest but before he could, Becky pressed on. 'My client has been given inadequate time to prepare his case and inadequate time to brief me. Should you do other than acquit him today of the charges against him, I shall have to advise him in the strongest terms to appeal to the Courts for justice.'

The speech was delivered with panache and conviction. Haynes studied the ceiling as though hoping for guidance, Osbourne doodled. Cottington, though, was close to losing his temper.

'Very pretty, my dear,' he said icily. 'But I shouldn't do that if I were you. I'm not a lawyer, heaven forefend. I've always been an honest man myself. But of course the Jockey Club does have lawyers, bloody expensive and usually a waste of

Counter Coup

money but there you are. And our lawyers advise us, with all due respect to you, that the courts are extremely reluctant to intervene in the proceedings of private disciplinary tribunals. The case law is extensive – but then, Miss Tregwynn, I hardly need to remind you of that.'

Brendan hoped that she would contradict him. Her silence spoke volumes.

The chairman continued, 'That reluctance to intervene is especially true of cases which involve the Jockey Club. We have elected several judges to membership. They have been good enough to explain to their judicial colleagues the difficulties under which we labour.'

Cottington was warming to his theme. 'In the sport we have administered so successfully for so long, it has always been a problem to get proof. Of course, these modern devices with which Mr. Dodgson and Mr. Simmonds are so adept do help, but it's not easy. Yet it is an absolute necessity, if our industry is to thrive, that we are seen to be maintaining integrity. The man in the average betting shop is suspicious enough about what goes on. If we fail on integrity, he'll put his money on something else – dogs, football, the election.' He paused, as if for the first time himself realising the appalling vista that was opening up. 'It's the punters' money that pays for the prize money for our horses, and the prize money that keep us paying our trainers and our jockeys. I am not ashamed to admit it. So we have to crack down on wrongdoing, and we have to be seen to be cracking down on wrongdoing. I know less about the courts than you do, Miss Tregwynn. But I am happy to take my chances and that of the Club in any court of law. We are good for as much as it costs. I understand your client has not been doing so well of late. Is he up to paying for a major action?'

Brendan remembered the little stack of unpaid mortgage reminders on his desk at Lambourn, and controlled the urge to wince.

Cottington glanced around him. 'Any comments, gentlemen?'

Osbourne and Haynes shook their heads.

The chairman's eye's narrowed, in a way that sent a shiver down Brendan's back. He turned to Kathy Brown. 'Switch off that tape a moment would you?'

He looked back at Becky. 'There's something else you might ponder before you take your client off to the courts, Miss Tregwynn. Yes, you might find a sympathetic judge on a good day who would give you your ruling. But where would that get your client, I wonder? Maybe, just maybe, we'd have to give him his licence back. But who would want a crook riding for them, even if he was allowed to do it?

'You can't take away a man's professional livelihood just like that,' Becky told him.

'Oh, yes we can. But we don't have to. I'll tell you exactly what would happen to any trainer who put Donoughue up on one of his horses. We wouldn't need to tell his owners what to do. They are not idiots. Next morning, half the owners in the yard would be taking their horses away. A friendly owner? Only if he wanted to be ostracised on every racecourse in the

Counter Coup

country. If even your respected father put him up for her beloved Majesty, that would be the last time he'd dare show his face round here. Mind you, given his politics that might not be a bad thing.'

Becky thought of arguing but realised that Cottington was going to enjoy throwing the book at Brendan, if for no other reason than having the hurt feelings of a betrayed Tory. His next assertion was disingenuous at best.

'You've been brought up to be in favour of justice, and good for you. In the right time, at the right place, I'm all for justice myself. But in racing, justice is - how shall I say? - a relative concept. If we worried about justice all day, we'd never get by.'

Cottington drew breath and began again with quiet finality. 'If you can prove your client didn't do it, fine. Our doors are always open. Just forgive me if I do not hold my breath waiting while you try to get your evidence. Meanwhile, if I may give you some free advice, next time you get a day off from court, spend it counseling your drug-dealing friends in Brixton. You're wasting your time here.'

There were a few seconds of silence. The other members of the committee seemed to be absorbed in their pencils, the walls, anything to avoid the eyes of the defendant and his lawyer.

'Tape on, please, Miss Brown.' Cottington announced with decision. 'Brendan Donoughue, this committee unanimously finds you guilty of behaviour likely to bring the name of racing into disrepute. You are therefore hereby warned off every racecourse, training ground and racing establishment in the country for ...'

Dodgson stirred in his seat by the window. Holding his finger to his lips, he vigorously shook his head. Cottington, who had evidently forgotten his brief in the excitement of his own oratory, noticed just in time.

Donoughue was to be given his fortnight to shop his co-conspirators before sentence was finalised. '...for a period to be decided when this tribunal reconvenes in two weeks. We'll tell the press that's to give you time to put forward any mitigating circumstances, which should deal with any fun you and Miss Tregwynn might be planning to have with them at our expense.'

He shuffled his papers. 'Goodbye and good riddance, Donoughue. And goodbye to you too, Miss Tregwynn. Do tell your father not to bother with this sort of case in future. I doubt if Her Majesty will put up with much more of it.'

*****

In normal circumstances, a drink in the Connaught with a lady like Becky would have snapped Brendan out of anything. He was, of course, monogamous these days, but the opportunity would have been delicious, even if he decided in the event not to take advantage of it. He could at least go through the motions, with the clever way he recognised the waiters by name, the large tip, the risqué banter. He would just omit the bit where he sidled up to his old friend, the head porter, and arranged

Counter Coup

for a bottle of champagne to be sent up to the usual room at the usual time.

However, the moments after your professional life had been brought to an ignominious close did not constitute a normal opportunity. The way he felt, Brendan could as easily have recited the Holy Bible backwards as make love – even to Becky. Especially since he knew that the chairman had been right.

It is an illusion of our times that the law can put everything back together again. It can't. If a man dies and his wife sues the hospital, who wins? Not the wife who has to go through years of legal agony without getting back what she most wanted. Not the health service which pays out. Not future patients, on whom doctors may neglect to try out treatments that might work but are risky. If a smoker gets lung cancer and sues the tobacco company, who wins? He dies anyway. And if a disqualified jockey sues the Jockey Club, who wins? The chairman's prediction of what would happen had a horrible ring of truth.

'What now, Becky?' he asked after they'd found a corner table and ordered a stiff drink each.

Becky was still shaking with rage. 'That patronising, sexist bastard! How can my father tolerate such people?'

'Because he has to,' suggested Brendan reasonably. 'He has to mix with them every day of the week. '

Becky glared at the innocent waiter approaching with their drinks. She took a sip and let it calm her before going on. 'The trouble is Brendan, the only thing that was not wrong was that arsehole's analysis. He's right about the evidence. You do look guilty. And he's right about the courts. We'd have a hell of a time getting you back into racing by using human rights legislation.'

'So that's that, then,' muttered Brendan.

'No,' said Becky. 'Not quite.'

'I thought you said...'

'I said the Club were right. So we have to play them on their own terms. This is just the start.'

Brendan looked forlornly at the confident young lawyer. 'What do you mean?'

'I mean the only way out is to prove them wrong - prove that you were somehow made to fall off that horse - with evidence that is incontestable.'

As Brendan morosely fiddled with a cocktail stick, he realised what the determination in Becky's face meant. She was going to stick with him. Not because she knew he was innocent; she could have no certainty of that. Not because she liked him, though she did. Not because she fancied him, which was too much to hope. But because she was a lawyer and one of a rare breed of lawyer who was devoted to justice. It helped that her whole life had been spent learning to loathe the sort of people they had appeared before that day.

In life, it is notoriously difficult to prove a negative - to prove that you have not done something rather than for someone else to prove that you have done it. And it was more difficult still in a case like this one. In a court of criminal law, it is for the prosecution to prove its case. The defence merely

Counter Coup

has to shed sufficient doubt on that case, without providing an alternative explanation or solution, and the defendant gets off. The test in civil law, however, is much less severe. Its test is set on the balance of probabilities.

That was the test which tribunals, such as the disciplinary committee of The Jockey Club, adhered to. And on the balance of probabilities from the evidence (the betting patterns, the tape of the race, let alone the tape of the phone calls) clearly Brendan was guilty.

How could he and Becky prove otherwise? Where would they start?

For fully an hour they got nowhere. The waiter kept the drinks and little plates of nuts, olives and biscuits coming. The circle of their reasoning stayed just as repetitive. Then, somewhere about the fourth drink, they saw a glimmer of light. In examining the facts from every possible angle, it began to emerge that something, after all, had clearly been up that day. The betting patterns proved it.

Brendan had to find out what and who was behind it. He and Becky concluded that depended on making what they could of the only people who could help them.

One was Dodgson and Simmonds' friend - the man in the photograph. About him, they knew what Brendan could remember, namely that he was middle-aged and had been at Cheltenham one day when Brendan had ridden a winner. As a third of the population was middle-aged and as Brendan had ridden 109 Cheltenham winners, those clues fell something short of precise.

David Lipsey

The second was the owner of one of the faces in that crowd by the penultimate fence at Bangor: not the young mother, obviously, but perhaps the man who looked like Fitzpatrick, or the fat man with the cigarette. And then somehow they had to work out how that person had managed to work the apparently magical trick of converting Brendan temporarily from a top jockey to a dunce. They had just under two weeks in which to do it.

Counter Coup

Chapter 7

A jump jockey had to be extremely lucky or extremely poor never to have made the pilgrimage to Norman Jones' surgery in Harley Street. Norman Jones was the king of orthopaedia. He had only to look at a broken limb for it to start to heal. That and his surname meant that everyone called him Bones.

Beneath a questioning, melancholic look, Bones was funny as well as learned. Some jockeys, particularly those with injuries they were trying to conceal from the racing world, claimed to visit him just for the jokes. For others, he was the only contact with culture they ever had. But he was a professional too. He knew very well that one couldn't simply tell a jockey to do what was in his own interests. Returning to the saddle too early might indeed lead to arthritis in old age but that was not going to stop him.

However, as well as his responsibility to his patients Jones had a responsibility to the racing authorities, who could not

David Lipsey

let racehorses be ridden by cripples. Often he had to tell a jockey that he could not ride, however tempting the chances of a particular mount might look. It said much for him that, after they had finished cursing and wheedling, the jockeys usually respected his decision.

Brendan was in no mood for either jokes or culture next morning as he climbed the familiar stairway to Jones's consulting room. If his shoulder wasn't healing properly that was bad news, not just for whatever subsequent employment he was able to find but for his future health too. Brendan had seen too many broken ex-jockeys to take that lightly. If it was healing as it should, that too would be bad news. It was hard enough not being able to ride when he was physically unable to. To be fit for the saddle and banned was going to be psychological torture.

It was a visit that could have no happy outcome.

Bones was sitting behind a huge desk, reputed to be modeled on one belonging to Hitler. But anyone less like Hitler it would be hard to imagine. As Brendan entered, he saw him hastily cover over the *Racing Post* with the *British Medical Journal*. Not much point in that, Brendan reflected: you could not drive round Lambourn without seeing the placards advertising the paper's headline - 'Donoughue to be banned'. Still, it was a kind thought from a kind man.

Bones's instruments of orthopaedic torture lined the room, together with his various libraries: 17th century poems, a collection of Swift first editions, the international history of anaesthesia. A *Test-Your-Strength* machine, recovered from

Counter Coup

some derelict pier, stood in the corner. Bones sometimes used it to check jockey's claims that they had fully recovered from some ghastly fall.

Brendan wondered why a man so learned bothered himself with jockeys. Then he remembered that an addiction to racing is something to which people of all kinds, at all levels, are subject.

'Well, let's have a look at you.' Jones the Bones smiled.

Gingerly, Brendan pulled off his shirt with his working arm. Dr. Jones began the familiar task of removing the strapping on the shoulder. At first, he nodded reassuringly, but then Brendan could not help noticing a puzzled frown.

'The shoulder's coming on fine,' Jones said, 'but you don't look all that well, I must say. Is your face always so red?'

'Well, the last few days haven't exactly been stress-free,' said Brendan, 'and the face? The outdoor life, you know.'

'Hang on a sec,' said the doctor, reaching for a needle. 'I'm just going to take a drop of your blood, if it's spare.'

He found a vein and sucked out enough for two or three tests. 'Thank you. And a quick look on the spectometer. Handy this new one: gives you the results in seconds.'

Dr. Jones peered at the instrument. He did not find it easy to look grave but he managed it this time. 'Sit down, Brendan.' Brendan sat down. He noticed his hands were trembling.

Jones laid his spectacles on his desk but remained on the patient's side of it. 'First thing, blood alcohol. If you drove with this in your system, you'd be banned. At ten o'clock in the morning? Second thing: liver function. Your ALT is above a thousand. Of course it can go much higher. You haven't got sclerosis.....yet. But Brendan, if you go on drinking like this, you will have. You've got.....four years, maybe five? And, believe me, it is not a pleasant way to go. No wonder you're falling off horses. At this rate, you'll soon be falling off chairs.'

'It's not that bad,' Brendan protested lamely.

'Yes, it is,' Jones said firmly. 'This is not advice, it's a straight warning. Give up the drink. Now. For ever, if you can't keep it right down - and I don't mean just to 21 units a week. I mean half that.'

Jones stood and made his way round to the other side of the desk. He wrote the details of a celebrity clinic - very respectable, expensive and discreet - on his notepad and handed the sheet to Brendan. 'If you take this seriously you'll spend some of your recovery time there in the next few weeks, and you won't be the first jockey through its doors.'

The doctor forced a smile. 'Booze aside, you'll be fit to ride in three days. Why not buy yourself a hack? Put him over a few jumps at home, and you can always pretend it's the real thing.'

He was a kind man, but even kind men make mistakes. Jumping a hack was not quite yet how Brendan saw his future. Nor was he ready to admit that he was an alcoholic.

'I'll forget the bill. After all, this may be the last time I ever see you,' Jones quipped.

Everyone said he had a tremendous sense of humour.

*****

Counter Coup

That night Brendan was staying in town. No judges had fainted in the past twenty-four hours, and so Becky was not available until after court. By the time she had changed, tidied up and they had done their business it would be too late for Brendan to set off for Lambourn. In any case Tanya was away, visiting her father. *Always Daddy's girl in a crunch*, Brendan thought.

Brendan, daftly, had suggested El Vino's in Fleet Street, just round the corner from the Old Bailey, before remembering its notorious resistance to the admission of women. A frostiness in Becky's voice warned him of his error. It had better be the Savoy. Brendan was relieved that the Head Porter at the Savoy was a stranger to him.

The American bar was already crowded at that hour. Rich Midwesterners somehow thought from its name that it must be a home from home, and came in for a couple of cocktails before dinner at 6:00.

'When in Rome...,' thought Brendan. He remembered Dr. Jones. Then he thought of a Manhattan, with a cherry dangling from its rim. Stopping the drink could wait until tomorrow.

Becky, work ahead of her, took Perrier. If Brendan were ever to ride again, the pair were going to need her finest detective skills.

In the absence of any obvious strategy to suggest, Brendan kicked off the conversation by telling her about his day. Bones Jones was a bit of a character after all. Unaccountably he omitted the bit about the booze from his tale. Instead, to help his flow he had another Manhattan. By the time he had drunk that, she needed another Perrier, and it would have been wrong to leave a young lady drinking alone. Already, being banned from riding was feeling less bad.

'Brendan!' The edge in her voice caught him by surprise. 'That's three Manhattan's in half an hour.'

Brendan looked sheepish.

She did not let him off the hook. 'Didn't Dr. Jones say anything about booze? Because, frankly, if the reason you're falling off horses is that you are an alchi, I'll let you get on along with it right now.'

Brendan was not a natural liar. He wasn't an alchi. Just a man who enjoyed the odd drink. 'Honestly, before this business, I hardly touched a drop.'

Becky, though, was by now in cross-examination mode. 'Drugs then? We've all heard about the weighing room.'

What had she heard? Quite a lot of the lads smoked because it helped to keep the weight off. And quite a lot of them supplemented the tobacco with a bit of spliff, except that tended to up the appetite; many a horse due to weigh out at 10st had had to carry an extra couple of pounds, courtesy of a few tokes of Acapulco Gold the night before. Some jockeys used amphetamines, which killed the appetite, and others liked the odd line of coke. Brendan among them.

Funnily enough confessing to dabbling with cocaine seemed a lot easier than confessing to being an alcoholic.

'Well, yes, I'll have the odd line. But never when I'm riding. I can't imagine what that would be....' Brendan's hand shot to his mouth. His face went pale.

'What?' Becky demanded.

Counter Coup

'It's just, well... the moment before Robber Earl fell. The clarity, the confidence. It was a bit like you feel when you've taken a line.'

'But you hadn't? At least you hadn't, if I can believe you.'

'Yes, but supposing someone had given me some without me knowing?'

'The effects would last some time,' Becky objected, 'not just for those few minutes - and anyway you said the last thing you felt was clarity and confidence. Half a second later, you barely had any sense at all.'

'But there must be different types?'

'Or different drugs,' said Becky, and pulled out her mobile phone. 'Hi Dad,' she said finally, after a long delay and explanations to parliamentary officials.

Lord Brecon didn't sound too pleased, for once, to be phoned by his daughter. 'It had better be good. You've just dragged me out of a debate.'

'Oh, sorry,' Becky's tone was only half apologetic. 'Was it important?'

'Actually, yes,' her father harrumphed. 'Our amendment to the Hooligans and Public Disorder bill. We want the caning which the Government is introducing to be administered by the policeman on the beat rather than after trial. Unfortunately, your lawyer friends are objecting. I've never heard such eloquence from them in the cause of liberty. It's amazing what a proposal that would take away their fees does to them.'

Becky was unimpressed. 'Oh Dad, shut up. If you had your

David Lipsey

way I'd starve to death. Now listen. You know that library of yours you're always banging on about. How is it on drugs?'

'No idea. You know me, fit as fiddle. I've never asked. But I expect it's pretty good. After all, health is the main topic of conversation around this place. Half of them are over ninety and complaining about their ailments to each other is what keeps them going.'

Laughing at his jokes was part of the price you paid for having Brecon for a father. 'Try the library on this one then,' demanded Becky. 'If you wanted to deprive someone of their capacities, just for a few seconds, without rendering them unconscious, and you needed to make sure that they wouldn't remember a thing about it, what would you use? Some kind of cocaine, maybe?'

'You don't ask much, do you?' Henry Brecon muttered. 'I'll ring you back, in an hour or so with luck.'

*****

Besides the attendants, the librarians of the House of Lords are its great glory. Other libraries in other places now merely refer inquiries to the relevant website. But the library of the House of Lords understands that, given the age and dignity of its members, that would never do. Many Lords and Ladies struggle gamely with the Internet. Training courses are packed with elderly peers determined to master this icon of the modern world. But a query to the library is rewarded with paper: paper you can mark, sort, file and keep. Many of the

Counter Coup

Lords' most accomplished performers owe their deadly thrusts to the impartial services of the library.

Underneath the old-world courtesy, it is quick and efficient too. Miss Burgess listened to Henry's query as if a peer asking about a peculiar drug was a daily happening. Perhaps, since the amazing day when a newspaper found traces of cocaine in the Lord Chancellor's toilet, it was. 'Yes, of course my lord. I'll see what I can do.'

Precisely fifty-seven minutes later, Lord Brecon was lifting a bulky brown envelope from the tray in the inner library. His daughter, he knew, was a hard woman to satisfy. But if she was not satisfied with this lot, he did not know what she would be satisfied with.

He called. Through the merry tinkle of bar conversation, he could hear his daughter's voice, cool, efficient, sober.

'Any luck?' she asked.

'Becky, darling, get yourself over here. And bring that client of yours with you. I have something here that just might interest you both.'

*****

Henry Brecon was lucky enough to have a small office in the Palace of Westminster, an unusual convenience for a peer who was not a government or senior opposition spokesman, chairman of a committee or holder of one of the grand offices of the crown.

So great had been the Labour whips' joy at his unexpected

allegiance, that they had shown unwonted generosity. Henry had spun the line that he could never be sure when Her Majesty might take it into her head to come round to talk horses. Utter rubbish, of course. Even if she had been younger, the Queen Mother would have summoned him to her, rather than venture from the comfort of her palace.

The Deputy Chief Whip in charge of allocating offices had been around long enough to see through that. But, like most socialists, he was a little in awe of those with Royal connections, and Henry got his office.

It was a good room too, reasonably convenient - which meant not through too many courtyards and up obscure back staircases - close to the premises of Hansard, the Houses of Parliament's journal of proceedings. Henry shared it in theory but with two distant, sickly members who were only likely to attend if summoned by the Leader of the House in person. Lord Brecon therefore had felt free to install all the necessities: a drinks cupboard, a fridge, a run of form books, rather than Hansard volumes of debates. Even when a vote was not expected until quite late, Henry was happy in his lair.

Although definitely Labour, Henry was not exactly *New* Labour in attitude. He didn't keep a computer in his office for the very simple reason that he hadn't the faintest idea how to use one. So he, Brendan and Becky were able to spread the fruits of Miss Burgess's labours over the desk - in practice, over all three desks - as they looked through them.

And an extraordinary collection it was too. There were extracts from obscure American medical journals. There were

Counter Coup

reports from select committees on the drugs laws. There were selected literary references to celebrated drug-takers: Coleridge, de Quincy, Burroughs. And there were a series of cuttings about recent drug-related court cases.

Brendan took what seemed to be the dregs of the research. Indeed, at first, he could not understand why Miss Burgess had seen fit to include an article on Aztec human sacrifice. He'd vaguely heard that that great civilisation chose to appease its gods by removing the hearts from living victims in their hundreds in front of huge crowds. He felt the Jockey Club had done something a bit like that to him, but he didn't find the analogy particularly comforting. He read on:

'One challenge for the Aztecs concerned the victims. The whole point of the sacrifice would be vitiated if they appeared to be unwilling. They had to appear gladly to be giving their hearts to the gods. Otherwise, they might struggle or scream: and that would offend the advanced sensibilities of the audience.

Cocaine was highly satisfactory for the purpose. It did not incapacitate the victim. It merely rendered him more cheerful about what was happening to him. And, by dulling the pain, it cut down on the screams.

However, that ingenious civilisation was not satisfied with simple cocaine. For example, it did not want a drug that gave the victims too much relief for too long. For the priests, if not for the public, the victims' sufferings in anticipation of their ordeal were part of the fun. It served as a constant reminder not just of the power of the gods, but of their own.

Cocaine might make them enjoy the hours before their demise and that would never do.

So that was the challenge: to find a strong drug that would enable them to satisfy their needs and those of the people. They wanted something that would last only the brief moments before the sacrifice, and which would not excessively incapacitate their victims.

In pursuit of this ideal, some Aztec civilisations achieved a degree of pharmacological sophistication that would amaze even the coke-cookers of the chemical laboratories of today's Latin America. For example, some tribes achieved a form of cocaine which would deprive the recipient of all capacity for decision or co-ordinated action, while at the same time enabling them to function with, what could seem to the untutored observer, normality. In some cases, it appears that the effects lasted only for a few seconds. A few of their detailed instructions for the making of such derivatives survive.'

For a moment, Brendan found himself caught up in the excitement of his reading. Since what had happened was seemingly inexplicable, even the most remote possibility of a solution seemed somehow plausible. And if he had been drugged, that at least would explain why he had seemed to be deprived of his powers.

But, of course, it wasn't possible. Aztec ingenuity or modern chemistry: no-one was likely to be able to design a drug which could be administered in advance to take effect precisely as a horse approached the final fence. It would only

Counter Coup

take a delay at the start for the jockey to fall off before the race began. And that would not only scupper the coup; it would undoubtedly arouse the suspicions of the security forces.

Besides, Brendan would know if someone had given him a jab. He read on through the sheaf of papers. Now and again Becky pushed a new one towards him while Henry grunted with disgust at the depravity revealed in his bundle.

One of the court cases concerned a nasty case of rape. The victim had gone out, against her better judgement, with a smoothie who had made his sexual intentions clear from the beginning. She resisted. The next thing she remembered was waking up in his flat, semen seeping from all orifices and with absolutely no memory of what had happened. He claimed that she had consented. He would have got away with it, except for a brilliant police forensic scientist who found traces of a date-rape drug in the assailants' heroin syringe.

'Could this explain why you can't remember being jabbed?' Becky asked as she watched him read it.

'I'm not sure. Perhaps it could.'

Becky wasn't convinced. 'That wouldn't account for the suddenness of it, though. A cocktail of drugs might be more likely than a single drug.'

'But who could have done it?'

'And when?' agreed Becky.

'Even if it is the explanation, it's not going to help me much,' complained Brendan. He thought of Sir Clive Cottington, the chairman of the disciplinary committee, sitting there staring at a note from Miss Burgess on Aztec practices. He didn't think it likely that this would represent the proof of innocence that the chairman was looking for. In fact, he was not sure if the chairman would laugh or scream.

Brendan wasn't sure he could blame him. This was the stuff of fiction, not real life.

The position remained precisely as it was before Becky had launched her pharmacological investigations. To have a hope in hell of getting off, he had to find much more than a plausible explanation. They were back to finding a perpetrator – the man in Hacker's photograph, someone in the crowd by the second-last fence, or both. Finding them, tracking them down, and proving that they were culpable - at that moment all seemed utterly impossible.

Counter Coup

Chapter 8

Most jockeys can sleep anywhere. From the age of sixteen, when they leave school and become apprentices, they are used to bedding down in dormitories, often noisy, often drunken, with the prospect of rising at five am to gallop first lot. There are overnight stays at racecourses, whose facilities for humans are as primitive as their facilities for thoroughbreds are supreme. There are catnaps by the motorway or in the racecourse car park if, for once, the traffic isn't heavy and there is time before racing. For the fortunate few there is the annual fortnight in the West Indies, usually spent on the beach wiping out a year's accumulated sleep deficit. The rest are lucky to get a weekend in Brighton.

Generally, Brendan was no exception to this rule. Admittedly he was roughing it tonight. He was aware that his earning power had fallen – to zero in fact. Drinks with Becky in the Savoy he could justify as a legal expense in his case. A bed upstairs he could not. So when finally they left Henry, he repaired to a cheap hotel near Victoria. Henry had recommended it because it was the one his more impecunious colleagues used. The overnight allowance for Lords in London, set so as to avoid public outrage, ran to nothing better.

Brendan couldn't really blame the welcome at the hotel, which was warm, or the reasonably quiet room, or the bed, which was soft enough. As he stretched out, he tried to think he was in Tanya's arms. Unfortunately, it was only too apparent to him that a strange translation had taken place, and it was a phantom Becky, not a phantom Tanya, who held him tight.

He did eventually slip off to sleep, but not for long. Some dreams are past bearing. In his first of the night, he was just settling down to a night of pleasure with Becky when the door flew open. In burst Dodgson and Simmonds, their eyes gleaming wildly. Dodgson was carrying a racing whip. Simmonds was wearing spurs.

Brendan sat bolt upright, sleep banished. He felt a cold shiver run down his spine. If he could not bear to dream about it what was the real thing going to be like? Only thirteen days remained now until the deadline for finding the man in the photograph expired. If he failed, he knew better than to expect any mercy from his tormentors.

Quite how the one thing led to the other, he could not afterwards recall. Indeed he could not recall at what moment, precisely, the extraordinary thought had come to him. All he knew was that one moment he was shivering with fear and the

Counter Coup

next moment he was basking in a revelation.

In his mind's eye, first he saw the man in Dodgson's photographs, his alleged chum from the winner's enclosure at Cheltenham, the one in the photograph sent to Dodgson and Simmonds. Then he saw the fat man with a cigarette, in the crowd standing by the fence at Bangor. The man in the photograph, the man in the video, they were one and the same.

This was progress, of a kind. Before, he and Becky had been looking for two mystery men. Now they need look for only one. The problem was that he still hadn't a clue who that could be. He couldn't be sure that it wasn't simply a coincidence. He couldn't even be sure that the obvious explanation was not the right one: that, for some reason, Brendan had made a catastrophic mistake at a moment when it was bound to be interpreted as a crime.

His moment of triumphant revelation swiftly passed.

Brendan tried to sleep, but sleep evaded him.

As the first light of the warm late summer morning seeped under his bedroom door, Brendan rose, dressed, and set off down the long familiar course of the M4 to the sanctuary of his home.

*****

The difference between a good jockey and a top jockey does not lie in their relative talents. At any one time, there are a dozen jockeys blessed with that rare ability to make horses run. They come every year out of Irish country towns with names like Rosgarden and Litherridden, riding tiny ponies before they can walk and on racehorses before they can read. They come from the racing towns of Britain, from Newmarket and Lambourn and Middleham, often bred small from jockeys, the trade handed down from father to son. And occasionally they come, totally unexpectedly, from places unconnected with racing where, for some reason, a boy or even a girl emerges with nothing in their head but a burning desire to be on a galloping thoroughbred and in the winner's enclosure.

During most years in the racing industry a little over 5,000 stable staff are employed by trainers. Of these, only just over 130 are apprentice jockeys. Of these only a few can expect reasonably regular race rides. Half are useless, and many of the rest spoil themselves with drink, drugs, women, men, or an inability to get up in the mornings.

What separates the wheat from the chaff for those who remain lies in their ability to take pains. Brendan could ride from the first, ride so anyone in the yard could see which of their callow apprentices had the potential to make it into the first division. In those days, he did not much like drugs, he was a moderate drinker, and he never stayed all night with his girlfriends two days running. But his exemplary behaviour was not what set him apart. What made him special was that he learnt as he went, absorbed every scrap of knowledge and experience that came his way.

From the first, Brendan had kept a book of his press cuttings. For every race in which he rode, he pasted the list of runners and riders and added detailed descriptions of each

Counter Coup

horse's performance that appeared in next day's *Racing Post*. The descriptions themselves were written in a special language, known only to the writers of form books and their punter students. Once you had learned the language, you had every race laid out before you with a skill and insight that made Brendan marvel. 'Sa; prog to chlng 4 out, not ro flat.' The horse had started slowly, had progressed to challenge the leaders with four fences remaining to be jumped, but had failed to run on when asked to go through with his effort between the last fence and the winning post. 'A prom until ur 15th.' Up with the leaders until he dislodged his jockey at the 15th fence. 'RFO' . An epithet reserved for the most incompetent riders at their most disastrous moments, and which Brendan had always avoided until that dreadful day at Bangor: 'Rider Fell Off'. Brendan, understandably, had not yet got round to pasting the coverage of that particular day in the book.

He himself lacked the skills of observation and compression of the trained race-reader. But he did his best to record what he knew. Below the *Racing Post's* description, Brendan appended his own detailed handwritten note of the animal's owner and trainer. Many good rides had come his way because he was able to remember the names of the owners in a syndicate for whom he had ridden, and flattered their ego by using them.

At £90 pounds a ride, and 10% of any prize money, it was worth the effort.

Below that again he noted exactly how the race had been run, the characteristics of the horse he was on, the bits he had

David Lipsey

got right, any mistakes he had made, any hints for next time. He noted the going and the weather and the horse's preference for left-handed or right-handed, up with the pace or held up, whether it might need blinkers or a snaffle bit, responded to the whip or not. A gambler keen to know about the best horseflesh on the National Hunt circuit would have wanted for nothing if he'd access to Brendan's notebooks.

Only after all the useful information had been minutely recorded was vanity allowed a little space, when Brendan added below any available photographs of the race and its aftermath. There were pictures of the owners, the trainers, the stable lads shaking him by the hand, slapping him on the back. There were pictures of Brendan with the big boys of racing, the Senior Steward, the head of the British Horseracing Board, the Chairman of the Tote. There were pictures of Brendan with monstrous trophies as big as he, with bottles of champagne so large that they would have fuelled a Bacchanalian orgy, with watches and cufflinks and silk ties. With the aid of these pictures, one day in tranquility, Brendan thought, he would be able to replay in his mind the glories of his youth.

To help in his review, the entries were carefully indexed and cross-referenced by the name of the horse, its owner, its trainer, the date. Unfortunately, the index was lacking one thing: the names of the racecourses. If Brendan was to track down a winner at Cheltenham, he had absolutely no choice. He would have to read through the lot.

He had one volume for each season, one page per ride. That

Counter Coup

made ten huge leather-bound volumes in all; each of some 600 pages, in a huge heap on the floor of the ranch-house, from which to find the Cheltenham race when he'd encountered the fat man in the winners' enclosure. There was no-one he could trust to help him. He had to do it himself. Still, Brendan thought, trying to force a smile, he didn't have a lot else to do.

Cheltenham 1993. It couldn't be that one. He'd been going well in second place approaching the tricky downhill fence three out when the jockey on the leader pulled a fast one and gave his horse a nudge, just as he was about to take off. 'Prom until f 3 out'. Cheltenham 1994. It couldn't be that year either. It was a winner all right, by a hard-fought neck: 'led until hdd 2 out, ro under stng ride flat to lead on line'. But it couldn't be that because that one had been owned by the Queen Mother herself. Men such as the one he was looking for weren't, even in these democratic days, likely to get within the same unsaddling enclosure as HM the Queen Mother.

The more he searched, the more hopeless it seemed. All that he knew was that the man had managed to get himself with the winner into the unsaddling enclosure. But that hardly narrowed it down much. There were the owners, sometimes as many as twelve to a horse. There were the owners' husbands, sons and friends, and their daughters' friends. There were the trainers of course, and the stable lads. There was the press, hanging around in the hope of a quote or a hint for the future. And there always seemed to be a few others too, who were not quite attached to anyone but who somehow in the excitement of the moment managed to infiltrate themselves into the winning crowd.

'Come on,' Brendan said to himself. 'This is no bloody good!' and braced himself to start again on a new tack.

The best detectives, like the best jockeys, are the ones who take the most pains. If he was to get anywhere Brendan knew he had to put in the work. Be systematic, he thought. Let's get the Cheltenham races first. Then the winners. Then the dates.

In most cases, the cutting told him which was Cheltenham. Besides, 109 winners notwithstanding, it was not every day that you booted one home at Britain's premier jump venue . Quite a few of them, Brendan found with satisfaction, he could remember perfectly clearly, not just the horse but the race and the connections too.

He marked each such race in his books with a little post-it note. He scrutinised the cuttings to see if, by chance, a photo such as the one Dodgson had given him was taken from the racing press. But if it was, then Dodgson would surely have tracked it down himself. Though he hoped for the best, he feared the worst.

1993 took him three hours. 1994, the year he won his first Champion Hurdle on King's Mill, took four. He calculated that at this rate, leaving an hour a day for eating and six hours a night for sleeping, three of the fourteen days he had left would be spent in this way. In his mind's eye, but only too vividly, he saw the day when he got the life ban creeping ever closer. Tanya returned from her father's, full of love and solicitations, while Brendan could manage only a half-friendly grunt.

Counter Coup

'Are you getting anywhere,' she asked gently, bringing him a cup of tea.

'Nothing so far.'

'You will.'

'Not at this rate.'

'Can I help?' Tanya stroked his forehead.

'I don't see how. You don't know the people round the courses like I do. I've just got to keep going.'

'You'll find them, but come to bed soon. You're still not as fit as you'd like to be and a little TLC might do you good.' Tanya offered, but her half-hopeful call to him went in one ear and out the other.

Time did not exactly fly in the small hours before he collapsed, exhausted, for a few hours on the leather sofa.

Tanya had been right, he realised in the early dawn, when he rose stiffly with his injured shoulder screaming after the distorted sleep. He should have gone to bed with her.

Henry rang. Brendan asked Tanya to put him off until he had something definite to report.

Becky rang. He asked Tanya to tell her too that he'd get back. Tanya did as she was told but there was something in her voice, a slight frost towards Lord Brecon's daughter. Brendan knew only too well that Tanya had often had plenty of good reasons to be jealous. She clearly wondered if his relationship with the lawyer really was entirely professional. He would have liked to be in a position to test the theory himself. Not now, though. For now he needed all the allies he could find and he needed them to realise it.

'What's she like?' Tanya asked.

It would have helped if he could have answered that she was round as an apple, forty-three and with six children.

'Very fierce,' he said instead, 'on the skinny side.'

Tanya's look was old-fashioned.

Noakes, the policeman, rang to say that he had spoken to Dodgson and he would not need to call Brendan for questioning until he was finished with the Jockey Club. No charges were being brought yet, but that was not to say that they wouldn't be. He and Dodgson went way back and he'd take his advice as to whether Brendan deserved pursuing further or not.

Gressop rang. He did not like to kick a man when he was down but Brendan would understand: an agent in his position not only had to be clean but had to be seen to be clean. Their relationship was therefore hereby terminated, as a letter from his solicitors would shortly confirm.

Futtnam rang, and laughed a maniacal, vengeful laugh into the phone, until Brendan slammed down the receiver. Apart from that, the phone which normally chirruped with rides to come and gossip to enjoy, remained ominously silent. A letter from his building society asked when it might expect this month's payment.

When he had taken a break from the trawl through his archives he returned Becky's call as he'd promised. Just his luck. It was Friday and the magistrates were in the middle of hearing her heart-rending plea on behalf of a Brixton bad boy who had been caught offering half an ounce of grass to a plainclothes copper.

Counter Coup

He rang Brecon, but by then His Lordship was racing with the Old Lady.

As for Tanya, she had tired of acting as his unpaid secretary, especially when the task seemed to include dealing with his new girlfriend. Whether she seriously believed he was having an affair already or not, she had decided that she was surplus to his immediate requirements and went off to see her family again, this time without leaving his dinner in the oven.

The immediate prospect facing him was pretty clear. He would have to sit all afternoon, in a ranch house he could no longer pay for, with a pile of information that was probably not of the least use to anyone, all afternoon, until one of his few remaining supporters was free to talk to him about it.

Despair was not an emotion that was familiar to Brendan. Suicide was a notion that didn't come readily to a life-loving man like him. But somehow the loneliness and the isolation were eating away at the natural sunniness of his character. Having thought of suicide once, when the life ban was threatened, he thought of it again that afternoon. The garden hose, the car in the garage, a few minutes with the engine on full throttle, and he'd not have to go on with the shreds of what used to be his life. It looked temptingly like the best way out.

The more he thought of it, however, the more determined he was that this wouldn't happen. He was not intending to bow before injustice. He hadn't become champion jockey by giving up when the going got tough.

However hard it might seem, however few the clues and however thin the evidence, he was going to find that man in

David Lipsey

Dodgson's photograph – the man who was standing by the second last fence in Bangor. From this man he would find out what had happened. He was going find out from him why what had happened had happened. And, God willing, he was going to clear his name. He now had just ten days to do it.

Chapter 9

No-one could have helped Brendan with the task of going through the 109 races, scouring the cuttings for clues as to the identity of the mystery man. It was slow laborious work, and Brendan had finished only another three years' worth before he finally retired to his bed that night.

It was a complete waste of time. He knew precisely as little when he finished as when he had started. A picture of the man existed. Dodgson had given him one. But that alone wasn't a great deal of help. There must be a dozen photographers in every winner's enclosure, every day of the week – and more at a big race course like Cheltenham. They would take hundreds of shots, of which only a few would ever see the light of day.

That was not the end of the story. Every race nowadays was televised, and more than once. As well as the old terrestrial channels, and the dedicated Racing Channel, there was the service which was beamed to the betting shops, SIS. There was also the service that was available to the racecourse, for the use of the stewards and which provided videos to owners and trainers, so they could take a record of their triumph home with them. Dodgson's picture could be taken from any of these sources. It could easily be a video grab.

That started Brendan's tired mind working again. For a photograph was a one-off, and likely as not would exclude people who were present. If, however, he could get hold of the videos of the race at Cheltenham, it might be a different story. The cameras panned hither and thither. It might easily at some point have caught the man he wanted. After all, he himself had caught his first glimpse of him in that charming video he had been sent of the race at Bangor.

All he needed was a set of videos of the 109 races and time to look. But from where? Not the BBC, nor Channel Four, its successor in conventional coverage of Cheltenham. He was not sure that either would go back far enough. And they were most unlikely to have made and saved coverage of the many, many races at Cheltenham which they hadn't broadcast.

Nor was he likely to get much cooperation from SIS. An approach from him for help was likely to be as welcome as a hailstorm on the beach. Allegations were still festering that it was the bookmakers who had paid Brendan to fall off. Though individual bookmakers knew that it was not them, they did not know that it was not a rival bookmaker. And the more the mud was stirred, the less confident in their integrity Joe Soap down the betting shop was likely to feel.

Counter Coup

Anyway, sentiment towards Brendan was not exactly warm among the bookmaking fraternity. They were glad that he had been warned off, since he had cost them plenty of money in their time, and they were glad that no-one had yet proved that his offence had been perpetrated at their instigation. The last thing they wanted to see was the case reopened. They wanted to forget Brendan as soon as possible – forever.

He could of course give Mr. Dodgson and Mr. Simmonds a ring, and ask for access to the Jockey Club archives. But not only was this a call that he would not enjoy making; he had a sneaking suspicion that they were on balance unlikely to hand over to him a pile of their most precious evidence. Besides, if he found the evidence in their archives, it would suggest some dereliction of duty on their part in failing to find it themselves. Their employers might not be amused.

So where on earth was he going to find the 109 tapes of the full proceedings in every race he had ever ridden on at Cheltenham? He brooded in despair. Perhaps Aunt Doris would have the answer. He emailed.

The answer came back promptly. 'How about Phil?'

Now the old dear really had taken leave of her senses. Who the hell was Phil?

Brendan couldn't think of a single Phil, until, in an abrupt and meaningful way, the penny dropped.

Phil Cowcross, the brains behind the nation's most successful tipsters.

David Lipsey

*****

Brendan was not sure that the head of Trueform would still be taking his calls but he had to try. Certainly, he and Phil had been friends. That was saying something, because Phil did not have so many friends. Admirers, yes; of those he had a plenty. You couldn't help but admire a man who could tell you from memory what weight the seventh in a selling hurdle at Sedgefield had carried 17 years ago. He had made a fortune backing the horses he had selected from the form book. Then, when one by one the bookmakers closed all his accounts, he made another fortune selling his expertise to punters.

Trueform had more competition these days. The *Racing Post* contained more information about each race than its predecessors had about a whole meeting. With the competition, Trueform's staff had grown too, until some fifty well-paid analysts were now crammed into its offices, working day and night to spot winners. Yet it survived, and even thrived. It survived because Phil had something beyond a great memory and a devoted analytical intelligence. Phil had genius.

Genius, however, can often be accompanied by other, less palatable qualities. Phil did not suffer fools gladly. He didn't think the opinions of others rated respect, unless they coincided with his own. And in an industry that thrived on gossip and doings just this side of the dividing line between right and wrong, Phil could not stand anything that hinted at cheating in his beloved sport.

His tool was the form book, the record of horses' past

Counter Coup

performances. Any hanky-panky that made the form book lie would incur the full heat of his wrath. It was not a popular stance. As few in racing were as Simon-pure as he was, few in racing had not at one time or another had their differences of opinion with Phil. And he never hesitated to parade his opinions, in purple prose, in public print.

Phil was only 5'6". He smoked and he drank and he did not look like a man who was in the habit of jogging. Even so, Brendan trembled to think what he would do to a bent jockey, for example, riding a certain winner, who deliberately fell off. It wasn't going to be an easy phone call to make. But Brendan had no alternative.

'Phil Cowcross, please,' he said, a touch more tensely than would have been ideal.

Phil's secretary responded with a touch of frost. 'Mr. Donoughue, is it? I'm not sure Mr. Cowcross is in.'

Brendan thought he heard something *sotto voce* that just might have been, 'to you, you bastard'.

There was a delay, the sound of muffled voices, a receiver being picked up without Phil's usual gruff greeting. There was nothing for it, Brendan thought, but to plunge in.

'Phil, I need your help. Before you ask, I did nothing wrong. I just need to prove it.' Still, there was silence. 'Remember that afternoon,' Brendan urged, 'when I came up to see you in your office in Bradburn? The time you showed me round? The evening we drank the local bistro clean out of champagne? Well, unlike you, I don't remember everything about that outing. But I do remember the archives you showed me. Every foot of coverage of every race, you told me: digitalised, indexed, sorted. Well, I need to use them. If I'm ever to ride again.'

'Brendan,' said Phil's voice surprisingly softly. 'I've watched that Bangor race a dozen times. I have to say it doesn't improve with study.'

Brendan braced himself. He could not expect Phil of all men to mince his words.

Phil's attitude sounded very similar to Gressop, the agent's. 'A man in my position has to watch out. For thirty years everyone has known that I steer clear of the crooked side of this business. That's why they trust me. If I were seen helping you, the tongues would wag. And besides anything else, I don't want to see fifty people here lose their jobs.'

Brendan heard Phil grunt, in the grip of fierce emotion. 'There's another thing you don't want to hear. A friend of mine, a very good friend of mine, took my advice and had forty monkeys on the Robber with an Internet bookmaker who hasn't yet sussed him out in Gibraltar. The value stood out on my ratings: seven pounds in hand, not bad for a 40/1 shot. Forty times £500: no tax; I make that twenty grand don't you? And I have to say, Brendan, my very good friend doesn't like giving bookmakers money.'

'Phil, I didn't want anybody to be a loser,' Brendan stuttered. 'But you have to believe me. I don't know what happened. I don't know why I came off. All I know is that I wanted to win that race and something went wrong.'

There was another silence. It might have been five

Counter Coup

seconds, though it seemed to Brendan more like five hours. He hoped that Phil was thinking about the race he had won for him at the Festival meeting in 1997 flogging home a brute of a shirker that under any other jockey would have been beaten the length of the proverbial street.

He remembered why he had had Phil for a friend when so many others didn't: his conviction that this was a man to whom loyalty mattered. Now was the time to test his theory. Now was the time for Phil to return the favour.

At last, the answer came. 'I don't want you driving in your state,' Phil said, though hardly softening his voice. 'I'll meet you at the station. The 14:13, and I'll book you into the Grand.'

*****

Bradburn is the sort of town of which they say it's good to get out of. The Dales countryside around attracts walkers from all over the world, when the farmers haven't managed to have it shut against foot-and-mouth. You could be in your office at five o'clock and half way up a deserted hill at six, though P. Cowcross was more likely to be in a bar.

The town itself was a different matter. The centre was done up in the mid '60s under a Labour leader of the council who may or may not have been in the pay of the developer. It was done again in the '80s by a Tory leader who didn't need to be in the pay of the developer, since he was the developer. He went spectacularly bust, caught by the Lamont hike in interest rates of the early 1990s. And since then there had not exactly been a queue of people waiting to take his place.

Urban revival under the new government had not yet reached Bradburn. The grimy estates and the broken-down tower blocks that surrounded the centre provided little custom to the shops. Hardly anyone went to the brave new civic theatre despite its programme of Alan Ayckbourn and one-man shows featuring men who had once played a barman in Coronation Street. Anyone with cash who lived in Bradburn watched telly and went to the out-of-town mall.

Phil could have afforded to have his headquarters anywhere. Some would have thought it quixotic to choose the town in England which, bar Penzance, was furthest from any decent racecourse. But Phil's mother had lived in one of those tower blocks, and he wasn't going to spit in her face just because he'd made a few million. After all, he had no-one else but her.

The 14:13 arrived half an hour late. The passenger service comfort manager announced that this was due to a shortage of drivers. A sign on the platform announced that it was due to 'operational difficulties'. Brendan remembered why he usually drove and tried to remember why on earth the government had privatised British Rail in the first place.

Phil Cowcross was waiting, the usual fat cigar hanging over his long red beard. So was the Rolls Royce, with the *Racing Channel* keeping him up with the action in the back.

Brendan shook Phil's hand, now with warmth, and he knew that, so far as Phil was concerned, on reflection, if Brendan said he hadn't done anything wrong he hadn't.

Soon they were in the basement of Trueform's

Counter Coup

headquarters. They were comfortably ensconced in director's chairs, cigars on one table, Taitinger on the other because Phil knew they could be there a little while. In the four hours Brendan had taken to get to Bradburn, the tapes had been found, sorted, and put together in a single compilation by the technical whiz-kids who helped preserve Trueform's edge.

In more normal times, Brendan would have enjoyed reliving every one of those 109 winners. The highs of racing are like no other highs, especially if you can enjoy them without having to endure the lows too. But the Dodgson-Simmonds clock was ticking away. There was no reason to expect the mystery man to appear while the races were being run. They had to fast-forward the videos as quickly as possible to the unsaddling enclosure if they were to get done in reasonable time.

There was nothing in the first five seasons. The sixth was the Festival when Brendan had won the Queen Mother Champion Chase, the Champion Hurdle and the Gold Cup by less than two lengths in aggregate. Nothing. The Mackeson meeting. Nothing.

Then he turned to the New Year meeting. Brendan remembered the race well enough. The four-miler was one of the most gruelling races in the calendar, even when the going was good. In the torrential rain that had made the course almost unraceable that day, it was an ordeal for man and beast. Bolshoi needed blinkers and the whip to keep him going at the best of times; which this was not. This was racing in the raw.

Brendan was hard at work with a circuit to run, twelve

lengths down at the top of the hill and four down at the last. But Bolshoi, though incurably lazy, was also fundamentally brave. He wore down an unfortunate creature from the bogs carrying all Ireland's cash on it, and won going away.

That day, Brendan did not so much dismount as topple off after he got back to the winners' enclosure. The saddle weighed a ton. He could barely stagger with it to weigh in.

The owners were enthusiastic as they should have been, but it took all Brendan's remaining strength to manage the smiles and the nods that they deserved. Especially the smile and the nod to the fat, nondescript middle-aged man, hanging around the back of the group but with a face that said he had won more than few bob.

'That's him,' Brendan gasped.

Phil Cowcross sat forward, scratching his beard and peered hard at the screen. He recognised perhaps two-thirds of the people in the picture: the trainer, the lad, and most of the owners. Not much worse a crew, as he recalled it, than most of those syndicates of Midland builders - and a great deal better than the hunting, shooting, fishing, racing crew who used to monopolise Cheltenham's best races. But the man at the back did not ring a bell.

Nor did he for Brendan.

They had got near. Yet they were still a long way from where they needed to be.

Phil paused. Then he opened the cigar box. Alongside the giant Havanas sat a miniscule mobile phone.

'Jane? Phil. Is Richard in? Send him down to the archive

Counter Coup

suite. Now, if you can.'

If Richard Potts had had Phil's genius, he would have been the greatest tipster in the history of racing. Phil could remember what weight the Sedgefield seventh carried all those years ago. Richard could tell you what place he had been at the first, second, third flights of hurdle, his time to half-way, the distance between him and every one of his rivals at the finish, and whether the wind had been westerly or easterly that day. If you had Richard on the staff you barely needed an archive suite at all.

Unlike most such racing *savants*, Richard could remember other things as well. Like the face and name of every individual he had ever come across on a racecourse, where they lived, their phone number, their wife's name, their mistresses' name and the name of the boozer they retired to when they wanted to be absolutely sure that no-one could find them. Jockeys' wives relied on Richard to help retrieve their husbands when they strayed. In return, they would supply him with their husband's pillow tips.

Only in racing would a man like Richard have found a niche. Only in racing would his shyness have been tolerated for the rich rewards it could yield.

'Who's that?' Phil asked, pointing at the man at the back of the unsaddling enclosure. It did not sound as if he was in any doubt that he'd get the answer.

'That?' Richard muttered, as he peered at the screen through old-fashioned health service spectacles, which looked as if they could do with a clean. 'That's Kantor. Mike Kantor.'

David Lipsey

He nodded to himself, certain. 'We haven't seen him for a few years,' he went on. 'You remember, Phil, he was all over the papers for that bit of business with the jockey and the two tarts and the snuff box of cocaine. The story hit the *News of the World*, if I remember rightly, the day after your birthday, Brendan.'

Brendan grinned. It had been a story with all the ingredients for a good read in bed on a cold January morning.

Richard Potts had more. 'Of course, that wasn't the first time he'd come to the attention of the authorities. He had previous. The old guard at the Jockey Club security department weren't like these new blokes they have now: all tough talk and no old-fashioned memory. They knew him like the back of their hands. It was pinning anything on him that was their problem. You wouldn't call an eel slippery if you'd met Kantor. Thank goodness for the *News of the World*.'

Once Richard started, it was not easy to get him to stop. The shyness fell away. 'There was talk of bringing him before the disciplinary committee, even prosecuting. But Kantor got himself one of those lawyers who prefer defending the guilty because they can charge more. They threatened the *News of the World* with a libel action, accused them of fiddling the evidence. And in truth the two lads from the *Screws* had, shall we say, taken steps to improve the quality of the tape.

'You wouldn't exactly call what appeared in the next week's paper an apology, but it's not the kind of situation which has the Crown Prosecution Service licking its lips. The Jockey Club generally has more guts than that, but it was one of those

Counter Coup

periods when they were under attack. Discretion before valour, eh?

'There was a lot of toing and froing and the last I saw Kantor was pictured getting on a plane with an Armani jacket heaving over his paunch, shades the size of dinner plates, and three young ladies who wouldn't have been as old as he was between them. South of France, he was off to, if memory serves. Somewhere near Nice – Grasse, maybe?'

'Have a cigar,' said Phil.

David Lipsey

Chapter 10

If all airports were like Nice, Brendan thought, air travel would be even more popular. There had been the usual grey take off from Gatwick and then the usual half-glimpses of a grey channel through the cloud. But just past Paris things had started to look up. The last part of the flight, high above the Alps (white-tipped even in late summer), before turning in low with all Cannes laid out beneath, was breathtaking. It was all Brendan could do to resist another of those little bottles of champagne that the attendants kept offering.

As the plane banked for the final approach, the manoeuvre forced Becky's upper arm tantalisingly close up against his. Why she had so readily agreed to come with him, he wasn't entirely sure. Was it because she fancied a touch of sun, or that she fancied a touch of danger?

How good it would have been if she had fancied him, though he doubted that was an option. Anyway, come she had, and he

Counter Coup

couldn't have been more pleased to have her with him.

French officialdom, unlike British officialdom, seemed to have realised that the European Union existed. Brandishing their little red passports, Becky and Brendan did not even have to break stride as the gendarmerie waved them through. Even so, their baggage was on the carousel before they reached it. They queued the usual half-hour at the car hire desk as the clerk made them suffer by crawling over the paperwork. Brendan pondered to himself why it was that in France the public sector worked and the private sector didn't - the exact opposite of Britain.

The wait hardly mattered. Brendan and Becky knew they had to go to Nice as soon as they'd mulled over Richard's intelligence and weighed up their options. That was Kantor's last known destination and they had nothing else to go on. What exactly they were going to do when they got there, they didn't know for sure.

Even Richard Potts had been unable to provide an address there for Kantor. His interests tended to stop at Dover. Miss Burgess, after Lord Brecon's request, had managed to borrow a Nice telephone directory from the French embassy, saying she needed it for a delegation of Peers to the Council of Europe. She trawled through every possible variation of Kantor's spelling without success. Like most people on the seedy edge of betting, Michael Kantor was evidently ex-directory, or living under an AKA.

Brendan and Becky knew that Grasse was no longer a small town with a few perfume factories. The ancient centre was surrounded now by an industry that smelt even sweeter to the greedier natives than perfume: tourism. So far as the eye could see, down half-way to the bay below, the lower slopes of Grasse were largely one big suburban sprawl of villas. Parisians, Germans, Italians, above all the English were all there. Becky and Brendan needed to find just one of them.

They knew very little about Kantor, other than he'd settled in Grasse, and he smoked. They could, they supposed, tour the *tabacs* of the area asking if they knew a fat, English smoker. Becky swiftly calculated that if they did fifty of them in a day, they would be halfway through by the time the Dodgson and Simmonds ultimatum expired.

Fat, there was a thought. How about the restaurants? On reflection, that did not seem likely to yield swift results. There was a restaurant every few metres and they did not have a clue where Kantor's gastronomic tastes lay.

The English were known to enjoy their golf. But with a belly like that, Kantor could hardly hope to raise a club. There were the beaches but surely even he would be too ashamed to expose his whale-like physique.

They even thought of putting out a request on Radio Riviera. That Nice and environs should support an English language radio station however only underlined that they were looking for a needle in a haystack. Anyway, it seemed unlikely that Mike Kantor, hearing a request for him to ring a certain number, would conclude that he was about to hear something to his advantage.

They were stuck before they started, in theory, but Becky

Counter Coup

had the legendary Tregwynn optimism and refused to be daunted by Brendan's accurate but dismal reasoning.

As they waited in the car hire office for the company to finish cleaning their vehicle, Brendan leafed idly through *Nice Matin*. It didn't take him long. He could just about make out the symbols on the weather forecast: all yellow suns down the Riviera where the rest of Europe was black clouds and rain. But the words were something else. He had a distant recollection that someone had tried to teach him French at school. Otherwise, how did he know to say *merci beaucoup* when he rode a winner for a French trainer? But that was all he remembered. He would have to rely on the fact that Becky, who had spent three months at the Sorbonne, was fluent.

His phone bleeped. Aunt Doris again. She never left off.

'Good journey? Going racing?' the text read.

That hadn't occurred to him. But a lot of things that had occurred to Aunt Doris hadn't to him and they invariably turned out to be good ideas. He grinned, showed the message to Becky, and leafed through *Nice Matin* with a good deal more purpose.

A racing card is a racing card in any language. Of course, the card for Cagnes-sur-Mer was far from identical with that for, say, Royal Ascot. Though the racecourse, he knew, had both grass and dirt flat tracks, and even an attractive jumping circuit, the local speciality was trotting.

The oddities of trotting form were immediately apparent. For some reason that Brendan could not fathom, the name of every horse began with the same letter. There was no handicap

David Lipsey

in the sense of a list of the weights each horse could carry. Instead, some horses got ten, twenty, thirty metres start. There were no bookmakers' prices, because in France, bookmaking was illegal. There were, however, estimates of the likely return on the *pari mutuel*, France's Tote. Page after page was devoted to the *Tiercé*, France's favourite bet requiring punters to predict the first five home in a tricky handicap. Brendan thought he would prefer to stick to the Tote's home-grown Scoop Six.

As Brendan struggled with the mysteries, one little corner of his mind must have had some thinking space left. If you were looking for a racing man, where else would you look but on a racecourse? Especially a man who clearly liked a bet, but was under suspicion in his native land. The South of France after all was full of shady characters. Kantor would barely stand out.

No doubt the English Jockey Club had warned their French counterpart, *La Societé pour 'l'Encouragement* of their suspicions about Kantor. But the two groups, British racing and French racing, were rivals as much as friends. Neither was all that enthusiastic about the other's security arrangements. It was entirely possible that his past had not followed Kantor to the shores of the Mediterranean.

If their luck was in, Kantor could be racing at Cagnes that very afternoon.

'It's a long shot,' said Becky, who had begun to hope that perhaps their first step might be to consider their options in the sun on the beach at Cannes.

Counter Coup

'This whole bloody quest is a long shot,' replied Brendan tartly.

*****

Racing wasn't due to start for another 90 minutes, and the course was only a quarter of an hour from the airport. That didn't leave time to find a hotel but shortly their rented Citroen Visa was making its entry into the huge car-park at Cagnes-sur-Mer.

Brendan visited racecourses every day of the week. He knew the rhythm of the day, the slow start, the build-up as the horses and the trainers and the jockeys arrived, and finally, their public. He did not expect Cagnes to be exactly pulsating at that hour. But this! He had known more atmosphere watching the hearse arrive for a funeral. Horse lorries trundled in and were unloaded. The lads did not smile. Nor did security on the gate. Nor did the old crone who let them in for a negligible number of francs.

The track looked lovely; no expense spared. That was what you got with a State monopoly on betting, whereby all the profits were ploughed back into the sport. That was what English racing would be like, if the British Horseracing Board got its way and the bookmakers were made extinct. But there was another way of looking at it that appealed to Brendan. Why should the poor punter in the betting shop subsidise the rich man's hobby? It was just another example of racing's snobbery that it despised punters as much as it despised

David Lipsey

bookmakers.

You got no row of bookmakers in France. You got no shouting of the odds. You got no characters. You got... Well, you got practically nothing.

There was no sign of Kantor.

The horses paraded in silence for the first race. Their owners were dressed up to the nines. But only the bright colours of the ladies' couture distinguished them from funeral guests. The horses went down to the post in silence. The commentator announced that they had started, to silence. And when, four minutes later, they paced off the final bend, whips cracking, four in line, 200 metres to the post and not one of them breaking out of the trot into a gallop, the crowd watched them in silence. Once they were past the post some went to get a drink and some to queue for their winnings, in silence.

Brendan searched the bars with Becky. By the time they had finished, Brendan had absorbed a few Pernods but there was no sign of Kantor. They looked in the queues. Perhaps there was something in the *tabac* idea after all. The kiosk was situated at the end of the grandstand, on the way to the paddock. Brendan asked for five cigars. Becky asked, with a passable trace of a Marseilles *patois*, if they knew a large, fat Englishman, as depicted in the grainy shot of Kantor at Cheltenham that Brendan produced.

The man shrugged his shoulders. Brendan proffered two hundred francs for his twenty-franc cigars. The man nodded, and became a trifle more expansive.

'*Il y a un homme comme ca, je ne sais pas son nom. Mais*

Counter Coup

il vient seulement les soirs.'

A man who comes only in the evenings? Of course! Brendan had forgotten. On Saturdays in the season Cagnes-sur-Mer held a second meeting under floodlights as well as the one during the day. It seemed they'd wasted the afternoon.

'Come on,' said Becky. 'Even you're bored, and you *like* racing.'

Brendan reluctantly agreed. 'So what do you suggest?'

'For one thing, you'll feel much better for a spot of sun on that poor old shoulder of yours.'

'You think so?'

'I do. And for another, I've been running around after you since dawn.'

'Sorry.'

'Don't be - but we are on the Med and I want to feel like it. Until your man starts watching horses, I'm going to be spread out on the beach.'

Brendan scanned her figure with more enthusiasm than he had felt all day. 'You've got something to wear then?'

Becky grinned, 'I might have and I might not. But then again this is the South of France.'

'So you don't mind going...'

'...and there are shops,' Becky announced firmly.

*****

Cagnes-sur-Mer at night was not the same as Cagnes-sur-Mer by day. By day, the racing was confined to the trotters. By night, out came the steeplechasers. That was more to Brendan's taste than the trotting. However, that apart, Cagnes wasn't much more of a pulsating hot-spot when it opened again at 8pm. Brendan guessed that most people preferred to go straight from the beach to the casino.

It wasn't hard to spot Kantor, lounging round the enclosures. He was wearing a linen suit that had clearly been cut for him by the kind of tailor who is practiced at minimising fat men's curves. He was sucking on the usual cigar.

Having found him, however, it was not clear what followed. Was Brendan to sidle up to him and ask him what he had been doing at the second-last fence on a racecourse in a country in which he no longer lived? He was not sure that he would get a helpful answer.

Then they noticed the two men following Kantor. In truth, it would have been hard not to notice them. They were as tall as he was short. They had shoulders which would be the envy of any prop forward. Their white suits were intended to advertise their presence. And anyone up to something would guess from the bulges that they were carrying something more than wallets in their breast pockets.

Introducing himself to Kantor was one thing. Introducing himself to these two characters would be another. Brendan was no coward, but even if his shoulder had been sound, discretion would have beaten valour - easily. Still, a cat can look at a king, and for the next few hours Becky and Brendan tried to look as inconspicuous as alley cats as they stalked their quarry.

Counter Coup

Kantor, it was clear, was not there just to soak up the atmosphere. Ten minutes before each race, one of his white-jacketed attendants would join one of the Pari-Mutuel queues. Sometimes, he would reach the head but nothing happened: a murmured *pardon* and he would slip back to join the boss. But sometimes, at the last moment, Kantor would join him. His inside pocket contained a different kind of ammunition. Drawing out a thick wad of francs, he would plonk them down in front of the clerk, together with his instructions, in a sort of amalgam of Brum and French.

Of course, he could not have done that in Britain. Big punters tended not to use the Tote pool. The way pools work all the money bet is added together, a deduction is made to pay expenses and profit, and the rest is then divided up among the winning punters. This did not appeal to the big players, because some of the money they won would inevitably be their own.

In France, however, there was no alternative. It was consequently the recipient of big bets as well as small. And nobody cared if something crooked was up. For the clerks, it was all the same to them – the *pari mutuel* took its share of every bet, irrespective of whether it was from a punter who knew something, like Kantor, or a punter who didn't. That he was going home with a great many francs belonging to the small guys round Cagnes-sur-Mer did not matter a stuff .

On the first seven races that night, Kantor had four bets in all. One fell when clear. One was beaten a short-head when his jockey ran into traffic problems in the straight. The other two won with their heads in their chests.

Had French racing employed plods, they'd have had to be hopelessly thick not to appreciate that something was going on. After all, Kantor was the gossip of the bars. But French racing too had gone over to a different kind of security staff, which preferred bugging phones to bugging bar conversation. And a man like Kantor had not got where he was today by blagging about his doings on the phone.

It was fascinating to observe. Still, it didn't really get Brendan and Becky very far. It told them only what they already knew, that Kantor was a man on the inside track who would make a lot of money out of betting.

Idly, they left him and wandered over to the parade ring. The next was a claiming hurdle, for four year-olds and upwards. The paddock was filled with representatives of the *selle francais,* the special French breed that has done so well in Britain over the last few years. Indeed, only one runner to Brendan's tutored eye, looked like an English thoroughbred. *Tout La Nuit* was a fine stamp of a horse, a flashy chestnut, nearly seventeen hands high and looking fit as a fiddle.

Brendan grabbed Becky's arm.

'What?' she asked.

'That horse. He reminds me of one I rode'.

'Which one?'

'The one I'm thinking off was a four year old - Outlaw Express. I won the Triumph Hurdle on him two years ago.'

Becky looked at the chestnut more carefully, not that she expected to learn anything. 'So what had happened to Outlaw?'

Counter Coup

'Don't know,' Brendan admitted, 'I never rode him again. He had a bit of a leg problem, it was reported, too good to rush. He's meant to be enjoying a good cosy feed.

The horse turned to walk towards Brendan. Then he saw a scar on the foreleg, now perfectly heeled.

There could be no doubt about it. It was the same scar as on Outlaw Express.

'Bloody hell, it *is* Outlaw Express.' he hissed at Becky.

'How can you be sure?'

'I know horses the way you know men.'

'Oh, thanks.'

Brendan ignored her protest. 'That scar. He could beat any of this lot by a hundred yards on three legs.'

He glanced down at his card. *Tout La Nuit,* a trainer he'd never heard of from a yard he'd never heard of, with an apprentice jockey he'd never heard of, but all with impeccably French names. *Tout La Nuit* was having his first run in public, no mention, of course of any former name.

'He's a ringer,' said Brendan. 'He was one of the best juvenile hurdlers England had seen in years.'

'Why's he here?' Becky asked. Clearly her father's horse sense had not been passed down to her.

'Why do you think? Because someone's about to pull off the gambling coup of a lifetime, and I can guess who. Come on.'

He tugged at Becky's arm, and ran back to the *pari mutuel* window. Kantor's gopher was just reaching the head of the queue.

David Lipsey

Kantor stepped forward, brushing his man aside. But this was not the wad that they had seen him with before. It dwarfed it. It was a whole handful of French bank notes that Kantor was carrying - 200 franc note on top of 200 franc note. There were thousands of them. It wouldn't do a lot for the price, Brendan thought, but better a short priced certainty than a long priced loser.

Brendan itched to get closer. But the more he observed the men in white suits, the more he concluded that a conversation with Kantor was a conversation better postponed.

Moments later and they were off. It was not a race. It was a procession. Outlaw Express's jockey had been ordered not to risk letting anything get in the way. He was ten lengths clear at the first, a distance ahead by half way; hard-held, jumping smoothly, enjoying his work, as he always did, even when the going was a lot tougher than tonight.

Only a fall at the last could rob him now.

He did not fall at the last. The apprentice chose sensibly to pop it, and pop it he did, nice and neat. It wouldn't have been the quickest jump in the world nothing like the leap Brendan conjured out of him over the last at Cheltenham when he'd won his Triumph, but it was quite enough to settle his one-paced rivals.

Kantor hadn't bothered to watch. He did not even smile as the result was confirmed. He merely moved himself around to the pay window.

By the time the weigh-in was announced, he was there, at

Counter Coup

the head of the queue, as the cashier began a long, careful count.

Brendan was not used to francs, but he knew enough to know that 650,000 profit was not bad for a night's work – or even for the year's planning that would have preceded it.

After the race, Kantor did not hang about. He walked to the car park where his chauffeur waited, his bodyguards ever watchful.

'Come on,' said Becky, 'this could be the interesting bit.'

Fortunately, Kantor carried enough overweight to make sure he didn't move fast. And Becky wasn't wearing heels. When the big Mercedes pulled out of the car park, the little Citroen wasn't far behind.

'Have you done this sort of thing before?' Brendan asked as Becky shot out into the traffic three cars behind Kantor.

She smiled. 'Not often. I'm a lawyer not a private dick. But enough.'

Even at that time of night, there was a steady line of traffic between the racecourse and Cannes. As Kantor pulled into La Croisette, the Citroen hung back, its lights indistinguishable from any others in the slow moving line.

The moon was casting a pale light over the gently lapping waters of the bay. But Kantor was not the kind of man who cared much for moonlight. He crossed the dual carriageway and pulled up outside on of the more elegant premises on the sea front. Becky drove passed and parked the car in the next side street. They clambered out and walked back.

From the way Kantor conducted himself as he entered *Le*

David Lipsey

Coq d'Argent, it seemed he was expected. He took the best table in the corner, back to the wall, eyes easily scanning the street. The two bodyguards sat at a respectful distance. Becky and Brendan made themselves as comfortable as they could on the low wall opposite.

'Hell, I'm hungry,' muttered Becky.

Brendan glared across the road. 'Could do with a drink too.'

Instead they sat and suffered, watching Kantor.

Fruits de Mer was very much the kind of thing jockeys enjoyed. You could hardly help eat them slowly, what with the cracking , the peeling and the picking out. At the end of it, you achieved a high ratio of appetite satisfaction to calories, which was every jockey's dream. Watching someone else eating, however, was rather less enjoyable.

Brendan groaned as they huddled inconspicuously in the street, and a waiter set a stand beside Kantor's table, followed by something which at first looked simply like a very large tray. Then he laid it on the stand. There were oysters, perhaps a dozen. There were cockles and mussels and limpets and winkles. Half a dozen huge Dublin Bay prawns sat on one side of the tray. Several sea urchins decorated the other. A crab topped the lot.

Then the waiter brought a second stand. It was followed by a second tray, only a little smaller than the first. On it was a crayfish, and a largish lobster. A third tray was needed for the champagne bucket. A fourth held the Chablis.

It was as well that Kantor's table was designed for four,

Counter Coup

because it also had to accommodate a white bowl of yellow mayonnaise, sufficient for three people; a basket containing a couple of cut-up baguettes, potato salad, beetroot salad, celeriac salad, and Russian salad. Also, as a concession to health, there was a plain green salad of dandelion leaves and rocket.

Kantor didn't eat fast. He ate methodically. And he ate everything.

The waiter removed the first tray as his client finished the last of the prawns. He arrived with the cheeses as Kantor stuffed the last of the lobster between his tireless jaws. A host of varied cheeses, unidentifiable from the street outside was accompanied by a bottle of *Chateauneuf-du-Pape*.

As the cheese moved off the first stand, the puddings arrived on the lobster stand. *Mousse au chocolat*, a raspberry *Barvois* and a bowl of *crème brulée* were offered. Kantor carefully selected the lot.

Maybe he was going easy that night. The Sauternes that replaced the champagne was a half-bottle only. He declined the *petit fours* in favour of an Armagnac.

Brendan was used to feeling hungry and thirsty, but Becky felt sick.

David Lipsey

Chapter 11

It was approaching one in the morning when Kantor rose from the wreckage of his meal, like a seal poking his head above the waves. He had paid for his dinner in cash, *pari-mutuel* cash no doubt, Brendan thought, and plenty of it. As he waddled towards the door, he and Becky slipped off the wall and ducked behind it. Kantor's two minders were soon, if unsteadily, on their feet, close behind the master. The purr of the Mercedes coming toward them could soon be heard.

When it drew up beside him, Kantor brushed the chauffeur irritably aside. 'Not now. At 2:30 sharp. *Rue D'Antibes*. And you two can bugger off as well.' The bodyguards nodded and turned back, brushing against Becky as she strolled along the pavement in Kantor's wake.

Kantor walked along the sea front. He hesitated at the doors of the casino before walking in. His followers slowed. Becky took Brendan's arm, comfortable lovers out for the last walk

Counter Coup

of the night.

They spotted Kantor throwing his jacket at a liveried attendant together with a 100 franc note.

Becky and Brendan ambled in, inspecting the casino like the neophytes they were. In the next room they saw Kantor sit down at the blackjack table. An air of expectancy settled around the table.

Kantor wasn't planning to stay long at the casino, but not because he was a loser. Quite the contrary - he had the rare ability to count cards, remembering precisely what had gone and what had not gone. At blackjack that tilted the odds between him and the dealer inexorably in his favour. Long-term, that meant that he would win money. Making sure that no-one wins money in the long run is one thing casinos are devoted to. Card-counting was against the rules.

Kantor had long since been excluded from every casino in London, and he knew it would not be long before he was excluded from every casino in Cannes. His only chance, he understood, was to bet in very small doses, patiently, letting lots of short runs build up to one long run. On occasion, he would lose deliberately and no small sum, betting like a mug punter on speed

Brendan and Becky lurked by the entrance. There was nothing unusual about that. There were many such visitors who either lacked the courage to sample the entertainment within or, more often, were too impecunious. No-one noticed them as they examined the plush wall paper and pushed a few ten franc pieces into slot machines that stood just inside the door.

The blackjack table was not easily visible from where they stood. So after a few minutes, Becky begged the commissionaire for permission to use the toilet. Had Brendan done so, he would assuredly have been told where he could go, and none too gently. But good looks got you a long way in situations like this. A smile and a hand laid gently on the arm secured Becky her request.

As she passed Kantor's table, the dealer had a large pile of chips by his side that he'd scooped from Kantor's box, and they weren't ten franc chips either. Gold chips at a thousand francs a throw were the kind of currency that was noticed even in a casino for big-spenders.

Kantor's pile was already noticeably smaller than the dealer's by the time Becky sidled out of the ladies'. She perched herself against a bar, out of Kantor's eye line but within sight of Brendan feigning interest in the machines in the anteroom. It meant shaking her head firmly from time to time as hopeful men twice her age offered her a drink and a stool next to them but she was practiced at inoffensive refusal.

After an hour or so, Kantor's pile of chips was exhausted. He rose rather unsteadily to his feet, pushing his chair back so firmly that it fell to the ground with a clatter. Without a 'goodnight' he headed for the exit.

He may not have been pleased. No-one likes losing, even if they are doing it deliberately. But he did not forget to leave a big tip for the doorman. This was a town where it did not pay to be a cheapskate.

Counter Coup

Becky followed Kantor closely while Brendan ducked behind a line of slots. He waited for ten seconds then strode out, careful not to catch up with Becky until Kantor had turned a corner.

Kantor struck off north on foot in the direction of the station. The houses remained quite grand even away from the posh hotels and the expensive jewellers of the front, but the shops became gradually less salubrious. Insofar as town the size of Cannes could boast a red light district this was it.

And indeed there was a discrete red light on outside the detached *fin du siecle* house at which Kantor eventually stopped. He looked to his left, and then to his right, and his pursuers were glad of the cover provided by a pair of large dustbins awaiting morning collection. Then he rang the bell.

The lady who emerged was an exotic specimen, even by Cannes standards. She set out to look forty though she might well have been sixty: long black dress with multi-colour sequins and a neck that exposed a dramatic cleavage, three-inch heels, blood-red lips and the kind of tan that requires hours of dedicated lying-about to acquire. She allowed Kantor to kiss both cheeks, no mean manoeuvre given the size of his belly, and then gave him one on the mouth.

'*Mon cher Michel. Et vous voulez Jacqui ce soir, ou Josephine?*'

Kantor replied in his grotesque Brummie French. '*Tout les deux.*' Both. Clearly he was not only a glutton for food.

The door closed, and Brendan and Becky could see no more, until a light came on in a first-floor window. For a few minutes, the pair awaited any move Kantor might make. But his chauffeur wasn't due back until 2:30. It was pretty clear that if they stayed where they were, they weren't going to see Kantor move before then.

Though the curtain was closed, a small chink had been left open at the bottom, just enough, perhaps, to catch a glimpse of the action within. Brendan spotted that Madame had also put out her dustbins, and fortunately they were of solid aluminium. They would have to provide the spying post he needed.

He was aware of every sound: his feet on the drive, the slight squeak of the dustbin as he carried it in front of the window, the metal on metal as he inverted the lid to stand on. He hoped that those inside had other things on their mind.

'See anything?' whispered Becky.

Despite his efforts he could see very little – not, he thought, that he would necessarily want to see very much. He did see a hand. It was clad in a long studded glove, it was female, and the arm to which it was attached was rising and falling methodically. It carried an implement which he too used professionally: a leather whip. He could hear suppressed groans and cries intermingled with sucking sounds that he didn't even want to identify.

It didn't require much imagination to know what was happening in there. But it didn't seem a wise moment to approach Kantor.

There was no point and some risk in remaining on top of the dustbin. As near to silently as he could manage, Brendan

Counter Coup

climbed down and rejoined Becky in the shadows.

The minutes dragged until at 2:29 the Mercedes swung round the corner, one bodyguard in the front, one in the back. At 2:30 precisely, a stiff looking Kantor waddled out of the building, looking as if he'd just spent too long sitting at his desk in the office. One of the bodyguards opened the door, and Kantor slumped on the back seat.

Becky wished she had gone back for their car during the long wait. But it was too late now. Once the bodyguard had ensured that all of Kantor had been shovelled into the Merc, his driver wasted no further time before speeding away into the night. He could be going anywhere.

With the benefit of hindsight, that would have been the time for Becky and Brendan to speed off into the night as well. It was pretty evident from what they had seen that Kantor was a man of regular habits - and there was racing next night too. They could have prepared themselves and come back with a car. Then they would have been in a position to follow Kantor home. But Brendan was a jockey, and jockeys are rarely patient. Besides, he hoped that Kantor held the secrets that would determine whether he had a life left or not. If he didn't, or if they couldn't be got out of him, Brendan would rather know sooner than later.

Grabbing Becky by the arm, he marched up to the front door of the brothel and knocked.

Madame appeared, wreathed in smiles.

'*Mon cher monsieur. Et mademoiselle aussi. Charmante. Sexy.*' Madame looked Becky up and down with professional appreciation. Clearly there was a job on offer if Brendan put her on the market. '*Vous aimez tout les deux le hanky-spanky?*' Becky saw that matters could swiftly lead down a path for which they were not prepared. '*Non Madame, nous cherchons un client.*'

Becky's accent was near flawless, but you didn't become the madam at a leading brothel by not being able to spot accents.

'Looking for a client?' The apparition's countenance darkened, until her face powder practically cracked. 'Fuck off the pair of you,' she said in tones that were unmistakably from one of Glasgow's less healthy quarters.

Behind her, Brendan spotted a pair of large Alsatians. They looked hungry and they were suddenly taking a close interest in proceedings. It was time for a gamble.

'Perhaps you recognise me,' said Brendan.

Even in Cannes a Scottish madam could be expected to have a passing interest in racing. And you would not have needed much of an interest in racing to recognise Brendan Donoughue, even before his recent unwelcome excess of publicity.

She looked at him more closely without giving away whether she knew him or not. 'And if I do - what of it?'

'If you do know who I am, perhaps you wouldn't mind if we discussed it inside for a moment.'

She thought about it. Becky shivered.

'All right. You've come this far.' She nodded them in and closed the door, careful to leave it ajar. 'Any bother and Sheba

Counter Coup

and Cleo there will have your scrawny genitals - and that goes for both of you. What do you want?'

If you are going to lie, lie big. The hardest people often fall for the softest trick. Adopting a polite tone that he usually reserved for the most difficult owners, Brendan plunged in.

'Your gentleman visitor, Mr. Kantor. He's doubtless a kind man.'

'Fuck me, yer joking, aren't you?'

'At least, a generous man,' Brendan pressed.

Madame looked as if Kantor's generosity might not be sufficient to pay for the wear and tear of his attentions on her most promising girls.

'Let's say, a man who by any standards is not short of a bob or two.' Brendan suggested.

At last, Madame half-nodded.

Brendan continued, 'Mr. Kantor is a gambler. But, not to put too fine a point on it, he is not a gambler like other gamblers. Mr. Kantor has a bet only when he is pretty sure that he is going to win. And the reason that he is sure he is going to win is that someone has told him something. As you may have heard, I am not riding just at the moment - a spot of bother with the authorities.'

'I did hear.'

'So you do know who I am, then.' It was a minor victory.

'Perhaps I do.'

'They can take away my licence, but I still know people and they tell me things. Things Mr. Kantor would very much like to know. I'm too closely watched to use the information in

England. Unfortunately my reputation is not what it was. I have to use it outside the country. We can't do these things by phone of course. The Jockey Club seems to manage to tape every single conversation these days. And we don't like to be seen talking to Mike either. Closed-circuit television is everywhere. Even at this time of the morning, Madame. Even here.'

He hoped that Madame might feel that the prospect of being on closed-circuit television was sufficient of an incentive for her to keep her salivating dogs out of things.

'All he needs is the name of a horse, on a bit of paper. All we need to give it to him is an address.'

Madame's look was hardly less suspicious. 'Give the name to me, then. He will be here again tomorrow.'

'Madame, you will understand that in our business, you do not give the name of certain winners to third parties,' Brendan replied. 'They might care to have a bet on themselves. That would tip off the bookmakers that a coup was looming and would spoil the odds for our client. Anyway, he needs the name tonight. The race is tomorrow afternoon. We are not talking peanuts here. He will need to get his team together to get the bets on. Even in England, a ten grand bet takes a bit of sorting out, Madame.'

Brendan was not sure whether he had carried it off or not. For a moment there was a hesitation. Brendan drew a 500 franc note from his pocket, and started to roll it between his fingers.

He soon realised that he had made a mistake. Madame

Counter Coup

looked at him with astonishment. Then she threw back here head and laughed uproariously.

'Laddie, you don't get to run the most popular house in Cannes by giving your clients' addresses to strangers. Not for 500 francs, not for 5,000 francs, not for anything. They come here because they know they are safe here. We wouldn't want anything to happen that changed that. In fact, if we thought anyone was spying on our guest.... You ken these dogs? They hanna had their supper yet. And besides the dogs, there are people around here who would nae be tae friendly to a spy.'

A wiser, more patient man than Brendan would have backed off. Instead, he raised the stakes.

'Look, I don't care what you get up to. If we can do this the civilised way, that's fine by me. But if not; the police would surely be interested to know precisely what you get up to here.'

Now Madame could not contain herself. She did not so much laugh as roar, so Brendan and Becky feared for the tranquility of late-night Cannes. 'Stop, stop. You're makin' me piss myself.' Then she turned behind her and beckoned. 'Ici, inspecteur.'

From a door behind her, someone emerged. He was on all-fours. He was wearing a red jacket such as poodles wear when out for a walk in the rain. It was buckled around his belly so he could scarcely breathe. His dog collar was surrounded by long steel studs, and a whip was tucked into one side.

'Inspector,' she said talking in English since it was the English she wanted to get her message. 'This pair want to talk to the polis about my establishment. Mebbe you'd help them?

And perhaps when you have, you can teach 'em a lesson? Perhaps your colleagues could offer 'em rooms for the night, the concrete ones without chairs or beds or toilets. They might ask 'em a few questions and encourage them in the normal way to give their answers. And if, my dear inspector, you would deal with them in the way I want, I just might have an extra-special treat for you later.' She thrust her hands on her hips and stared at him as if she was not expecting a refusal.

The inspector stood up. He suddenly looked much less comical. He picked a mobile phone out from under his poodle's jacket.

Brendan and Becky swapped glances.

'Madame,' said Becky. 'We had no intention of upsetting you. Naturally, Mr. Kantor will be disappointed not to get his tip. We hope that he does not come to blame you, or your house.'

The door slammed behind them with a bang that did not suggest it would be reopening swiftly.

*****

By now, Becky and Brendan felt they deserved a bit of luck, and they got it. Normally, even in Cannes, the restaurant that Kantor had almost emptied of shell fish would long have been shut by the time they got back to *La Croisette*. But not this time. It was the run-up to that year's autumn film festival, and the town was starting to pack full with big shots who kept peculiar hours. They also ran up peculiar bills, and some

Counter Coup

Cannes establishments stayed open late in the hope of picking up an unexpected share of a whole lot of dollars.

Le Coq d'Argent was still doing respectable business, even if the majority of tables sat empty and the waiters looked dead on their feet.

It occurred to Becky that Kantor would surely have reserved a table at the restaurant at this time of year. And they might, just might, have a note of his telephone number. Becky led the way in, even at three in the morning looking as if she was in the film crowd. She smiled sweetly at the head waiter. 'May we reserve a table for dinner for tomorrow?' she asked with just the right touch of diffidence.

Again their luck held. The bookings were held in a large book, one page per day. Fortunately tomorrow was on the right hand page of today's bookings. They pretended to argue between them what time they should eat: 8:30, 9:00, 9:30. Meanwhile they scanned the page opposite for that night's bookings until they reached '*11:00 Table pour 4. M. Kantor seul.*'

Alongside it, praise be, was what they'd been looking for - a telephone number. You couldn't master a brief in hours the way Becky could without being able to remember a telephone number, even when your heart was beating like a rapper's bass line.

M. Kantor. Residence: 49 55 67 08.

It was not much, but it was enough.

David Lipsey

Counter Coup

Chapter 12

The restaurants in Cannes may have stayed open in the hope of top dollar customers. Its hotels hadn't. That night, their overnight accommodation, assuming that the inspector did not catch up with them, was going to be a choice between the car and the beach. Brendan and Becky chose the beach. They were not alone. Little groups of hippies crowded below the concrete skirt at the top of the sand, fires and joints burning. Between the groups, lay the odd drunk, the last of the French consumers of the *vin ordinaire*. Even the down-and-outs seemed to have rugs to lie on. Brendan and Becky had to make do with two small towels.

The weather had been hot enough during the day. But, that late in the season, there was a chill on the night air. They huddled close to each other for warmth.

Sleep seemed unlikely, and it came but briefly. Only a few minutes seemed to have gone past between the moment they lost consciousness and the moment they were wakened by a roar in their ears. The engines of the giant beach sweepers, removing the last remnants of the rubbish of the night before, had not been designed to be quiet.

Yet the scene they woke to provided some compensation. To their left, a giant orange sun hung low over the palm trees. You could just see the edge of the mountains beyond Nice. To the right, one of the world's most sought-after landscapes stretched away, the Esterel Massif still in partial darkness overlooking the indented coast. It was a pity that they were not here on holiday.

Cannes, they quickly discovered, was not a great centre for public lavatories. Eventually, Becky found an old two-franc piece in her bag and risked getting trapped by going into one of the French round loos with a sliding door. They had only the one coin. Brendan managed to slip in as she slipped out without getting caught in the door.

Neither was Cannes yet open for breakfast. A few workmen were getting into gear, pouring coffee out of flasks and gnawing on *baguettes*. Not many years ago it would have been *un café* and *pastis* in a local *zinc*. No wonder everyone was living so long. No wonder France's pension scheme was going belly up.

The approach to Kantor was not going to be easy. Seeing how he had spent the previous night, they did not think it likely that their cause would be helped by calling him early. Indeed late afternoon might be the best time, after the long sleep he must surely have taken after lunching and before he left for the races. They had time to fill.

Counter Coup

Becky collected the car from its precarious parking spot of the night before and they headed through the town to the railway station. It was early enough to find a space to leave the car and they made for the station bar, the one place guaranteed to be open for coffee and croissants. She bought *Nice Matin* and settled down to read while Brendan settled for *Turf Matin*.

*****

After an hour and three coffees (chased, in Brendan's case with just a small *vin rouge*) they tired of the station. The commuters were beginning to throng the concourse and the shops were opening. It was time for work.

'Thank God for mobiles,' Brendan muttered as he thought of the old alternative: finding a French *Telecarte* and crouching by a public telephone in the station trying to fathom how to make the damn thing work. Besides, the background noise of trains and announcements would hardly help their pitch to Kantor either.

They returned to the car and headed back to the beach, this time finding a space that was at least vaguely legal. Now, they could sit on the sand and make the crucial call in relative comfort, whenever they were ready. There was no hurry. After his exertions of the night before Kantor would not be rising early.

They had gone carefully through the options. They thought that Brendan should make the call, offering inside information on a horse. Then they remembered how that excuse had bombed when they had tried it on Madame, not many hours before, and thought again. They thought of a direct approach. After all it was Kantor's Bangor-on-Dee performance they wanted to find out about, so perhaps they should just ask him. 'Listen, Kantor, we want to talk to you about Bangor-on-Dee.'

Becky ruled that out. 'Kantor's not going to want to talk to a pair of strangers about Bangor-on-Dee.'

'Who says we're strangers?'

'Makes no difference. If he knows anything at all he certainly won't talk on the phone to the jockey who had lost his job as a result of what happened there.'

A deception was needed. While they considered the options, they had to decide who should do the deceiving. Brendan pointed out Becky's qualifications.

'You're a lawyer. All lawyers are liars, by profession.'

'Thanks a lot. And what about jockeys? Professional liars from their caps to their arses. All the lies you tell to owners who are in danger of discovering that the horses they fondly believe are swans are in fact geese – and very slow waddlers, at that.'

Eventually, they found a coin and tossed for it.

Brendan called tails.

It came down heads.

Becky shrugged, resigned to her fate, but she had other things to do first. She left Brendan and strode across to a boutique, bought a small bag and two pieces of cloth that, at a pinch, could have been called a bikini, changed expertly in

Counter Coup

the back of the shop and stuffed her dress, bra, panties and purse into the bag which she dumped at Brendan's feet as she ran passed him to the water.

She bathed for a while, too far away for Brendan to enjoy anything but a general view. There was no shortage of alternative bodies to admire though. Eventually she returned and flopped down on her stomach beside him.

'Don't just sit there gawping,' she commanded, 'be of some bloody use and go get me some sun lotion. Heavy on the screen factor.'

Brendan lumbered to his feet and did as he was told. A few minutes later he was allowed the intense and singular pleasure of applying the lotion to as much of his lawyer as she was prepared to allow. To his surprise, that seemed to be most of her.

Spot on eleven, she dialled the fat man. The phone rang and rang - that irritating French beep - with no answer. After twenty it cut off. Perhaps Kantor wasn't up yet.

She paused, took a deep breath and dialled again. This time, a voice that could not possibly be that of a Frenchman said 'Allo'.

'Allo. Monsieur Kantor? It is here Delivery Direct. I 'ave a pacquet for you. Cigars, perhaps? But l'addresse monsieur; I cannot read it.'

She was aware that she was something of a ham act. It did not help that Brendan in the background was holding his hand over his mouth in a desperate attempt to fight back the hysterics.

David Lipsey

There was a pause. Becky thought she had blown it. Then she heard a loud belch.

'Chateau le Bouzy, La Forestiere, Grasse. After four.' And the phone went down, with a bang.

'Yesssssssssss!' cried Becky, as if she had just got a murderer off scot-free. 'Five hours. Let's get out of Cannes. How about *Tahiti Plage*? Even with the traffic round here, we will be there for early lunch.'

Brendan felt like neither *Tahiti Plage*, nor lunch. But he hadn't a better plan.

*****

The season was past its peak, and the year-round South of Francers had long thought the only way to the beach was by boat. So it took only an hour for Brendan and Becky to clear the traffic, skirting St Tropez, going over the hill via Ramatuelle, and descending to the great beaches below.

It had been years since Brendan had been to St Trop. Like most jockeys, he preferred holiday destinations where the waiters spoke English. But Tahiti could hardly fail to make an impression, even on a man with as much on his mind as Brendan. They paid the statutory 50 francs to park the car. They paid the statutory 50 francs for each lounger, and another 50 for the umbrella.

As far as the eye could see, there was flesh. Brown, roasted, uncovered flesh. The standard uniform was a gold pendant over the neck, half a dozen rich bangles on each arm and a

Counter Coup

leather thong. Brendan was relieved to see that the men were not uniformly handsome. Some were old, and many were fat, with bellies that were like miniature versions of Kantor's.

But the girls! None was much over thirty. All had legs miles long, thighs like iron, firm breasts, hair straight out of a shampoo advertisement.

'Half an hour more sun, then we'll go and eat,' said Becky, sensibly.

Brendan caught a sniff of burning fennel leaves, coming from the grill in the makeshift open-fronted restaurant overlooking the beach, and with it fish (sea bass if he was not mistaken). The plop of a cork being drawn from a bottle could be heard through the laughter.

Becky slipped off her dress again. And then the bra of her bikini. That left only the tiny piece of cotton thong that threaded up between her buttocks. Where was Brendan to look? If he looked at the beach, she might think he was eyeing up other women. If he looked at her, she might think that he was about to make a move. Perhaps he was. He was a man, wasn't he? Was it his fault if his focus on the job in hand was disturbed by the tiny penumbra of Becky's bare breasts?

She lay on her back, eyes closed, letting her skin soak up the warmth of the autumn sun. He compared this confident and brilliant girl to Tanya. Their bodies were so different. Tanya would have filled the beach bed, her breasts voluminous enough to stand comparison with any of the Dutch and Germans littering the sand around them. Becky in contrast hardly seemed to be there. Yet she was perfect in every detail and Brendan noticed that he drew the envious stares of many of the men who strolled by, just closer than was strictly necessary. Becky Tregwynn, it seemed, met any standard St. Tropez cared to set.

With an effort, Brendan lay back, closed his eyes and thought of the last fence at Bangor, and of Kantor standing by the track.

Counter Coup

Chapter 13

It was nearly three by the time they drew up at Chateau le Bouzy. They had thought that their prospects of getting in would be much improved if they actually had the cigars. A box of twenty five had been acquired which would pass muster, and with it, brown paper. It took a little while to spill sea water over the address so the name and telephone number was readable but not the address: a nice touch that, the pair thought.

The slopes below Grasse were a navigational nightmare. Signs to La Forestière suddenly appeared and then suddenly disappeared. The road narrowed without warning. Becky and Brendan did not know afterwards how they had squeezed between the wall and a bread van without a collision. Requests for directions were met by blank looks, profuse apologies usually in English, and machinegun-like eruptions of *a gauche, a droit, tout court* which even Becky struggled to keep up with.

David Lipsey

Eventually, a red sign announced the entry to La Forestière. The village was tiny. On the right of the road was the church, with the school at its side. The school was now closed, they noted; a sign that this was a village where very few people actually lived. On the left was a large set of gates which seemed to be the way into a substantial estate. It seemed unlikely that a village this size would have more than one Chateau.

They parked. On the gate was the usual warning "*Chien méchant.*" In case anyone thought that this was bluff with nothing more than a lapdog inside, someone had scribbled an 's' after chien, and appended a photo of three large Alsatians. They pulled the chain. After a second or two, in which they were acutely aware of the security camera above their head, the gates squeaked open.

The property was not enormous but it was more than big enough for one. To their left, the olive groves were terraced down the hill, behind which they could see the glinting of the bay. There was a large swimming pool surrounded by recliners and tables. A few damp towels were draped on a low white fence.

They noticed a fridge-freezer, humming softly to itself. Evidently Kantor did not like to stray far from a cool drink.

To the right was a long low white building, presumably the old stable block, but now converted into primitive sleeping accommodation. A man in Kantor's way of life, Brendan thought grimly, was unlikely to sleep sound a'bed without knowing that his security men were close at hand. Not to

Counter Coup

mention the Merc, whose bonnet could be seen poking out of the garage.

Kantor evidently did not keep the same hours as the rest of the human race. A table had been set for breakfast on the terrace. Coffee, *croissants, pain au chocolat* and a restoring bottle of local *eau de vie*.

There Kantor sat. As they came through the door, Kantor made as if to stand, thought better of it, and beckoned them over without looking at Brendan. His eyes were firmly on Becky.

'Takes two of you Froggies to deliver a few cigars these days does it?' he said. 'Not hoping for a tip, I trust?' He emphasised the point by spitting brown phlegm on the floor at their feet.

The ease of their entry had caught Brendan and Becky by surprise. In truth, what with dreaming up the cigar yarn, preparing the parcel, and conducting a tour of Grasse villa-land, they had not considered their next step with as much care as they might. As with lying to owners and judges, they were going to have to busk it.

Brendan knew he lacked feline skills. Directness was his strongest weapon, and he had found his fame had done him no harm in tight corners in the past.

'I think you know me better than that,' said Brendan.

Kantor cast a not-very-interested glance in his general direction. He looked as if he was meeting a perfect stranger.

Brendan shrugged. 'Though you usually see me wearing, say, a yellow silk shirt and a peaked cap.'

David Lipsey

Kantor looked again, more closely. If he was in any way phased by Brendan's arrival, he certainly didn't show it. This was what the term poker-faced meant, and it went with being a professional gambler.

'Brendan Donoughue. Fancy that.' Kantor at last said without extending a hand. 'A privilege I am sure. And perhaps you would like to introduce me to your young lady?'

'Elizabeth Tregwynn,' Brendan announced without elaborating.

'My word, there's a mouthful,' Kantor grinned. 'Well, what brings you two lovebirds to these parts then? Not to deliver cigars to a poor old ex-pat like me, I feel sure. Perhaps though you thought you'd like to meet me, now that you have no cause to worry about contact with the kind of people who get racing a bad name.'

He guffawed at his own joke. 'Come to think of it, Donoughue, you're about to be a banned person yourself now. We're two of a kind really, aren't we? Except I can't help but think that my little difference of opinion with the authorities has left me quite considerably richer than yours has.'

Brendan was seething but knew this wasn't the time to show it. He stared at the pool behind Kantor to control himself.

The obese gambler was enjoying himself. 'To think they got you and not me! Doesn't do much for one's confidence in the system, does it?'

At that witticism he could hardly contain himself, until he was forcibly reminded what rocking with laughter does to a hangover.

Counter Coup

Kantor bit into a *pain au chocolat*. A little chocolate oozed out and hung for a moment on his lower lip before landing on the top of his new white shirt. Kantor brushed at it, so that the smear spread more widely.

'Anyway, you might be very welcome, now we are on the same side, as it were.'

'What did you have in mind?'

'That's the spirit boy,' he reached across for some coffee. 'She your bit of stuff these days? Bit on the dainty side for me but I can see why she'd fit on a jockey.'

'No,' began Brendan, 'she's...'

'Whatever. I'm more interested in that four-year-old Futtnam is introducing in the National Hunt Novices Hurdle at Nottingham next week. Some of my informants tell me he's been working quick enough to catch pigeons. Others say that, but they also say that Futtnam has hired a jockey who can be sure to pull him. Or fall off if necessary. You know the type, Donoughue. You'll know I want to back him if he's going to win. And a few of my bookmaking friends will pay me good money to let them know if he's going to lose. Which is it do you think, old son? Only if you don't know, don't try to bullshit me. As you might imagine, I do not much care for making losing bets.'

Brendan remembered the casino. He could imagine. 'Don't know much about him, I'm afraid.'

'Oh, don't you old son?' Kantor was into his bullying stride. 'The collar bone you did, wasn't it? Funny, they usually knit after a fall but after a good kickin, - I'm not so sure. Besides, we have other ways in case you feel a little brave.'

One of the Alsatians sniffed over towards Kantor, who gave him a hunk of *pain au chocolat*. Something about the way the dog scoffed it persuaded Brendan that he wouldn't want it to be his leg that was on the menu.

Kantor changed tack. 'I expect you are looking for a job at the moment. That girl must be expensive, so long as she stays with you.' He turned philosophical. 'Funny things women. When you're in trouble, they swear undying love. Then, when they find you're hurrying them past the jewellers, something goes wrong with the undying bit.'

He looked Becky in the eye, after he'd looked her everywhere else. 'Darling, believe me, he ain't worth it. Come to Daddy.'

Had Brendan thought things through more carefully, he would probably have resisted his next move. He tried not to let men like Kantor get to him. But Kantor had got to him all right, got to him so that he would happily have attacked him with the butter knife and taken the consequences.

'You're right Kantor,' he began with a hint of steel in his voice that was rarely there, 'I am looking for a job. You know why. And so you'll also know why, I want to know what were you doing standing by the second-last fence at Bangor-on-Dee racecourse on September 13th?'

To the watching astonishment of Becky and Brendan, Kantor did not explode. The dog was not unleashed, nor did he call for the bodyguards. Instead, a look of what seemed like genuine puzzlement crossed his face. He seemed not to know

Counter Coup

what to say.

'Lost your mind as well as your job, have you?' he replied eventually. 'I haven't been back to England in months.'

Brendan wasn't having that. 'I saw you there. I've got a film of you there. And I intend to prove why you were there.'

Kantor did not seem to be impressed. But it was clear that his patience, not his strongest suite, was by now exhausted.

Slowly almost casually, he reached into the pocket of his dressing down. Brendan did now know much about guns, but he had a strong suspicion that Kantor did.

'Jean-Pierre!' he rasped. 'Quickly, si'l vous plait. I want you to look after someone for me,' Kantor paused and transferred his gaze to Becky, 'while I look after his friend.'

Jean-Pierre had been, no doubt, selected partly for his looks. Even Kantor did not need to feel jealous of him. His belly might have been a mite smaller. It takes a long time to get back to full strength after 15 years of prison food. But that was not the only mark that prison had left. A scar, still livid, spread right across his neck, where a cellmate had not responded as expected to his advances. His eyes had shrunk with the darkness of solitary, so that bare pinheads of hatred shone from them.

He was obviously used to swift summons to action too. He had his own gun. He also carried a length of wire.

Within seconds, Brendan was strung to a chair, a dirty dishcloth between his teeth to muffle his shouting. If he breathed, the wire cut into his chest. If he tried to look towards Becky, he was in danger of an unscheduled garrotting.

David Lipsey

'Now fuck off, Jean-Pierre,' he heard Kantor rasp. The Frenchman was gone.

Kantor took a step towards Becky, 'Now my dear, I know all about you laah-di-daahs. All the same, you types. Like a bit of rough.'

He seized Becky by the wrist and pulled her away from the pool towards the bedroom that opened straight onto it. He pushed open the glass door. The room was not a pretty sight. There was a bed all right, still unmade after Kantor's afternoon sleep. There was an ice bucket, containing two bottles of Bollinger, the empty one upside down. And there were other things; manacles, whips, handcuffs and many gadgets in steel and rubber that Becky didn't recognise and just then had no wish to.

Kantor did not always go out for his pleasures.

Brendan could see all this out of the corner of his eye. He waited for Becky's scream. But it did not come. Instead he heard a voice that he hadn't ever heard from her before, half innocent schoolgirl, half practiced whore.

'Oh, Mr. Kantor. I'm not sure....'

'Oh but you will be sure, my dear,' said Kantor. 'Just come over here to me and we'll slip that dress of yours off.'

Brendan could not see properly, what with the door and the garrotte. But what he could see he could scarcely believe. He saw the dress falling down Becky's legs, ending up in a little pile at her feet.

'And if I do, is there something in it for me?' she purred as she stepped out of the cotton, 'A little ride to the airport

Counter Coup

perhaps? For both of us?'

At first Kantor said nothing. He was clearly disarmed by Becky's unexpected acceptance. Brendan saw the dressing gown join Becky's dress on the floor.

'Maybe,' Kantor's voice was husky with lust. Brendan saw him move closer and slip his hand under Becky's thong, 'just maybe.'

Brendan closed his eyes.

He never knew how Becky found enough room to grab the gun off the floor or had the strength to hit Kantor so hard with the butt that he fell to the floor like a shot elephant.

Becky's control was remarkable. Her dress was on and tidy before she ran outside to Brendan's rescue.

Kantor looked out of it: the accumulated drink alone might keep him down. But neither fancied his waking; nor making the acquaintance of Jean-Pierre again. To get away was the priority. Equally, all they had done so far was to prove what they already knew; that Kantor was a villain. They were little further forward in their quest.

Anything that would help they needed now. They were not likely to be visiting again, and they did not imagine that Kantor would be assisting them in their inquiries.

They looked around. The detritus of a degenerate lay everywhere. Half-drunk cups of coffee. Empty bottles. Odd piles of change, a wallet, his diary.

His diary.

It was something. They could look up September 13th. It could show the flights he had taken, the train to Bangor. It might not of itself be enough to persuade the disciplinary committee that Brendan was innocent. But at least it would help nail the man Dodgson and Simmonds wanted nailed – and that might mean a shorter sentence for Brendan. He grabbed it. As he did so, they heard what sounded like the beginnings of a groan from the man-mountain at their feet.

They ran as the groan began to turn into something more articulate. They could hear Jean-Pierre starting to respond. And then there were the three Alsatians, sniffing action, pursuing them down the path. If the car failed to start first time, they were dog meat.

The car started. In the passenger seat, Becky shook. Only the need to drive – and drive fast – stopped Brendan doing the same.

He was pretty sure that by now Jean-Pierre and his colleague would be in the Mercedes, but he thanked God for the network of little roads that snaked up from the sea and scattered among the villas. Kantor's men would assume they were heading for the coast, where their options for escape would be widest. But they were already heading for the mountains, along the old *Route Napoleon*, climbing until the snow-white tips shone brightly ahead of them.

To their right, just below the snow line, they saw a little wooden chalet serving drinks and snacks. During the ski season it would have been packed. But now there were only a handful of tourists taking a break from the heat and dust of the coast. Brendan discretely parked the small anonymous vehicle.

They both eschewed alcohol. This was a job for clear heads.

Counter Coup

Two steaming hot chocolates arrived but a few minutes passed before the trembling of their hands stopped long enough for them to think about opening the diary. At last Brendan put his hand in his trouser pocket, and drew it out. Too late, he wondered if he should be wearing plastic gloves so as not to smudge the finger prints. He opened it.

At the front were the usual pieces of useless information: public holidays in Muslim countries, a table for dating Easter into the 22nd century, useful telephone numbers in Paris and a vintage chart. Then, the pages, one per week. He turned to the one for 13 September. The curiosity about what Kantor did for the rest of the year could wait.

Kantor's writing hand was worse than a scrawl and it took Becky's practiced eye to decipher, 11:00 Doctor. 12:00 Notary. 1:00 Cagnes-sur-Mer. 5:30 Drinks, Inspector Juste.' There was no point in reading any more. Kantor seemed to have his alibi as stitched up as a doped favourite in a selling hurdle at Southwell.

Donoughue was unlikely to persuade Dodgson and Simmonds that he had seen Kantor at Bangor when there was a doctor a lawyer and an inspector ready to swear that, at precisely that time, he had been something over a thousand miles away.

Could this be all? Feverishly, they turned the rest of the pages. Some, like the one they had read the previous days, were all too innocent. Lawyers figured a lot. So did doctors and dentists. So did financial advisors. So did a well-known specialist in obesity. So did days at the races and nights at the

David Lipsey

Casino.

On others, however, something else figured, and not only at night.

'9:30 pm. Elsa, 4,000 francs.'

'Noon, Petrushka, 3,000 francs.'

'11:00pm Felice and Hortense, 10,000 francs.'

He paid the girls well. His little secret was safe in their hands, so long as the cash went on flowing.

Beside the entries of dry times and amounts of money there were other little details added. Elsa had 'forty lashes, bit of blood'. It wasn't immediately clear whose.

Felice and Hortense's description made it clear enough. 'Nipple clamps and grater. F likes the hot wax and needle. H bruises too easily. Cried nicely.'

'I need the loo,' said Becky suddenly.

A minute later Brendan heard deep retching sounds came from the lean-to at the end of the chalet. Only a few minutes earlier the same treatment could have been applied to her. While she was away Brendan scanned more pages. There was plenty to keep even the most salacious tabloid happy.

When she reappeared some minutes later, nothing was evident of the tan Becky had acquired the previous day.

The diary had failed to prove what they wanted it to prove. Kantor, it was true, would not want the diary to be widely circulated. The French were famously liberated on matters sexual. They were much less hung up than the English about people paying for what they could not get free. On the other hand, serious assaults on women were a different matter.

Counter Coup

No doubt, the Cannes police were well suborned by Kantor. That had been clear at the brothel in the early hours of the morning. But there were other things for him to worry about. The French papers for example. They had always been fascinated by what in French was known as 'le vice Anglais'. They might not take kindly to an Englishman who went about beating up their women, even if he paid them handsomely for the privilege.

So far as the locals were concerned, Kantor was a reasonably respectable man - no less respectable certainly than the retired Mafioso who made up a goodly proportion of Cannes's population. He would not want the staff in his restaurant whispering to each other before they brought his *fruits de mer* or his staff gossiping to their friends about his nocturnal habits. He would not want to be sneered at by the clerk at the *pari mutuel*. No, Kantor would certainly not want his diary to be in wide circulation in the Cannes area, or anywhere else come to that. While they had it, they had something on him.

It did not take long for the corollary of that to dawn on them. Kantor would be eager - very eager indeed - to get it back. Thoughts of an afternoon riding the ski lift to the top of the mountain and staring down on the coast below were banished. It would be a beautiful view, yes. But if Kantor guessed they were there, they might not be the first people to fall from the summit to their deaths.

It was impossible to know how many men Kantor would have on the job, how many cafés he would inquire after them in. Towns would be watched, petrol stations covered. And, though there were many roads down at the bottom, there was only one road up to the top, all hairpins. A car could easily skid. It could so easily leave the road, and bounce two thousand metres down to the valley below.

The Riviera had suddenly lost all the attractions it had held when they were lunching at *Tahiti Plage* the day before. Now, if they hurried, they could still catch the easyJet afternoon flight back from Nice and be home for dinner.

If they got home. It seemed unlikely that a man who wanted something as much as Kantor would fail to post a watch on the entrance to Nice airport. Muggings took place outside the airport quite regularly. There had been one killing that year already. No-one would be unduly surprised by two more, although the early hour, just before sundown, would cause a few heads to shake at the state of modern France.

It was a thousand kilometres from Grasse to Calais. In that small hired car it would be a long drive. But then, in his working days, Brendan had got very used to long drives. He knew that if you kept going long enough, you would eventually end up in your own bed.

'Which is the shortest way to the Autoroute du Soleil?' he asked Becky.

She could sense the ordeal he had planned for her but she had neither the will nor the strength to argue.

Counter Coup

Chapter 14

Racing in small cars turned out to be more tiring than racing on horses. Some 150 kilometres short of Calais, Brendan found himself swerving dangerously towards the central reservation. He realised that he must have nodded off. They were in enough danger of death already without risking a smash.

He looked at Becky to see if she might take over the driving. Once glance told him what he needed to know. She was so exhausted that she barely looked pretty.

Neither of them was accustomed to staying at a *Cavotel*. Where hotels were concerned, until recently at any rate, four stars was Brendan's idea of slumming it. But a *Cavotel* was all the motorway offered, in only another five kilometres. Neither of them fancied pulling off in search of something more congenial.

A pall of exhaust fumes lay low over the car park. The ground shook as the heavy lorries passed. Barely thirty seconds went by between horn blasts. Still, someone had planted two tubs of flowers by the entrance, and Brendan could see an ice-making machine up against the wall. It would have to do.

'*Deux pour nous*,' said Brendan to the receptionist, brandishing two fingers in a sub-Churchillian gesture lest his rudimentary French failed to convey the right meaning.

'*Très bien, monsieur*,' the receptionist replied with what looked like a wink. '*Un lit matrimoniel, bien sur?*'

Evidently, the *Cavotel* performed the same function for illicit couples as the more salubrious hotels Brendan frequented in London. The receptionist might have been the Chief Porter at the Ritz, and she did not even have to be tipped. Brendan glanced half-hopefully at Becky's face. She did not need to shake her head for him to get the message. Ah well. They were both too tired to have fun.

'*Deux chambres, Mademoiselle.*'

The receptionist looked crestfallen. Had it not been for her error in interpreting their motives, she might have persisted in her native tongue. Despite the construction of Europe, the French do not easily concede the need to communicate other than in their own language. But Brendan's accent, and the small misunderstanding that had already passed between them, convinced the receptionist that English would be easier in the long run.

'I regret infinitely monsieur but I have not two rooms. I have only one for two persons, at 300 francs. Perhaps that would fit you and your...your sister?'

Counter Coup

Again, Brendan glanced at Becky. Again, he did not really need to. Sister or not, she was not going any further that night. 'OK, a room with two beds. Here's my credit card.'

Brendan at least had the strength to slip into the little shower room to undress for bed. He already knew from her performance on the beach that Becky was not as modest as he was. As he emerged she was throwing off her clothes. Further north they may have been, but the night was still stuffy and their budget room did not boast air conditioning. Not troubling with a nightie, she flung herself under the top sheet. Soon she was dead to the world.

He was as tired, but not as ready to drop off. Fortunately, the mini-bar was well stocked. He began to feel woozy. As his eyelids closed, he dreamed of a naked Becky. Only the dream was not the pleasant one he had enjoyed on the beach. This Becky was screaming. And leering at her was the unmistakable form of Michael Kantor.

Waking was just as bad. It was not just the raging thirst that made the new day seem unattractive, or the beating of his head. A couple of aspirin would see to that. It was the realisation that he was now even further behind the game than when he had begun his quest. His chief suspect had turned out to be in another country at the time of the Bangor race.

Yet, despite the fact that Kantor was plainly not the man they wanted, they had turned him into an enemy who, on form, was quite capable of hunting them across the continent. All their French expedition had yielded them was a diary that was no more than a defence for Kantor.

David Lipsey

Brendan thought seriously about giving up. And even when he dismissed the thought, he was reminded that there were just eight days to go until Dodgson and Simmonds's deadline. Nearly half his time was up, and so far, he had achieved precisely nothing.

*****

Nothing about the *Cavotel* tempted them to linger long once the sun shining through the thin curtains finally got them up in the morning. They went without the free if stale-looking croissants and stewed yesterday's coffee in order to get back a little earlier. Despite their exhaustion they were on the road again soon after six. Becky had a case on.

Brendan looked forward to Lambourn, and Tanya. Perhaps because of the glory of the bodies he had gazed at but not been able to touch over the last two days, the thought of a bed with Tanya and no restrictions on his exploration pulled him home.

For once, there was no delay in the tunnel. Even the rush hour traffic was relatively co-operative. The clock on the fascia showed only a little after nine am, English time, when Brendan dropped Becky outside her chambers. Fortunately she kept a change of clothing as well as her wig in her rooms. She would yet have time to remind herself of her client's case before the court went into session at the earliest hour by which a judge could be expected to be *compos mentis*, that is to say, at ten am.

Driving against the traffic, Brendan made good time to the

Counter Coup

airport. He did not give the hire company time to make a fuss when he told them that he was returning a car he had hired in Nice.

'You did promise unlimited mileage,' he pointed out. As he strode off to get his own car, he could hear them calling 'sir, sir' after him like bleating sheep.

By 10:30 he was back in his own car; by 11:30, he was letting himself into his own house. It was then that he regretted that he had forgotten, in the excitement of the past two days, to phone Tanya.

Tanya was a loving and a loyal girl. But her love and her loyalty came at a price. She expected some back. When Brendan was in trouble, she expected to be told what was happening. When he failed to tell her, she felt temporarily released from her obligations.

The note on the kitchen table did not mince words.

'Brendan. Since you appear to have lost interest in our relationship,' it read, 'you will forgive me if I get on and have a life of my own.'

The words stung. Surely a relationship such as his and Tanya's could not be over this suddenly? Not when he had not so much as touched another girl?

'You know I was talking about going with Jen on Safari to Africa,' the message continued. 'You know you weren't sure you could manage without me. Well now you are going to have to. I don't expect the telephones will be as good there as I am told they are in the South of France. So don't concern yourself if you don't hear. I may see you in a fortnight.'

David Lipsey

He felt unreasonably angry with her. Then he felt angry with himself for feeling it. Then angry that he had not, after all, taken advantage of the temporary pause in his established love life to see if Becky was as tasty as she looked.

Jen was Tanya's best friend. Indeed, she had sometimes said that Jen was her only true friend. At the moment, the word 'only' seemed to exclude Brendan.

She was talking of coming back, at least, if she survived the bugs and the crooks. He could expect a couple of weeks of feeling anxious, but he felt so anxious anyway that it would make little difference. And at least she would be out of the way if Kantor and his friends came visiting. He did not think that they would scruple at involving an innocent person if that innocent person happened to be his girl.

He realised he was gasping for a cuppa, perhaps even for a bite. Tanya had clearly been very angry. But it would have been out of character for her to leave him entirely without supplies. Soon he gathered cereal, tea bags, milk in the kitchen. Life looked up.

It took little longer than it took him to put the kettle on for any illusion that he too might be safe to be shattered. Literally shattered in this case, for the half-brick flung through the window smashed through the glass, spraying him with shards. Instinctively, though unwisely, he rushed to the door and threw it open, hoping to catch the intruders red-handed. They had left the scene as quietly and as quickly as they could. Lambourn was as sleepy silent as ever.

Metaphorically Brendan saw red. Then he realised that he

Counter Coup

was literally seeing red. Drops from a deep gash across his forehead spattered down into his eyes. He rushed into the bathroom, grabbed a sponge, and wiped himself with cold water. It looked nasty, but Brendan had seen enough gashes to know that it was nothing too bad. Nothing even that needed stitches. Nothing, by an inch or two, that would affect his eyesight, and thus his career.

His career. What career?

He made his way slowly back to the kitchen. The brick was lying on the floor. And attached to it by an elastic band was a piece of paper. He picked it up and unfolded it. He didn't expect it to be headed or signed and it was not, but he didn't expect it to be quite so stylish.

The message was even less welcoming than Tanya's had been. 'This is a present from a friend of yours. He was pleased that you and your delightful companion were able to drop in on him yesterday. Perhaps he did not make her feel sufficiently welcome, and that accounts for your swift departure. Another time, you must allow the lady to become more closely acquainted with him.'

Kantor obviously had friends who were a good deal more literate, in a quaint old-fashioned sort of a way, than he was. Polite too.

Brendan read on. 'He hopes that you will forgive him for mentioning it but he could not help but wonder if, by any chance, you had inadvertently picked up his diary when you left? He has discovered that it has gone missing, and he does rely on having it available. Were you to have it to hand, perhaps you would care to leave it under the rubbish bin on Lambourn Green tonight, as soon as it gets dark, so that I may retrieve it for him. Please don't think of involving the police. I rather feel in the circumstances they would be more interested in your stealing diaries than in my throwing this brick. He asks me to add that should this prove impossible, the next present he sends you will surely be one to remember.'

Even the threat at the end was elegantly put. Brendan's brain was working fast. His first thought was a cheering one - at least the note suggested that Kantor has no idea who Becky was. 'Delightful companion' sounded anonymous enough, though when Brendan remembered what Kantor had planned to do with his delightful companion he felt sick. Anyway, while she remained anonymous, she remained safe.

His second thought was born of a certainty, something remote from reason. He was absolutely determined that he would not let the diary go. While he had at least it he had something on Kantor, something that might make him think before he acted. And his third thought at last contained an element of self-preservation. He must leave, leave Lambourn, and leave fast, for a place where Kantor and his hirelings were unlikely to find him.

There had been times in the past when Brendan had felt he could have done with somewhere to hide out from some girlfriend whom he had let down insufficiently gently. But in the end, he had faced them like a man. His was not a profession, like writing or painting, which required solitude. Partying was more the name of the game, and his idea of a weekend hideaway

Counter Coup

was somewhere where he could be joined by a few dozen of his closest friends. In this crisis he needed help.

Something about Lord Brecon told him that he was a man who would not let you down in a crisis. He had barely left a message for him on the Lords answering service before his lordship called back.

'Becky's fine,' Brendan began, cutting off the anticipated question. 'I expect she'll fill you in when she sees you.' As he said it, he hoped she would spare Henry the less savoury details. He did not want his Lordship realising just how dangerous a person Brendan was to be around.

'Glad to hear it,' Brecon said, 'I was going to call her after court.'

'I'm looking forward to telling you all about it too.'

'No doubt. Is that all you called to say?'

'I'm afraid not. I've had a bit of trouble here. I think we may have provoked a reaction over in France. Can you think of anywhere private I could stay? I need it fast. I hope it will only be for a few days.'

Brecon sounded doubtful. 'Just a few days. How do you know it will be?'

'Well, for one thing, it'll have to be over soon,' Brendan pointed out morosely. 'Dodgson and Simmonds's deadline expires pretty soon.'

His secret worry was that if Kantor's crew had not caught up with him by then, they would hardly give up. They would wait for his eventual return and take back the diary without worrying at all about any collateral damage they might inflict on him while they did so. On the other hand, if he could shake free of Kantor's attentions, perhaps, just perhaps, he would uncover a clue as to what was going on and bring the whole terrible nightmare to an end. So just a few days it would be.

'Very well, give me a minute.' Brecon answered cheerily. 'Let me see. There's a cottage on one of my estates, just a few miles off the M4, Abergavenny way, a few miles north of the town. It's empty at the moment. The old boy that had it has just died and we're going to do it up for weekenders, but he was one of the old school, I'm afraid – not much of a one for comfort. There's no central heating, just a gas ring, and no phone.'

'It's OK, I've got my mobile,' said Brendan.

There was a chuckle. 'I very much doubt if it works up there, old thing. It's on the Brecon estate. I'll ring the estate office and tell them you will be round to pick up the key. They'll tell you how to get there.'

*****

From the hunter Brendan had been transformed into the hunted, and he was not sure that he liked it. Even Lambourn, that idyll of rural peace, somehow seemed different, threatening.

It probably was threatening, to him. Somewhere out there Kantor's man was waiting to see if he would put the diary where

Counter Coup

he had been told to put it and if Brendan didn't, shove something worse than a brick through his window.

As his car rolled down the drive Brendan waved goodbye to the house as if Tanya was still there. Surely an explosion or a fire would not go unnoticed, even in Lambourn, and Kantor would not want to gamble with police involvement, Brendan thought.

Or would he? Perhaps his pursuers would save whatever they had planned for it for later when they realised that he and the diary had gone. Brendan thought of Tanya's expensively-assembled wardrobe, burning away. He wondered whether he might then find it easy to convince her that she had been better off, the past fortnight, in Africa, or whether she would be furious at him for abandoning her precious possessions to their fate.

He patted his jacket pocket just to make sure the diary was still in it. He did not know why but call it a jockey's instinct; he had a strange feeling it might yet have something in it that would help.

Usually he liked driving west down the M4. The high downs at the beginning with the occasional glimpse of a horse, then the long views as the road swept off the escarpment towards Bristol and the Bristol Channel refreshed him. Even the glimpse of Bristol dockland had its charms for him.

The old bridge alone seemed worth the toll for the views down the Severn. And the racecourses that he went to that way had always been happy hunting grounds. In his heyday, he had won three consecutive Welsh Grand Nationals at Chepstow. Then there were a couple of Welsh champion hurdles, and a host of smaller prizes at Hereford and Ludlow. But he didn't like driving with half his attention on the mirror. Could that be someone following him? That van? That sports car? That motorbike? So far as he could tell, none of the vehicles which temporarily aroused his suspicion stayed long enough with him to be likely candidates. As he was travelling at 110 mph, that wasn't surprising.

He wondered how it would sound if a policeman pulled him over. 'Officer, I'm just trying to get away from someone who wants to kill me.'

*****

It was past three when he arrived at the cottage after a flying visit to the estate office. Brecon had been as good as his word and the secretary had handed him the keys without demur - and even with a welcoming smile.

Usually, he would have liked the little house, with its picturesque wooden clapper boards and the metal arch, bearing clematis, around the door. A few bottles, a couple of friends, and it would be a great setting for a good time.

It had been built at around the turn of the century for a labourer on the estate. One down, two up, with an outside toilet; Brendan trembled to think how that might have felt to someone with a wife, a cow and half a dozen strapping sons. But done up for a London couple, it would be just right.

At this point however, one virtue of Lord Brecon's cottage in particular commended itself to Brendan. It was a long way

Counter Coup

from anywhere, and, as he had just discovered, it was the devil's own job to find, even with a sketch map and solid directions from the estate secretary.

Now he was there, though, it took only the flask of whisky he had brought with him to find that, for the first time in several days, he could really sleep.

David Lipsey

Counter Coup

Chapter 15

In extreme exhaustion, the body imposes its own priorities. Although Brendan had hardly eaten or drunk for nearly two days, he didn't wake until the dawn chorus hit his ears and the early light was peeping in through a hole in the curtains. He felt a little light-headed but clear-headed too. The peace of the country was beginning to work its balm. For the first time in days, he could now admit to himself, he wasn't shit-scared.

Kantor wouldn't find him here. Nor, surely, would Dodgson and Simmonds, though he was aware that their deadline was now looming uncomfortably close. Only Brecon and his estate office knew where he was to be found, and they were likely neither to be asked nor to tell. Henry, bless him, had arranged for supplies to be left for him at the cottage: a crusty white loaf, butter, tea, milk in a jug and half a dozen brown speckled eggs.

Brendan made himself tea and egg-on-toast almost like a

normal man.

Freed from the immediate fear of capture, he could see clearly to the heart of where he stood. To have any hope of getting out of the corner, he had to find who had been responsible for his fall at Bangor. To find them he had to identify the culprit from among the crowd by the second last fence. He thought he had found him when he'd found Kantor. Except he had turned out not to have been by the second last fence at all, but a thousand miles away. Kantor was the clue that had turned to dust before his eyes.

So where was he to go from here?

He reached for his mobile and dialled the one person he always turned to when stuck for direction - his Aunt Doris. Inevitably the mobile didn't have a signal, just as Henry had predicted. But Doris had found the answer last time and Brendan realised, somewhere in the middle of the second cup of tea, that answer still applied.

His best bet was another session with Phil Cowcross. It made plenty of sense. If a trail leads to a dead end, the thing to do is to go back to where you started.

Brendan walked out of the cottage and up the track onto the hill behind, hoping the elevation and the view out over the borderlands would somehow breathe life into his phone. However far he could see across the landscape, though, there was only a glimmer of a signal, not enough to call with.

He spent a few moments relishing the warmth of the autumn morning and watching the lasts wisps of mist lift from the river, then strode back decisively to the cottage, tidied up

Counter Coup

the kitchen, locked up and set off for the north. He might be in hiding but there was no time to be lost either. Once out of the Herefordshire blind spots and onto the M5 he rang Cowcross and warned him he'd be there just after lunch.

He had not expected to see Bradburn again so soon, or Trueform, or Phil or Richard Potts, but he was more sure of their welcome this time. They had, after all, helped him already. He did not altogether look forward to their conversation, though. He was coming to tell Richard that his identification was wrong. Phil certainly, and Richard probably, were not people who found it easy to admit to being wrong.

Over the phone, Brendan had asked Phil to set up the viewing suite and when he arrived, he told them the story of his encounter with Kantor, dwelling particularly on Becky's ordeal and bravery. Cowcross and Potts were intrigued and set to work.

There was no question of having to flick through 109 tapes this time. Before returning the video to its box, Phil had taken the precaution of attaching a little red sticker, like the "sold" sticker on a painting at an exhibition. He went straight to it, and pressed play until Brendan appeared in the winners' enclosure.

'So Richard?' Phil inquired of the memory man.

'Kantor. Mike Kantor. I told you last time. No doubt about it.'

Brendan shook his head but Richard was certain. 'He's not exactly a man you would easily mix up with anyone else. Even if he didn't have that cauliflower ear. Apparently it took him

two days to wake up after the punch that gave him that one.'
Phil pulled back his director's chair, and looked at Brendan. Brendan sighed, a deep, defeated sigh. He seemed to be going round in circles. Then a thought struck him.

'I'm sorry to impose this on you, but could we just have a look at Bangor-on-Dee, 13th September, the day when...'

'You don't need to remind us, Brendan," said Phil tartly. The familiar tape whizzed through the gate: the start, the early stages, Robber Earl's smooth run, the second-last. The quality of Trueform's tapes was naturally higher than the quality of the one so kindly sent to Brendan by his fan at home, and you could see the crowd standing by the second-last fence reasonably clearly.

'Well, Richard? Anyone there you recognise?' Brendan asked more in hope than expectation.

Richard stared hard at the frozen frame.

'Well that one for a start,' he said, 'the jockey-sized bloke. Well, he was a jockey, though not a very good one. Tom Jeffers. Lives in Widnes now. He acts as a sort-of gopher for Sean Fitzpatrick. Don't know much about his form nowadays, but he wasn't the kind you liked to lend a tenner to in his riding days. Wouldn't have thought he was up to much in the way of subtle plotting though.'

Richard peered even harder at the screen. 'And him?' He looked strangely puzzled. 'That's Kantor again. No doubts.'

'It can't be,' exclaimed Brendan. 'I've proof here in my pocket that he was more than a thousand miles south at the time.'

Counter Coup

'Never mind your proof,' said Richard, who was not used to having his identifications queried. 'It's Kantor. But if you say it isn't Mike, it must be...,' he stared even harder into the screen, 'it must be Matt. Matt Kantor. Mike's younger brother. The spitting image isn't he? Chip off the old block. They say their dear old mum couldn't tell them apart. Except that Mike was the one who usually had a fly in his fingers to pull the wings off.'

Potts was into his stride again, vindicated. The strange thing is, when Mike was in trouble all those years ago, they thought for a while Matt might be involved too. Not big time though, just on the side. If Matt did anything, he was just the little brother, the one who took the orders. He wasn't one for trouble, Matt, but he was scared to death of Mike. Anyway they never got the evidence to get Mike. So the chances of finding enough to get Matt were near to zero. And in those days, the Jockey Club didn't do people without hard evidence.'

That rang bells with Brendan.

'They might as well have warned him off though for all the difference it would have made,' said Richard, 'because until I saw this tape, I would've sworn Matt had never been seen on a racecourse since. It's not very often that people get to see the error of their ways before it's too late. But, once Mike had headed off for France, Matt did, apparently. A changed man. He didn't have an "O" level to his name - there'd never been a graduate from the school he and Mike went to, unless you counted graduates in the school of advanced criminology. But next he was applying to university. Lampeter from memory.

David Lipsey

It was somewhere the old, bad crowd weren't likely to venture. Clean air, no clubs, lots of theology, a funny language and a range of mountains between him and the nearest racecourse. The University was not exactly stacked with famous undergraduates at the time and they thought Matt might lend a bit of colour. He did more than that. Four years later, he graduated with a first in South American history. He hasn't been seen on our patch since. They say he's been writing a book.'

'So where is he now?' Brendan asked impatiently.

'I don't really know,' Richard admitted. 'I've no reason to keep him in the memory bank now that he's given up racing. But I'm sure he stayed in Wales though. Somewhere on the border. Near Hay-on-Wye it was, come to think of it. The nearest betting shop's half-an-hour's drive away, so he's keeping away from temptation. It's bookshops not betting shops round there, and that's what they say he lives for. Come to think of it, I think his boyfriend runs one. He turned out to have very different tastes from his brother. Anyway, I'm sorry I cannot be more helpful,' Richard said with regret.

Brendan breathed out, and shook him warmly by the hand.

'Encyclopaedic,' muttered Phil. 'I told you,' and reached for the champagne standing ready in its bucket.

'Can you do anything with that?' asked Richard, beaming at the compliments.

'I don't know yet,' admitted Brendan, 'but it shows there was a Kantor close at hand when I came a cropper, even if it isn't the one we expected. In a way it vindicates both me and

Counter Coup

the Jockey Club. If there's any Kantor at the scene of a fiasco, then there's something else going on.'

He had a long drive ahead so, with a discipline he would never have shown only four days before, he took only a glass of the Bollinger. 'Thanks boys. If I ever I get back in the saddle I owe you.'

*****

Brendan was back in the cottage soon after dark, convinced that doors that had closed were opening again. He hoped he would have Becky with him before he set off in search of Matt Kantor. She seemed to have a knack that he lacked of finding a way into inaccessible places that he found daunting. A few inquiries around Hay first would do no harm, though, to prepare the ground.

The next morning he headed into Hay-on-Wye along the roads that wound through the hills to the south. It was not the sort of place in which Brendan naturally felt at home. The last real book he had bought was *Lady Chatterley's Lover* when he was at school and Hay seemed to be overrun with bookshops, hick ladies' boutiques, trendy gift shops and cafés serving organic cakes. His idea of a charming town was one that had a couple of bars with full-thumping techno, and perhaps a lap dancer or two. But he could see that Hay had something appealing about it for those of gentler tastes.

He managed to find a space in the old market square, where the last of the stalls were just being packed up. He liked a place where you could still park for free. Without any clear idea of where he was going, he walked downhill, towards the town hall, past the parlour selling sheep's milk ice cream, the wholefood shop, towards a clutch of small bookshops.

A cosmopolitan crowd filled the narrow pavements: Americans soaking up what they would call typical England (though it was yards into Wales), absent-minded professors, walkers complete with backpacks taking a break from the Offa's Dyke path, and young couples dreaming of buying a cottage and installing an Aga.

He could start anywhere. But his eye was caught by a sign in one shop window saying 'Antiquarian Racing a Speciality'. He went in and began to browse. There was the Lonsdale Library's *Steeplechasing*, apparently dating from the late 1950s, edited by Lord Willoughby de Broke, MC, AFC. It was full of names that resonated with steeplechasing's past, all titles and decorations, a blend of history and practical instruction. The photographs of Golden Miller reminded him there had been good horses even before the great Arkle.

There was the Sporting Life form book of 1936: in its way a monument to change. It was not only the dead racecourses for which Brendan mourned: for Gatwick, now an airport, for Manchester, for Derby, for Buckfastleigh. Buckfastleigh in particular, though it had gone before he was born: for he remembered the familiar, woeful sight of the Buckfastleigh grandstand from the A30, mouldering away in a field not far west of Exeter, as he drove to the surviving course at Newton Abbot.

Counter Coup

You might have thought that the bookmakers were less transient than the racecourses. But it appeared that they were not. In those days, the only legal way to have a bet except on a racecourse was to have an account. *Hoi poloi* had a deposit account or a postal account where you paid for your bets with a postal order. Nobs had a credit account, or rather several. Gambling debts could not be recovered at law, so some bookmakers had ended up subsidising the British aristocracy. But when things moved on, and betting shops had opened, that was the end for many of the bookies of the day. Brendan scanned the advertisements in the old form book. No more Thomas Cook (Turf Accountants) Ltd. of Preston then 'trusted for 35 years' or J. John, Commission Agents Ltd., of Piccadilly. McLaughlan of Edinburgh had gone too. As for Diana Fairgood, the original lucky lady advertising expert racing information by wire at £5 for 6 days - there were no more wires, and he assumed that by now the lucky lady's luck had run out.

He even found a hardback copy of Dick Francis's classic fourth novel *For Kicks* with an intact green dust jacket of a blinkered horse under pressure and a steel bit. At 16/0d originally it had evidently been a bargain. At the £27.50 he had to pay for it, Brendan was not so sure.

If Kantor retained any interest in racing, surely they would know him here. He could but ask.

Brendan carried his Dick Francis up to the counter, produced the money, and followed with his question, asking for a, 'large man. Middle aged. Lives near here. Looks very like this.' He proffered a grainy picture of the man in the paddock

David Lipsey

at Cheltenham.

The bookseller did not look up but he gave a flicker of recognition. 'Sorry, not him. He does look vaguely familiar, but then you see a lot of vaguely familiar people around this town. Local, is he?'

Brendan's heart pounded.

'I do know the jockey, though,' the man sniffed, 'Diver Donoughue, the bookies' pal? I wonder how many times he did it before they caught up with him? Bastard.'

Then his eyes caught Brendan's. He was embarrassed, Brendan could see that. But English arrogance got the better of English politeness. He was not going to apologise.

'I'll just put that in a bag for you, sir,' he said.

Brendan left seething but knowing it would be a long time before he could shake off comments like that. He wished he'd had the conversation before parting with good money.

That there could be such a thing as a racing bookshop Brendan could just about believe. Like most people involved in the sport, he found it difficult to take seriously the notion that there was anything very much else in the world but horses and owners and trainers and jockeys. But a South American history bookshop: that was surely impossible. He couldn't believe it until he looked into the cavernous converted warehouse next door. And there duly listed in its list of specialities, between Snails and Spain was South America: its geography, history, lives and lore.

This time there was no hesitation from the man behind the counter.

Counter Coup

'Mr. Smith, indeed, he is one of our best customers. Buys and sells a bit, but mostly he buys. He must have one of the best collections on South America in the world. If you see him, could you thank him for his cheque? Very welcome.'

The 'Smith' did not put Brendan off. If you were going to change your whole way of life, it seemed only prudent to change your name with it. Smith seemed a bit unoriginal; it was true; appropriate more for a Brighton boarding house in the days before same-sex couples could openly share bedrooms than for a noted expert on the history of the South American continent. Perhaps Smith was the real name of Matt Kantor's boyfriend and Matt had changed names as if he was part of a married couple. Sweet really.

Brendan's upbringing had not been calculated to render him sympathetic towards homosexuality. His father had been of the old school, not above smacking a nancy-boy about a bit on a Saturday night. But he was pretty sure that he was going to prefer Matt's sexual preferences to those of his brother.

He wandered round the town, accumulating in the process a pile of books he did not very much want, Brendan soon found that the man in the racing bookshop was about the only bookseller who did not know Matt. Wherever he went the tale was the same. Mr. Smith was an expert, and much-valued, customer. He did not confine himself to South America. One shop knew him as a keen amateur lepidopterist. Another knew him as the man who would snap up just about anything on the engineering works of Brunel. His bent in psychology was towards Jung rather than Freud, he was assured at the Cinema

David Lipsey

Bookshop. He had collected a complete first edition of Trollope, according to the antiquarian bookshop next door. Something in the bookseller's character predisposes him to gossip, especially gossip which is indiscreet.

'He's not just a collector,' the owner confided to Brendan. 'He really loves his books, loves them like children. A few weeks ago, there was a bit of bother round town about him. He'd been buying more than he was selling, some of them very costly. A cheque or two bounced, or so they say. Anyway I told him that I could get him a five-figure sum for the Trollope, no problems. He wouldn't hear of it. "My Trollope? I couldn't live without it." Goodness knows how but this month it's all straight again. His cheques are honoured, and he seems to have piles of cash too. Came in yesterday and walked out with an 1853 collected poems of Tennyson. £125, though I have to say it's a bargain at the price.'

Even the religious bookshop knew Smith-Kantor. 'Strange, he never used to come in here, though nearly every other bookshop in town knew him. But it's all changed these last few days. He suddenly seems very interested in forgiveness and redemption. At this rate, there will be a choir of angels to welcome him when he passes on. A good day for heaven, that will be, but a bad day for this town, my friend. There're not many like him about these days.'

Brendan began almost to look forward to meeting him. But he did not want to ask where Matt lived. It was one thing to ask people if they recognised someone. It was another to be looking for their home address. If there was a spot of bother,

Counter Coup

and a spot of bother seemed odds-on, they would remember who had asked. He needed an address all the same; and he needed it soon. He tried the local phone directory. There were too many Smiths and Kantor was not listed.

Brendan sat over coffee and flapjack in café full of pine tables and adverts for therapies. A crystal ball would have been more use just at that moment. Then it struck him that there might yet be something - a number, an address - in Mike Kantor's diary. He was suddenly glad he'd hung onto it, even though it seemed likely that a firebombing was his most likely reward for not handing it back.

He pulled it from the pocket of his jacket. At the back was a list of addresses and phone numbers. There, under "K" was Matt. 13, Church Road, Felindre, Brecon, Powys.

Brendan leaned over and grabbed the map. A quick glance showed that it was only five miles from Hay. The temptation to rush round immediately was great but Brendan's record with unplanned visits was not encouraging. It was time to think things through.

David Lipsey

Counter Coup

Chapter 16

Brendan was not accustomed to loneliness. A jockey's life is usually full of people: trainers, owners, agents, journalists and, most of all, fellow jockeys. Usually, even for the long ride to the racecourse it is possible to find another rider who is going that way who will share the driving and help relieve the tedium. And for most of the year a top jockey was working a six day – sometimes a seven day - week. Brendan did not spend his evenings alone either. He liked to catch up with the recordings of the races he had not watched that day but other than that, he found television deeply boring. The local pub, buzzing with racing gossip, somehow seemed more attractive than an evening by the fireside. Once, of course, when he chased every ride in his bid for the championship, he used to nurse fizzy waters. But now, somehow, a pound or two overweight seemed a price worth paying for a few whiskies or a vodka-and-slimline. He could always make up for it by going easy on the grub.

David Lipsey

Brendan had to admit that he specialised in another way of avoiding loneliness. Even before Tanya, there had been satisfactorily few nights where he did not, one way or other, have the benefit of female company. The booze might be showing around his waistline, but, he flattered himself, the fillies did not yet mind.

To a more cerebral man, used to living with his own resources, Henry's cottage would have been bliss. He could read, gaze out of the windows, stride the grounds, listen to the birds. But for Brendan, the charm of isolation soon wore off.

Brendan could imagine how it could become bliss for him again. He could imagine the pleasure if Becky could be lured down to share it with him. Perhaps it could be on a rather different basis than their relationship had been on thus far. He would see. And he was expecting to see her soon.

Fortunately, the courts were about to rise for the weekend. Judges of course needed to break nice and early. As they explained, they had such a lot of paperwork to get through at weekends, and besides, nothing was as good for clearing the mind as eighteen holes on a course yet to be invaded by the weekend hordes. Recreation was the price of justice.

It followed that, with any luck, Becky would be free soon after lunch. And, he felt sure, she would want to be in at the death, finding Matt Kantor and solving the mystery that had absorbed them. He looked forward to planning his visit to Matt with her and an evening and night that fired his imagination as he thought of her naked in the motorway hotel.

He rang on her mobile around noon, when the court rose

Counter Coup

for lunch. She was in a rush, he could sense that. But she listened to the story of his trip to Bradburn and his researches in Hay, and promised to come down and see him as soon as she could. 'You're staying where?' she snorted. 'I would have thought that Dad could've found you somewhere better than that old hole! I've got to go home and change, then deal with Friday traffic hell, but I'll do my best.'

Brendan kept telling himself his intentions towards Becky must remain entirely honourable. Having driven all that way, though, she had every right to a glass of champagne, pink if possible. The cottage was a rather less smart than some she was accustomed to but a few flowers would help brighten it up. He guessed she liked oysters, which meant a drive down to Abergavenny, the home of the famous grocers, Vin Sullivan's. Two dozen *Fines Clairs* and a pair of partridges wouldn't stretch even his limited culinary skills. He reassured himself as to his intentions by making up the single bed in the small bedroom. She, of course, would have the double. And to celebrate, he helped himself to a double from the newly-acquired bottle of malt on the fireplace.

At 3:45 the doorbell rang. Good girl, he thought, a driver after my own heart, though three hours from the centre of London on a Friday would be pushing it, even for a speed maniac like him. High on anticipation, he opened the door. Dodgson and Simmonds stood in front of him.

The two men looked almost dapper in their regulation issue Jockey Club suits. Behind, he could see the outline of a BMW 5-series. The Club obviously understood that it was wise

David Lipsey

to pay well those who you wish to catch criminals. Temptation was ever present, and a fat salary cheque was the best antidote.

'How in God's name did you find this place?' Brendan gasped.

The question died on his lips. Had he not already established that the Jockey Club taps every jockey's mobile phone? They had probably been following his every move since he set off to find the man in the photographs after their interview. At least he would have been safe in the South of France. He couldn't see their telephone company co-operating with the Jockey Club as ours apparently did. But here in England, whatever the law might say, jockeys' phones were apparently fair game. There was no signal at the cottage, though, so there must have been some detective work involved. It probably explained why they had taken the best part of three days to find him. They would not be pleased.

'Nice to see you again, Brendan,' said Dodgson. 'We were a concerned not to have heard from you. After all, it's only a couple of days until the time you asked for runs out.'

'There's another thing. It occurred to us - you will forgive us I'm sure - that if you didn't find the man in the photographs, you might think it a good idea to go AWOL. Perhaps you might find yourself a tiny cottage on a big estate in the middle of Wales, where nobody knows you except the owner and his manager. You might think you would be well out of the range of the Jockey Club there.'

'That would have been a mistake,' added Simmonds. 'We wouldn't want you under any false illusions. So we thought

Counter Coup

we'd just pop by and say hello.'

'I don't suppose there is a chance of a nice cup of tea?' suggested Dodgson affably.

'Only if you want it over your faces,' said Brendan. The door slammed.

A minute or two later, he heard the BMW setting off down the drive. Dodgson tooted the horn to say goodbye.

It was another two hours before the bell went again.

'Sorry I'm late,' said Becky. 'Bloody traffic all down the M4.'

'It's good to see you,' said Brendan, kissing her enthusiastically on the cheeks. 'I'll just get your bags from the car, and take them up to the bedroom.'

Something was evidently not quite right. Becky paused for a second or two. 'Sorry, did you think I was staying here? Usually I'd stay with Dad over at Dolmaes but I thought that things might get too complicated so I'm booked into Dragoyd Hall.'

Brendan knew the place. A fine 17th century mansion near Hay, it had been redesigned in the 20th century by Sir Clough Williams-Ellis, famous for designing and building Portmerion, the Italianate village in North Wales. Dragoyd Hall was rather less exotic but very posh. The huge but fake Great Hall was lined with deep sofas facing the baronial stone fireplace, the morning room boasted a fine Blüthner grand piano. The library featured a perfectly maintained snooker table on which he had once or twice played late into the night after a successful afternoon at Hereford or Ludlow.

David Lipsey

It was the kind of country house hotel where the waiters lifted domes to uncover your dinner plate. A suite could be had for high hundreds a night. Breakfast was famous for the black pudding. Brendan had watched several young women friends of his whom you might have expected to be conscious of their weight finding that irresistible. Something the night before must have stimulated their appetites. When he came to think of it, and now his hideout had been blown to Dodgson and Simmonds, he was really going to enjoy his night with Becky there.

'John can't get away until later,' she said. 'He's joining me there for dinner.'

John. There was no ambiguity in the way she said the name. Brendan remembered the familiar feeling of being kicked in the solar plexus.

Why hadn't she mentioned John before? But why should she? She was his ally, not his girlfriend. She was helping him because her father had asked her to. Her personal life was no business of his.

He tried to give nothing away, but intuition is intuition and she could sense his disappointment.

'You've probably not met John Scadding before,' she said, letting him down as gently as she could. 'He's not very interested in racing, I'm afraid. He's a pharmacologist, a top one too. The champion jockey of pharmacology, they tell me.' Brendan absorbed what she was saying with as much equanimity as he could muster.

Becky went on. 'If you're theory about what they might

Counter Coup

have done to you at Bangor is right, he might be just what we need this weekend. I've asked him to bring a little equipment with him. Just in case anything needs testing. I'm sure you'll get on well with him. If it weren't for the fact that he keeps on about getting engaged, he'd be just about perfect for me.'

Brendan at that moment didn't care a jot whether he got on with the man or not. Either way it wasn't going to be the night he had hoped for.

'So, are we off to find the other Kantor now?' asked Becky.

'As soon as you're ready.'

'OK, get me a cuppa and let me pee and we'll go for it. Where's he living?'

'Felindre.'

Becky frowned. 'Wouldn't be his brother's style.'

They set off along the back roads at six. Becky drove. This was her territory - literally, since her family owned most of the land on either side - and she had known the obscure lanes all her life.

*****

Felindre was not one of those semi-English villages that surround Hay. Though it was in the National Park, it was not treated by the park authorities with the on-your-knees deference accorded to its posher counterparts. Permission had been granted for a large council estate at the top of the village and so there later seemed insufficient justification to resist corresponding private development. You could not call it a beautiful place, which meant the locals could still afford to live there.

At the bottom of the village the pub hung on, through good times and bad, its fortunes fluctuating with those of agriculture and local builders. But the village was not the kind of place that captured the heart of the retired and causes them to devote the rest of their lives to keeping the Post Office going. The school had long closed. The village hall had a faded and unused air. Occasionally it might host a whist drive for the WI but even the occasional young farmers' dances were sad affairs.

Felindre looked an unlikely venue for a criminal operation. A village lad might let down the odd tyre. Perhaps on a Friday, with the boys on a binge, a punch or two was thrown at closing time. Otherwise there wasn't much to be done without the whole village finding out. It certainly wasn't the obvious place to get involved in betting shenanigans. The nearest betting shop was in Brecon, a dozen miles away. Most of the local betting was on the little Welsh pacers, where the odds were as skinny as a fashion model, and £25 was a big bet. Felindre certainly wasn't anybody's candidate for betting capital of the universe.

The trouble with Becky's arrival was that it got Brendan's blood up. Until then he had been cautious, determined to keep his head down until they had a plan of action and the tactics to realise it. But Brendan, now his plans for the evening had died,

Counter Coup

had nothing else to do and felt the need for distraction from brooding on what might have been. Besides, he realised not without guilt, he was hooked on adrenalin, and now he wasn't getting it from race-riding. The chase had its own attractions. They walked around the village pretending to chat.

Just as Felindre was a nondescript village so 13, Church Road was a nondescript cottage. Semi-detached, it had been built at the turn of the century for the agricultural workers from the estate. That made it now much too small to house a modern family, and cramped even for a pair of weekenders. So alterations had taken place. What had been the smallholding was now a garden of some size. A conservatory had been added and the stable had become a spare room attached to the garage. It was just right for a couple, who might occasionally have their ageing parents to stay.

No car was to be seen, which seemed a pretty fair indication that no-one was about. The garage door had been left half-open. Fortunately, a high hedge protected the short drive leading to the garage from being seen from the house. Bidding Becky to watch out for him, Brendan set off up the drive, trying to think of a plausible tale he could tell if challenged.

What he saw under the door were books. Not just one or two books, but thousands of them. Some were on steel shelves, others were in packing cases, others again were simply lying in piles on the hard concrete floor.

'Keep watching, Becky,' said Brendan. 'I'm going to see what this lot is.' The garage had a foldaway door. He pushed it back, ducked under it and started to look through the titles.

David Lipsey

Brendan was not a literary man. He had heard of nearly none of the authors, and few of the subjects. But it was clear even to him that this was a very peculiar collection indeed. It did not have everything in it, far from it. One wall, for example, bore a cardboard placard proclaiming it was South America. But there was no corresponding placard for Asia, Africa or Europe. Another was headed 'philosophy'. But every book in it was by an Englishman. He picked up a few. Had he been educated that way he would have found that nearly all of them were by Englishmen at Oxford: Ayer, Strawson, Warnock. It was a tiny and desiccated area of philosophy that it covered, but clearly none other interested the books' collector.

The range of subjects was rather what you might expect of an obsessive autodidact: random but not scattergun. The man clearly knew what he liked, and what he didn't.

Every book was perfectly in alphabetical order by subject. Each had a label inside: *ex libris: Matthew Kantor.*

Brendan emerged, and looked through the window over the stream into the spare room next door. More books, many more, on shelves, in heaps, in boxes. He beckoned for Becky to join him, on the grounds that he would look less guilty with her by his side.

Gingerly they walked down the garden path and peered into the house. Even the kitchen was stuffed with books. From what they could see it was a collection of herbals of various kinds from various countries. The front room was evidently devoted to the South American history obsession for on the walls, as well as books, was a case containing what looked like

Counter Coup

a collection of South American blow pipes.

Felindre was the kind of place where no-one locked their doors. Somehow, they were drawn on way beyond the point where caution should have cried 'enough'.

At first, it seemed that there was really no more to see once they were inside. Brendan was just inspecting the case containing the blow pipes as a diversion from the dusty volumes when something caught his eye. He saw a small bowl of a white, sticky substance on the shelf immediately to the right.

Brendan had not been as keen on drugs as many of his colleagues, but that didn't mean he'd gone through life without any experience of them. He had a pretty shrewd idea of what was likely to be something potent when he saw it.

Becky's friend John might have destroyed his other plans but perhaps he could make up for it in the way Becky had suggested - by telling them what was in that bowl. He stuck a finger in, then scraped off a good dollop into his handkerchief.

'What are you doing?' a man's voice asked, behind him. The enquiry was soft and on the warm side of neutral – certainly not what you would expect if you had just been found helping yourself from someone's front room. Clearly, its owner had just come round the corner, missing the moment when Brendan was taking his sample.

He turned to see a short figure, slightly bowed, bald between two shocks of grey hair, and spouting a long, untidy beard. The phrase absent-minded professor sprung instantly to mind.

David Lipsey

They needed to take advantage of surprise, and Becky didn't hesitate. 'Mr. Smith, I believe?' she said and smiled. 'We're looking for Matt.'

For a normal person, this would have seemed a less than full answer. On the whole, people looking for others did not let themselves into the house and poke round. Certainly not a beautiful young woman and, what you would have expected to strike Smith more forcibly, a palpably fit young man.

But he didn't seem bothered. He just smiled back at Becky and said, 'Matt? He's down the road, at the drumming.'

They thanked him and strolled out. Indeed, as they turned into the garden, they could hear the sound of drumming: insistent, waxing soft and loud on the wind, almost hypnotic.

They followed their ears. A hundred yards away, on the road to Hay, stood a farm building in the early stages of disrepair. 'Rose Farm, organic farming and spiritual centre,' said a hand-painted notice outside. The windows were thick with dust and cobwebs. Brendan risked pressing his nose against them.

The sight was unexpected. There in a circle sat perhaps a dozen people, varying in age between 12 and 80. Some were in Laura Ashley skirts, some in dungarees or gardening jackets. Perhaps two thirds were women and one third men.

In the middle stood a tall, middle-aged man with a vague air, even through the glass, of spirituality. He was directing the drumming, looking as if he was transported to some far-off and better world. The faces of the devotees were fastened on him. *Pom pom pom pom pom pom*. And so it went on,

Counter Coup

unvaried, unaccented, weirdly compelling.

Any one of the faces would have stood out. But only one interested Brendan.

Matt Kantor was sitting on a small stool. The cheeks of his capacious bottom drooped down each side of the seat. He was wearing what looked like a schoolmaster's old suit, an open-necked and decidedly grubby white shirt, and an ancient pair of rimmed national health spectacles. His feet were bare and dirty. He had the largest drum in the ensemble, and the stare most fixed on their leader. Matt looked the epitome of benevolent goodness.

Physically, he was the spitting image of his brother. But otherwise it was hard to believe that he could possibly have anything in common with Mike, other than a father and a mother. He could not possibly be a doper and the cause of Brendan's downfall, surely?

David Lipsey

Counter Coup

Chapter 17

John Scadding had chosen the allegedly fast train to Abergavenny via Newport rather than the allegedly slow train to Hereford via Oxford, and, as usual, it was late. It was nearly eight pm before the three of them met up in Becky's room at Dragoyd.

The room was one of the hotel's best. It commanded sweeping views over the gardens, across the fields and down to the Wye, where the awake and the brave could take an early morning swim. They could see the rod of a salmon fisherman, still sweeping the pool in the hope of a late-evening rise.

Brendan was not sure that he wanted to like John. Half of him thought that he could be another ally, and allies were still remarkably few on the ground. Half of him thought they were rivals. However it was soon clear even to his prejudiced mind that Becky had not ended up with the man by accident. He looked good. He sounded good. And at least as much of his

David Lipsey

charm was directed at Brendan as at Becky.

The bedroom made an unlikely setting for a miniature laboratory, but that was what John had brought. Brendan did not pretend to know the names of the various items of equipment assembled on the chest-of-drawers, let alone their purpose.

'Just smear the white stuff here,' said John, holding out what looked a glass slide that looked vaguely familiar to Brendan from school. He took the handkerchief out of his pocket and smeared.

John pulled switches, and turned on plugs. The slide disappeared into a small box with digital instruments on the top. Nothing smelled, nothing burned, hummed, buzzed or whirred. Modern science evidently wasn't test tubes and Bunsen burners any more.

'Well?' said Brendan, after watching not much happen for a minute or two.

'Don't be so impatient.' said John. 'Once upon a time, a test like this would have taken a week, and even then you could not have been sure of the result. If we have dinner, and if we have plenty of courses, with luck it will be ready by the time we come up again.'

'I've got to get back to the cottage,' Brendan said, aware that he had still not entirely eliminated a sleep deficit which was large even by jockey standards. Even at that time of night, it was a good 45 minute drive.

'I can't guarantee exactly when we'll be done,' John said. 'If I were you, I'd book here if you still can.'

Counter Coup

A top pharmacologist knocking round with a rising lawyer clearly did not have to worry about money, in the way an almost ex-jockey should. Moreover, Brendan was not exactly thrilled at the idea of being under the same roof as the couple. He imagined waking in the small hours to the sound of Becky moaning, and suspected that dropping off again would not be so easy. Neither, however, would driving back be easy, especially with the return trip in the morning. Anyway, he wanted the result of John's test. And he wanted several stiff drinks with his dinner. What the hell. He booked.

Dinner was as good as they expected. Becky, with her background, took the fuss in her stride and enjoyed the chef's artifice. Judging by the way he handled the wine list, John was evidently accustomed to the lifestyle. Brendan, who secretly would have preferred steak-and-salad and a few beers, tried his hardest to be convivial. Fortunately, despite Brendan's predisposition, John confirmed Brendan's initial impressions. Indeed, by the time they got to the bottom of the second bottle, Brendan was starting to think that he might have made a lifelong friend.

It was well after eleven by the time they went up to look at the experiment. John examined a few dials, printed out a little graph and muttered to himself.

'It's as you thought. I've never come across this precise blend before. There seems to be a bit of curare, a little cocaine-derivative, and one or two bits-and-pieces of that ilk. Enough to stop an ox, but only for a few seconds. And then there is some rohypnol, you know, the stuff they call the date-rape drug. Not a lot, but probably enough to blur the immediate memory of anyone who got a dose.'

'That might explain a lot,' agreed Brendan.

'Anything else?' asked Becky, peering over the jockey's shoulder.

John paused, his smooth brow revealing just the hint of a wrinkle. 'There's just one thing that puzzles me. On their own, the ingredients would last months without losing their power. But once you've mixed them up together like this, they really would not last very long. The coke eats the curare you see. Twenty four hours, yes. Thirty six hours, very probably. Forty eight hours, pushing it. And the price of some of these today, you wouldn't think they'd want them going to waste.'

He thought in silence as he reread the print-out.

'This isn't the dose they used on you,' he concluded. 'This is a new mix. I wonder what's going on?'

Brendan's brain started to tick. Like any jockey, Brendan carried the racing calendar in his head. Even while John was speaking, the thought had flashed into his head. Tomorrow was racing at Hereford, 28 miles to the east, first race two o'clock. Kantor was at it again. Suddenly, his sleep deficit did not seem important any more.

'Right,' he said. 'You two lovebirds go to bed. I'm just going to pay another quick visit to Felindre.'

Before they could protest, he was gone.

*****

Counter Coup

He could not be sure that Kantor would still be up. He knew that Matt's brother kept late hours, and it was possible that reading into the small hours was Matt's equivalent of the casino and the brothel. But Smith looked as if he would be scared by the dark. Lights out at 9:30 for that one, he thought.

Brendan was worried for a moment that Smith would have asked Matt if his visitors had caught up with him at the drumming. But Matt was probably out of it, in a world of his own after the ritual. He could hear Matt asking 'what visitors?' He doubted that Smith would be the ideal person to give an accurate description. Probably Matt would think that it was all a figment of his partner's imagination.

Brendan left the car below the pub and walked as silently as he could up the lane. The lights were still on in the Kantor-Smith sitting-room. The wall provided him with cover and he could be reasonably sure that neither car, man nor beast would pass that way so late. He crept nearer.

Eavesdropping is not a habit that country folk much guard against, and the night was still warm enough for the window to have been left ajar. Brendan was lucky too with the wind direction. Matt Kantor was speaking. Straining only slightly, Brendan could hear every word.

'I won't do it. Not again. I was scared rigid last time. That poor jockey. Broken shoulder. Warned off. He will never be able to ride again. What had he ever done to me? For you it may be all right to destroy people. You've been selfish all your life.'

Smith's little voice piped up. 'You made Matt so unhappy

with that Donoughue business. For a fortnight he hardly read a thing. Just leave him alone.'

The third man had his head turned into the room. He was barely audible, and Brendan could not at first identify the voice. 'Shut up, poofter. You keep your nose out of this, you filthy little pervert. Or I'll make sure you don't have a nose left to keep out of anything ever again.'

Then the speaker turned towards Matt Kantor. Brendan strained to see him. He could only manage the top of his head. But that was enough. That cauliflower ear could only belong to one man. Mike. He was not staying in the South of France and leaving it to his henchmen this time. He was here to supervise operations in person.

'Now Matt. What would mum say if she could see you now?'

For a moment the bully was on hold. Mike Kantor's voice was quiet, soothing, insistent. 'Do you remember what it was like when you had that spot of money trouble? How it was? First you couldn't go into one bookshop without being harassed for a cheque, then another, then only cash would do? Then the ban? Took more than the local travelling library to keep you in what you need, didn't it?'

The elder Kantor waited for a moment while the memory surfaced. 'And the selling too. That collection of books on the railways of India under the Raj. Taken you years to get that together, you said. Saying goodbye to those must have hurt. And only a couple of hundred pounds for the lot. Chickenfeed. What would it have been next if I hadn't come up with this little proposition? South America? The Trollope?'

Counter Coup

The best Matt could manage in protest was a whimper.

'Anyway, you've done all the hard work already. You've made up the dope, found all the ingredients.

'That wasn't easy,' protested Matt, 'not round here.'

'I know that,' Mike went on. 'Bangor was just the rehearsal, though you didn't seem to mind the £1,500 you got for it. It cleared the bills around Hay didn't it? No it was only after you read all that crap about Donoughue in the newspapers that you went weepy on me. But tomorrow is the real thing. The big money. The pay-off for life.'

'Why tomorrow? Why me?'

'Because I can't go near the place, can I?'

'I've made the dope, though. Why can't you get someone else to do it?'

'I only trust you Matt,' Mike told him with uncharacteristic patience. 'Ever since Bangor, Futtnam has been aching to get his money back. And tomorrow is the day he is going to do it. A horse of his called King Omni. This time his team won't be betting in tenners and scores. It'll all be monkeys and grands.'

Still listening in the dark Brendan could imagine the piles of notes being pushed across betting shop counters up and down the land. He could see Futtnam and his friends working their credit accounts, relishing their coming win. And he could also see the faces of the bookmakers in the know, the ones who were paying Kantor richly to make sure that King Omni got beaten.

'If the horse wins, Futtnam will never have to train a donkey again. If it loses, Siberia wouldn't be far enough away

David Lipsey

for him to be safe from the boys, with gambling debts like he's got. He's even promised his jockey a proper present - just in case of a repeat of last time, when a bribed jockey fell off. Or at least that's what he still thinks happened last time.'

Mike chuckled. 'Hasn't told a soul who doesn't need to know. Except the wife. Big mistake, telling the wife. She may seem all blonde hair and big boobs and blow-jobs in the back of the horsebox. But women like that cost money, believe me. He should never have closed her Harrods' account. Now she has to get her wherewithal elsewhere, and there's a bookie friend of mine who is only too happy to oblige. He gives her a seeing to and the dosh, in return for the right information. Which is why I know that King Omni will be backed off course tomorrow at every betting shop in the country by Futtnam's agents, a few seconds before the off so no-one has time to cut the price.'

Mike was in his stride now, demonstrating his scam whether Matt and his partner were interested or not. 'At the same time, on-course, Futtnam will be loading it big on the favourite to win to improve the price on King Omni, just like he did that day the Baron came down. And why, if the plan works, the betting industry will be two million pounds lighter. Only thing is, it isn't going to work. I intend to make sure that King Omni won't win - in return for a little share in the proceeds from some of my bookmaking friends. And with a little help from you, Matthew my old mate.'

Brendan heard a loud thwack of fist on table as Mike emphasised his point. Then there was silence for a moment.

Counter Coup

'Mike, please don't make me,' said Matt eventually in a low, tremulous voice. 'Get someone else, I'll not tell. I got away from all that, I got a life, a home, a friend, my books. Yes I know I'm an addict, but *books*; surely I don't have to have my life ruined just because I like books too much. Leave me alone, Mike.'

Mike snorted derisively. 'Make you? How could I make you Matt? You're your own man, aren't you? Free will, I think they call it in that philosophy stuff you read. You can do exactly what you want. And so can I, Matt, so can I. For example, I could go to the car now, get a tin of petrol and take it out to the garage - put a match to it. Those books, old books aren't they, they must be dry as dust. A lovely fire they'd make. And I don't think you'd be calling in any police, not after what you did to Donoughue,' Mike paused, for effect. 'Not even if Smithy here got stuck in the toilet and went up with the books.'

He could smell his brother's fear. Now was the time to press home his advantage. 'And mum. I know you couldn't have her to live here, not with her views on gays. I respect you for that. But you found the best home you could, overlooking the river. Angels the staff, you were telling me, angels. And you visit once a week. It costs, though, that kind of care though, doesn't it Matt? I know because I sign the cheques. And if I found myself a bit short, because I didn't collect tomorrow, I might not be able to sign the cheques any more. I wonder how long they'd keep her there when the bills stopped being paid?'

Matt started to moan. Brendan could see him, arms clutched across his chest, rocking to and fro like a baby.

David Lipsey

'First time, yes, that was difficult for you. Then, you were selling your principles and that is hard. But you can't sell your principles twice, any more than you can lose your virginity twice. This time'll be easier. Of course I'll make it worth your while. Very worth your while. And I promise you, you will never have to do it again. I can't say fairer than that, can I?'

From his pocket, Kantor drew a copy of the *Racing Post*, already well thumbed. He turned to weekend entries. '3:30 Hereford. 3m 2f novices hurdle for 4-year-olds and upwards. Number one, King Omni. 8 to 1.'

He could be shorter, Brendan knew, if most of the bookies failed to get the message that steps had been taken to make sure the horse lost. He could be longer if they didn't and Futtnam repeated his trick of backing the favourite. Either way, the bookmakers were going to end up making a whole lot of money.

Brendan couldn't tell if any of Michael's threats were real. Burning the books would be easy. With Smith locked up with them? He thought probably not. Mike Kantor was not a nice man, but murder would be a bit dangerous for his liking. Getting mum evicted? Well, that could hurt Mike as well as Matt, and even Brummie crooks were a bit sentimental. Anyway the point was not really whether the threats were real. The point was whether poor Matt was likely to think they were.

Matt lived in the world of books. He imbibed fiction as well as fact, as the Trollope showed. A good author can make even a far-fetched plot plausible. His brother certainly had a touch of the persuasive author's gift: the plausible detail, the

Counter Coup

uncompromising tone, the sheer, consistent inhumanity of every word. Brendan felt sure that Matt was sitting there thinking burnt books, dead lover, homeless mother. The injustice to a jockey he didn't know would by now seem a minor problem beside all that.

Matt had got away with it last time. So far as he knew he had still got away with it. The day after the race, he had been back in Felindre, same as ever, except that he was *persona grata* in the bookshops again. He could remember the purchases he made that day, and felt the warm glow of ownership creep over him. If this was the big one, what desirable volumes might not, in 24 hours time, be within his grasp?

The conversation inside the house might still have hours to run. But however long it went on, Brendan was quite sure what the outcome would be. At three thirty five the next day, as the horses approached the second last hurdle, there would be a middle aged, fat man with a blowpipe, and there would be another ghastly fall.

Brendan turned to leave. His foot struck a stone that clattered against the wall.

For such a man-mountain, Mike Kantor moved fast. The curtains opened.

'What the hell was that?'

Brendan, lying now behind the low wall, froze.

'Just a sheep, Mike. Just a sheep,' Brendan heard Smith reply wearily.

Fortunately the sheep in the field opposite heard the

voices and set off a confirmatory 'baa'.

Kantor looked as if he was thinking of giving them a bit of a hiding for their pains. Then he thought of the effort involved, effort he might still need to expend on his brother and the boyfriend before the night was out if they continued to be awkward. Grunting, he returned to the task in hand.

Brendan drove to Dragoyd Hall. He had half-hoped that Becky and John might have stayed up for him. As he climbed the stairs and passed their room, a gentle fugue of male gasps and female moans showed that his hopes had been dashed. It took several large whiskies to banish the sound from his head.

Counter Coup

Chapter 18

The habit of a lifetime's early gallops dies hard. Brendan's sleep deficit did not stop him waking before seven am. The birds were singing, the sun was shining and his situation still stank. By now he had a good idea what had happened to him. But proving it seemed as hard as ever, and the deadline was moving relentlessly closer.

For a few minutes, he lay motionless, staring at the ceiling and feeling rather sick. The whisky repeated on his breath. He wondered about a hair of the dog, and then decided, with an effort, that it was too soon for that, even for him. Eventually Brendan concluded that nothing was going to be made better by lying in bed. A swim might help get him going. He grabbed one of the hotel bath towels and flung on shorts and shirt.

A 'do not disturb' notice hung outside Becky's door. There was no need to listen at the keyhole. Even from across the corridor, it was evident that the couple were not asleep.

David Lipsey

Brendan suffered a repeat performance of the one he had heard only a few hours before.

Once downstairs, he heard the sounds of silver being laid on tables in the dining room and waiters talking in low tones. For a country house hotel, this was very early. There was no smell of coffee, no sizzle of frying bacon. Reception was unmanned. Except for Brendan, not a guest stirred.

He walked through the garden, across the fields to the pool above the weir by the fishing hut. A farmer was already at work, ploughing the field on the far side of the valley, but down by the river all was quiet. The solitary fisherman of the night before was not there. The season was all but over and the hut was locked up.

At that time of the morning, in the middle of the countryside, modesty did not require swimwear. Brendan much preferred the freedom of nakedness, the intimacy of water on flesh.

He waded out across the rocks, towards a patch of quiet water and a deeper pool. He took a deep breath and plunged in. For a moment, at the shock of the cold water, his problems seemed distant. He swam a few powerful strokes of crawl, then breast-stroked round for a few minutes before lying on his back, barely bothering to kick. A heron stood on the bank upstream, oblivious to him, watching for fish. He heard a gentle splash as small trout rose for flies, the insistent call of a moorhen, and the distant bleat of sheep.

The water was low and the sound of the weir just beneath him was soothing music in his ears. But the blissful seconds

Counter Coup

where no worries stood between him and the water soon passed. His was not a predicament that even cold water could easily wash away.

He knew where Kantor was, that was something, and he knew broadly what was planned for that afternoon. The trouble was that he had absolutely no proof for any of it. He could imagine the sceptical look on Dodgson and Simmonds' faces if he was to tell them what he'd heard. With time running out, they would think that he was desperate, making up any yarn, however implausible, to buy time. Anyway, they'd want more than Kantor's identity and whereabouts.

They wanted to get him once and for all. That meant providing a crime. The only way of doing that was to catch them in the act. The only place to do it in time was at Hereford.

Brendan's problem was going to be getting anywhere near the scene of the action. He had been warned off and there were few more familiar faces round a racecourse than his. Any attempt to get into Hereford was bound to be spotted, and be followed by ignominious eviction.

That thought had only just dawned on him when another, more immediate and disquieting, overtook it. He realised that he was not alone.

Jockeys are born with a sixth sense. It is a sense they need in their profession - for the trainer who is going to promise rides and then give them to someone else, for the owner who blames you every time his horse is beaten, for the journalist who swears eternal fealty as preparation for doing you over. It is the sense that tells when a rival behind is going well and

David Lipsey

you need to put the pressure on; that warns them that a horse is about to make a mistake and throw you out of the saddle and prepare to roll into a ball, while you wait for the rest to go by and hope you avoid a kicking.

As he clambered out of the water, Brendan was aware of a tingling feeling at the nape of his neck. He knew that feeling. It meant that someone had eyes on him. Looking up, he caught a flash of early morning sunlight off a pair of binoculars. In a moment's fantasy, he hoped that it might be a tasty maiden, surveying him in all his glory. The trouble with fantasies is that they do not last long.

He heard the tell-tale noise of a snapping twig and the rustle of dead leaves. He was just able to see, slouching away with bent backs, two heads. They were not tasty and they were unmistakably male. Even from behind, at a distance, there was no mistaking Dodgson and Simmonds. They may not have been much good at catching criminals, but they were no slouches when it came to following him.

The peace he had acquired during his swim rapidly drained away. The sickness in the pit of his stomach – like the feeling when the starter mounts his rostrum – returned, but with none of the compensating excitement of the race to come.

Brendan dried himself, dressed, and walked slowly up to the hotel, which was still almost silent. The 'do not disturb' notice still hung on Becky's door. This time, however, there was also a tray that bore the remnants of croissants and coffee, a pitcher that had contained freshly-squeezed orange juice, nearly all gone, and an ice-bucket with an empty half-bottle of

Counter Coup

champagne. It looked as if he would be breakfasting alone.

Four notes had been pushed under his door from reception. Suddenly, he seemed to be a popular man.

The first was on Dragoyd's own headed paper. It was from Becky. 'Came to check you were all right but you seem to have gone out. What time shall we meet? And where?'

How delighted John must have been when she returned to bed to report Brendan's absence.

The second was headed with the red lion and unicorn logo of the House of Lords, crossed out and the address: Pen-y-rhoel Castle, Crickhowell, Powys.

'Dear Brendan,' Henry's brief scrawl read. 'Do let me know if I can be of any further assistance. I trust you are not placing my daughter in any danger.'

How did Henry know where he was? He would have thought that beyond even Ms Burgess. Had Becky phoned him? Had he happened by? Or were the staff of the estate under a general instruction to keep an eye on a well-known ex-jockey and to report anything they saw to Henry personally?

The third was on Jockey Club paper. 'Brendan,' it began, without feeling the need for 'dear'. 'The fourteen days are up. We didn't specify any particular time, so we won't bother you again until this evening. However, perhaps you feel like telling us who the man in the photo is now. If so, give us a call on 07971 465 391. Then we can arrange something more agreeable for ourselves for the evening than following you.'

Brendan took some satisfaction in tearing the last note into shreds and tossing it and the phone number into the waste bin.

The fourth message was in a brown paper envelope. The hand in which it was addressed was decidedly shaky, but not, Brendan thought, an old person's hand. Perhaps it belonged to a heavy drinker? The note itself was on a piece of cheap lined paper, torn off a pad such as people use for shopping lists. It did not bother with courtesies, and was littered with four-letter words.

Its author had been given to understand by some friends of his brothers in Hay that certain inquires were being made in the town. He had decided to take the precaution of ringing round the local hotels to see if they had a guest called Donoughue, and Dragoyd had.

'Shit,' said Brendan. He realised how foolish he had been to check in under his own name. Sure, he would have been recognised if he had used a pseudonym, but hotels like Dragoyd do not thrive by failing to realise that famous people sometimes want a hideaway.

Kantor's letter stressed that the attentions that Brendan was giving him were not welcome. He could, of course, have him seen to. Or perhaps he might have his girlfriend seen to. *Such* a pity it would be to spoil that pretty face.

Brendan was not sure that he could reassure Henry about his daughter's safety.

Kantor's final words were to the point. 'Brendan, it's time you disappeared. Now. For ever.'

There was studied ambiguity in the phrase. Perhaps Kantor meant no more than that Brendan should take a flight, to

Counter Coup

somewhere a very long way away, without ever coming back. Or perhaps he meant something even more permanent.

If Brendan's body was found, no-one would be very surprised. It would be pretty obvious really: suicide. After what he had been through. After what he had done. Even Becky might not be that suspicious. He had to admit that it was neat. The tabloids would enjoy a lurid weekend, exposing his past loves and excesses. The coroner would express his regrets. And that would be that. Kantor would be safe back in Cannes. Becky would weep a tear or two and then get on with her love life and the law. Tanya would soon find someone else.

He was almost tempted to co-operate.

The condemned man thought that he should first enjoy a hearty breakfast. Muesli, for the roughage; a bowl of exotic fruit salad, for the vitamin C, and eggs, bacon, sausages, tomatoes, fried soda bread, potato hash and mushrooms, for the what-the-hell. Toast, marmalade, coffee: he felt a new man. Dragoyd was a first-class hotel, used to dealing with the special requests of guests. While the rest of the tables read their *Times* and *Daily Mails*, the *Racing Post* was sitting waiting for him.

He ignored the big race preview on page one, and turned to Hereford. It was mostly as he had expected. 3:30 Lord Omni, in a field of twelve chasers, none of them outstanding: fourth favourite at the predicted odds in the betting. The only new information, however, was unwelcome. Whereas yesterday the horse had no rider against its name, today, it was down to be ridden by Peter Marston.

Peter Marston was Brendan's best friend in the weighing

room. He always slapped you on the back, whether you had beaten him a short head or he had beaten you the same. He was the last to turn in every night and the first to rise every morning. He had a mordant joke for every situation and an appetite for life that lifted you every moment you were with him.

He, only he, of the other jockeys, had rung Brendan to commiserate after his warning-off. Only Peter had said 'see you soon, mate - all the best,' as if he meant it.

That afternoon, just after three thirty, Peter was going to be in precisely the same situation as was Brendan now. He was facing a couple of seconds which would effectively mean the end of his life as it was. And the end of that life for Trixie, of whose delights Brendan had his own knowledge from the days before Peter came on the scene, and for the two daughters on whom he doted, and the three retired greyhounds around whom their off-course lives revolved.

It could not be allowed to happen. He must ring him. Warn him. Before he got hurt, got killed, or at least turned into racing's public enemy number one in succession to Brendan. It was his duty as a friend to save him from the fate which the Kantors had lined up for him.

If Brendan did that, though, Peter could not just disappear. He would have to explain himself. The authorities would be notified. The lid would be off the plot. Probably, the trainer would just pull King Omni out of the race. Why run risks? Even if he ran, the racecourse would be swarming with security men. Matt Kantor was not so unworldly that he would get up to any

Counter Coup

tricks in that situation. Peter would be fine, thank God, and so would King Omni, and some people would win a lot of money and others lose it. But Brendan's own life would still be wrecked. There was only one way in which he could save himself, he understood. That was by finding hard evidence of what he knew to be the case, but which he was, as things stood, quite unable to prove.

He had to save Peter Marston. But he also had to save himself. He had to find another way. If that meant, for starters, getting into a racecourse from which he was banned then he would have to do it. How to do it was another matter.

Brendan scanned the *Post's* coverage of the day ahead at Hereford. In normal times, it would have sounded like a fun day. True, the races could have been of higher quality. Brendan reckoned he could have won the selling hurdle on most donkeys off Skegness beach. Half the horses in the three mile chase had failed to complete in their most recent outing, and the rest were as motley a crew of non-stayers and rogues as he could easily remember.

But Hereford on an autumn weekend always attracted a good crowd. And under its new ownership, Brendan read, the course was putting on a show. There was to be dancing after racing. A jazz band was promised. Free tastings of the local cider were laid on. And the children were not forgotten: not just the usual bouncy castle, and the crèche for under-fives, but free ice creams and a visit from Chico the Clown.

Brendan had an idea. He wished it did not involve Becky but it couldn't be done single handed. Besides, and whether she realised it or not, Becky was in deep already. So he shoved a note under the lovebirds' door, asking them to meet him for coffee at Oscar's in Hay at eleven thirty AM, and to bring with them the substance he had borrowed from the Kantors.

More than an hour before that, he reached Hay himself. Not for the first time, he thanked God for giving him powers of observation and memory which compensated for his deficiencies in the intellectual stakes. There was, as he remembered, a children's book shop at the bottom of the town. For all the popular adult belief that children only watched television these days, it was evidently doing a thriving business. Milly-Molly-Mandy and the Famous Five weren't dead in Hay. Four year-olds were led by the hand in and out, each emerging with a little pile of picture books. The odd teenage girl slouched in, glancing furtively from side to side in case any of her friends noticed what she were doing when she should have been ogling boys from outside the public convenience across the road. And older couples in their fifties and sixties came out with the biggest collections of all. The boom in grandparenting was obviously sustaining this part of the Hay economy.

A gaily painted notice outside the shop, advertised its wares. 'Thousands of books for children of all ages. Also: vintage toys. Hornby Dublo model railways. Original Mecanno a speciality. Children's parties catered for. Magic tricks. Entertainer's outfits for hire.'

Brendan remembered ruefully how often he had been called a clown by trainers who had not thought much of the

Counter Coup

ride he had given one of their horses. Dressing up as a clown would be appearing in character. A visit to the chemist's shop opposite the market completed his errands.

A little to Brendan's surprise, John and Becky arrived at Oscar's punctually as they had been asked. No stamina, today's young people, he thought as he remembered their night of activity. If it had been him, he would have been in bed through lunch and tea. Then he remembered that Becky had been prepared to give that up to fit in with his plans, and felt appropriately chastened.

He was sitting with a cappuccino when they walked in. By his side was a polythene bag, containing a small disposable camera and a very large, old-fashioned looking brown-paper parcel.

He did not make them contain their curiosity long. He undid the string and laid out the contents. Inside was a pair of bright pink pantaloons, a pair of black shoes three feet long with curling green toes, a jacket in orange with huge red rose-shaped buttons and blue spots, and a clown's mask and hat. The package also held three balls for juggling. Brendan had never actually tried juggling except when trying to fit his rides into an impossible travel schedule, but given the clowns who seemed to manage it, he imagined that it couldn't be very difficult. There was a gaily-painted old-fashioned peashooter in wood and an envelope containing dried peas. Through each pea, Brendan had stuck a pin so that just the last few millimetres of the tip poked through.

The colour scheme of his outfit might not have been all

that Becky wished for but she could imagine what the ensemble would look like on Brendan and laughed. John laughed too.

'What on earth is that lot for?' asked Becky.

'We're going to the races,' replied Brendan.

Counter Coup

Chapter 19

Hereford didn't rank among Britain's most scenic racecourses. True, from the grandstand the Eastern scarp of the Black Mountains was visible in the distance and, closer to, a glimpse of the top of Hereford Cathedral where the *Mappa Mundi*, the most ancient map of the world, is housed. But an unappetising industrial estate and a shopping park lay between course and cathedral, giving the scene an untidy look. The traffic going in could be bad. The traffic out was terrible.

Hereford managed a jolly atmosphere, despite this, especially when full. And there was a right crowd in that day: beery coach-loads from the Midlands, red-faced Herefordshire farmers, and town families up for the children's entertainment as much as the racing. You couldn't get a drink unless you were prepared to push. The best of the food had gone an hour before racing started and the queues at the on-course betting shop were long enough to deter all but the most desperate.

David Lipsey

Brendan was used to wearing odd-coloured clothes. His clown outfit was only a little more garish than the silks he carried for some owners. He'd also taken a practice run round the car park in Hay, trying to perfect his juggling, amazed that he was completely ignored by the crowds of arriving bibliophiles.

When he'd first put on the clown's uniform he felt like a prat. But he was surprised to find how quickly self-consciousness evaporated. Indeed, as he drove through the gate of the racecourse he nearly made the mistake of heading for the trainers' and jockeys' car park. He gathered himself in time and found a space for his car at the bottom of the field.

Becky and John were travelling separately. They didn't want to risk suspicion by being with Brendan, particularly Brendan in clown's uniform. Their plan of action was agreed and it included an understanding that they would not meet again until after racing.

Moving about as a clown was more problematic than he had thought. He longed for his usual loafers rather than the monstrous ill-fitting clown's shoes, which threatened to trip him up at any moment. The children were getting into the party mood around him. There were cries of "Oy, mister'. Daring little ones touched him and rushed off giggling. Toddlers hid in their mothers' skirts. Used though he was to being a focus of popular attention, this was something else. He didn't think he would take to clowning if riding did turn out to be barred to him. However, his disguise worked, and that was the main thing.

Counter Coup

When he got to the entrance, Brendan was ushered without question past the punters queuing to pay and through the gates. Free entry: once the day's work was done, perhaps he could hire his outfit for a modest fee to impecunious would-be race goers. Being a clown, it seemed, got you a long way.

Before long, he was surrounded by familiar faces; jockeys he had weighed out with a thousand times and their valets, owners he had pleased and not pleased, trainers, bookmakers and bookies' agents, gatemen, barmaids - above all the cheery Tote girls of every age in the smart red uniforms that he used to enjoy unbuttoning after racing in the changing room at the back of the Tote Credit office. He knew them all but that day they didn't know him.

He even saw Futtnam who stared straight through him. Futtnam, evidently, had something big on his mind. Brendan thought of having a sandwich but then decided that a clown with a sandwich in his mouth might attract unwelcome attention. He thought of a drink or even two drinks. He cancelled the idea. He needed all his wits about him and a drinking clown would attract even more attention than an eating one. Thank God for the Dragoyd Hall breakfast.

As the horses arrived in the paddock for the first, he wandered over. Normally he would have been looking to see what looked well, and what didn't; what seemed to have been laid out for the race and what hadn't; what, if his mount was fancied that day, might be the danger. But that wasn't needed today.

The first race was soon up, off and over; then the second

and the third. The crowd seemed to enjoy it, but he had to admit that he found it hard to concentrate on the horses. Even when a nice chaser he knew took a fall, and both the vet and the paramedics were summoned, he remained disengaged. He had too much on his mind – what might be the biggest event of his life so far. But it didn't help that he'd collected a Pied Piper's following of little ones, begging him to do tricks.

'Hey, Mister!'

'Hey, Mister Clown!'

'Hey, Big Feet!'

'Give us a juggle - else what you got them balls for?'

'Bet they're the only ones he's got!'

He resisted the urge to take on one particularly persistent brat and smack his cheeky face for him. He thought that might be unwise, what with the youngster's approving mum and his particularly chunky dad looking on with a smile.

Finally, the horses came into the parade ring for the fourth, King Omni's race. Even as a jockey, Brendan had never found it particularly easy to fill the nervy twenty minutes before a race. But as a jockey, he had his little routines; checking his whip and giving it a smack on his boot by way of a warm-up, making sure the lead was in the saddle cloth, the cheery 'how do?' to the owner, crossing himself just as his horse left the ring. Today, he had to make his own diversions.

He watched Futtnam give Peter Marston his instructions, followed by a leg-up into the saddle.

Futtnam looked anxious. He kept staring at the horse's legs, as if he suspected that something might be wrong with

Counter Coup

them. He even felt a forelock up and down, looking for heat. The old trainer's trick, thought Brendan - make them think something's wrong with your hotpot and the price usually improved. Peter, however, seemed not to have been briefed on this part of the affair. He didn't look like a man who was sitting on a horse with a problem. He looked like a man who was looking forward to a winner.

Brendan followed Futtnam as he sauntered down to the betting ring.

At Hereford, there were only three rails bookmakers, none of them big names. The market was strong enough with tenners and scores – a working man's sort of a betting market - but there were very few thick bets. So when Futtnam placed £1,000 on the favourite, the price tumbled down immediately from 6/4 to even money. King Omni, which had opened at 8/1, was pushed out to 10/1, then 12/1.

How many thousands at how many betting shops had Futtnam had placed on him through his agents, Brendan wondered? How many bookmakers accepted the bets with a smile? They knew what Futtnam did not know. They knew arrangements had been made to make sure that, whatever Futtnam might think, there was no way that King Omni was going to win that day. How much did Futtnam think he was about to win and how much in bookies' bribes did the Kantors stand to make for ensuring that he didn't? Both sums included an awful lot of noughts.

Futtnam had another monkey on the favourite: £500 at even money. The horse immediately went to odds-on. King

David Lipsey

Omni drifted to 14/1, even 16/1 on one board. On course, at any rate, it seemed he had few friends.

It was time to get moving. If he left it too late, he wouldn't get across the course until the horses were going down, and the crossing was closed. A clown trying to dodge security men to get to the other side was not likely to go unnoticed. With his trailing party of children, he could be easily get arrested for putting them at risk.

Even in clown's shoes, it was only a brief walk from the lawn sloping down from the members' enclosure to the second last. That fence at Hereford is just before the final turn, the short straight and the run-in. The course is a sharp one, said to suit nippy types. Certainly it's rare for any horse out of contention two fences out to get involved in the finish.

Brendan didn't need to have heard Futtnam's instructions to Peter Marston to know what they were. By the time he got to the second-last, if Brendan had it right, Futtnam would have ordered Peter to lead. By the time he was over it, the race, bar the last, would be in the bag, and Futtnam's agents round the country could get ready to collect the proceeds of the biggest payday of his murky career.

As Brendan walked up to the fence, the last of the children peeled off, at last scared enough at being away from their parents' to resist the lure of the clown. He felt suddenly alone. Then he spotted Becky in a short summery dress and a too-smart handbag. She was leaning with a dozen or so other spectators against the rail, trying to look casual. A yard or two away stood John, keeping a watchful eye on her and him. The

Counter Coup

gaggle around the fence meant that he had to get a little closer before he saw what he had really expected. On the landing side of fence stood Matt Kantor.

He looked pale. He seemed to be shaking and shifted from foot to foot. 'You really don't like doing this, old son, do you?' thought Brendan. 'Not like your brother at all.'

'They're off,' the race commentator announced, and soon the horses were past the fence where Brendan and Kantor stood, on the first circuit. The pace was a fast one. That should suit King Omni, who stayed a bit further than the two miles of the race, thought Brendan. King Omni was soon handy, despite the pace, going well, just a couple of lengths behind some tearaway with an apprentice up, and alongside the favourite. Brendan couldn't help but admire the professional skill that enabled Peter to present him perfectly at every fence. It was as much to the credit of the jockey as to the horse that he jumped like a stag.

Four fences out, the favourite was going well too and it looked anyone's race. But King Omni put in the better leap at the third last, and Peter had only to give him a nudge to take it up on the flat after the fence.

The jockey on the favourite began to look anxious. His motions became more urgent. He kicked and shoved. He gave the horse a slap down the neck with the whip, then a crack behind the saddle, then several cracks, each more compelling than the previous one.

He wasn't play-acting, that was for sure. The horse was trying to win that afternoon but King Omni clearly had his measure. Approaching the second last, Peter took a quick look over his right shoulder. Already he was a couple of lengths clear, and knew that he had the race won, bar a fall.

At that moment, Matt Kantor reached into his pocket and took out a small white tube that looked like a cigarette. He didn't light it. Instead there was a flurry of movement as he shoved what looked like a pellet into it. He breathed in deep, and lifted the tube to his mouth, aiming at the spot where he could see that King Omni's jockey would be as he touched down after the fence. Becky raised her camera, focused on Kantor and pressed the button.

A fraction of a second later, Brendan aimed his peashooter at Kantor and blew hard.

Neither of them could believe the suddenness of the effect. At one moment, Kantor seemed like a man in full possession of his faculties. At the next, his co-ordination seemed to have vanished. His hand shot up to the spot on his neck where Brendan's poisoned pea had struck him. He dropped the 'cigarette', stumbled without quite falling, and muttered an oath.

Quite something, this white stuff of the Kantors, thought Brendan.

Kantor's recovery was as swift as his malaise, a matter of a few seconds only. But it was not quick enough. For one thing, John seized the white tube where he had dropped it, and transferred it in a flash to his inside pocket. For another King Omni was now over the second last, with the favourite toiling now in his wake.

Counter Coup

The lead round the final bend began to lengthen - four, six, eight lengths. Kantor could only watch, open-mouthed, impotent, horrified.

King Omni and Peter approached the last. Should he fiddle it or go for it? That was the question in the jockey's mind, as it had been for Brendan that afternoon at Bangor weeks earlier - before his ability to decide was taken away from him.

When a horse is going as well as King Omni was you don't want to risk unsettling him. Taking a tug can unbalance a horse, or shake his confidence. Besides, the exhilaration of victory was already pumping adrenalin around Peter's body.

No matter how many winners you have ridden, there is nothing quite like it, time and time again. And the more spectacular the way you do it, the greater the thrill.

Peter went for it. He kicked King Omni hard in the belly a good half a dozen strides from the fence. King Omni stood back a mile, but he met the fence perfectly. A huge roar of appreciation went up from the crowd as he soared over.

King Omni might be an average horse in a moderate race at a minor racecourse, but it was a jump a Gold Cup winner would have struggled to better.

Peter rode him out with hands and heels to the line, not even bothering to look behind him. The favourite scrambled over the last, and followed him home at a respectful distance, still well clear of the third.

'First, number one, King Omni,' came the dispassionate voice of the official announcement over the loudspeakers.

Back by the second-last, Becky didn't suppose that Kantor

had seen her and her camera. He was in any case scrabbling about in the long grass, looking for his missing tube. But there was no point in taking any risks. She winked at Brendan, beckoned to John, and made for the racecourse exit.

Brendan was tempted to follow immediately but he felt that a bustling clown taking off from the racecourse in a hurry might arouse suspicions. They might not alert Matt Kantor, who was wandering around staring at the grass in a daze, but if he was there and saw it, they'd certainly alert Mike.

Whistling a merry tune, Brendan drew the balls from his pocket and tried to look as if he knew how to juggle.

As he crossed the course again, he could see Futtnam rushing out from the Members' Enclosure to greet his winner. He was a bastard, thought Brendan charitably, but he was the kind of bastard you could forgive because he's only climbed out of the gutter in the first place by being one. And Futtnam was now a rich bastard. Say £100,000 on King Omni at a likely starting price of 16/1 at worst. Towards £2m the richer – that was knocking a hole in the bookmakers' profits that would hurt some of them for months. A nice day's work if you could get it.

As for the bookmakers, they knew they were stuffed. They might suspect foul play but they couldn't refuse to pay out. The straight bookmakers knew what the public really thought of them. They couldn't afford to seem bad losers. They might have their suspicions, but they had to keep them under their trilbys. And the crooked amongst them had been part of the Kantor plot. They wanted an official investigation into the race like a hole in the head.

Counter Coup

Brendan, who knew what it was like to fall out with Futtnam, now saw what it was like to do him a favour. The trainer positively bounced with joy. His weathered face seemed to be one big grin. He seemed unable to stop clapping Peter on the back, so that eventually the jockey had to tear himself free to walk away with his saddle. Futtnam retired to the trainers' bar with the owner and his chums. Brendan could hear the pop of champagne corks as the loudspeaker proclaimed 'weighed in'. The runners for the four o'clock were announced. Somehow, Brendan in a clown's uniform could not raise much interest in a five-runner, two-mile claiming hurdle for some of the slowest horses in training. It was time to go.

He passed the top end of the paddock, beside the saddling boxes and the pre-parade ring. The horses had already gone through to the paddock itself for the race, and the area was almost deserted. From behind the low block in front of him, Brendan heard a series of dull thuds, and what sounded like stifled yelps. Taking off his clown's hat and mask, he poked a tentative face around the wall.

On the ground lay Matt Kantor. Above him stood his brother.

Michael Kantor was administering a kicking. It was quite methodical. He began on the arms and legs, moved to the ribs and stomach, then concentrated with practiced accuracy on the testicles.

Matt wasn't built to curl up easily in a ball. He clutched his arms around his head, moaning hopelessly.

'Please, please!' he cried shrilly. 'It wasn't my fault!'

David Lipsey

Mike didn't deign to reply. It was clear that giving people high-class kickings was something he had done before. It was also clear that the fact that the victim was his younger brother was not going to make him lay off.

That was more than could be said for Brendan who, with whatever justification, was nonetheless part of the reason for Matt's beating. The stress of the day and the heat of his outfit didn't help. Anyone entering the gent's loo by the exit would have noticed from the cubicle the sounds of a man vomiting. If they'd peeked under the door to see if the man was all right, they would have seen he was dressed as a clown.

Counter Coup

Chapter 20

Brendan knew what he ought to do - drive to Hereford police station, explain the whole story and leave it to the professionals to sort out. He also knew what held him back - the thought of facing a ruddy-faced policeman, Hereford born and bred, thick in the arm and head. It was not an interview he looked forward to.

He did not suppose that clowns walked into Hereford police station every day, or that conspiracies to dope jockeys were the stuff with which they regularly dealt. Brendan doubted that they would listen patiently to a clown telling them he had that incontrovertible evidence, currently in the hands of a lawyer at Dragoyd Hall. They would certainly not shoot off into Wales and another police force's jurisdiction to interview her. He also remembered that he had a peashooter in his pocket with a number of peas and needles dipped in a substance that he strongly suspected of including a Class A drug.

David Lipsey

Talking to the police had better wait until he was in more normal garb, and had some way of proving what he was saying. Otherwise the most likely outcome was a night in a cell – or the funny farm.

It did occur to him to worry about Mike Kantor and what he would do next. He had just seen what the man was capable of doing to someone who crossed him. If his own brother got a beating like that, what on earth would he do if he got his hands on Brendan? But maybe he was worrying too much. If Kantor really knew what had happened he would hardly be wasting time kicking his brother's guts in. Most likely, Kantor believed that his brother's expensive miss at the second last was just that. Nonetheless it might be sensible to check.

He turned off the main road west out of Hereford as soon as he could, stopping briefly to strip off his clown's outfit in a field. With his own clothes back on, he began to feel positively cheerful. It was now that Brendan made a mistake that might easily have turned out fatal.

The little B road across the Wye valley to Hay had rarely looked so lovely. The sheep baahed hither and thither and the Black Mountains looked down on the scene like indulgent parents observing their offspring. He passed the point-to-point course beside the river at Bredwardine where he had ridden several winners in his amateur days and thought, not for the first time, that this must be the most beautiful racecourse in the world.

Brendan was normally a fast driver. But in surroundings like this, 40mph seemed unnecessarily fast, even when there

Counter Coup

was important business to complete. Or at least, it did to Brendan. The driver of the vehicle behind clearly thought otherwise.

Everyone in Chelsea and Mayfair kept a four-wheel drive nowadays. If they wanted to pay huge sums to make it look as if they owned a rural estate, that was up to them. But the Cadillac four-wheel drive behind Brendan would have stood out in Park Lane. It was an enormous beast, in garish metallic blue. The driver was perched so high that Brendan couldn't at first see his face in the mirror. All he could see was a bull-bar that would come in handy for crushing children.

The driver was as close behind Brendan's flimsy back bumper as he could get, revving his engine. His horn was blaring. He weaved to and fro as if to overtake even on the blind corners.

Brendan lowered his eye line so he could see the lunatic's face. It was unmistakable. Mike Kantor.

Only then did Brendan remember Sean Fitzpatrick's mucker, Tom Jeffers. If he'd been around to keep an eye on Matt last time at Bangor, perhaps he'd been around this time at Hereford too. There were probably rides of Peter's that Fitzpatrick would like to get his hands on, just as he wanted to get the ride on Grey Finch off Brendan.

Now he came to think of it, there was someone looking like Jeffers in the crowd this afternoon. He kicked himself for not having noticed at the time. Probably it had not taken long for Kantor to get his breathless report, and to put two and two together. Whether that was before or after Matt got his unmerited kicking, Brendan did not know. However Kantor had found out what had happened, he clearly knew it was Brendan at the root of it. For just after Brendan saw Kantor, Kantor saw the reflection of Brendan in the mirror. Brendan saw his face go even more livid, as a wave of pure rage passed across it. Then he felt the bull-bar bash into the back of his car. He put his foot hard down.

There was no doubt that Brendan was the better driver. Brendan drank too much but he had only been doing it for a year or two. Kantor had been at it for decades and had probably had several that afternoon, unlike the sober clown he was chasing. And alcoholism, years of alcoholism at any rate, blunts the reactions even as it enhances the confidence. Kantor had drunk too much for too long to be Formula One behind the wheel.

Brendan may have been the better driver, but Kantor had the faster car. For a couple of miles they raced, Brendan gaining on the braking round the bends, Kantor catching him on the straights. Brendan was just keeping the edge. He was within a couple of miles of the safety of Hay, and the crowds. Once they got there, not even Kantor would dare try something.

Brendan rounded a tight right-hander fast. Sheep. About a dozen had escaped from the field, and were spilling along the road grazing as they went. Had the road been wider, he might have got through. As it was, there was nothing for it but to brake, and brake hard. As he did so, Brendan felt the bull-bar smash into his rear and his car spun to a halt.

Kantor looked like a man who was in the habit of crashing.

Counter Coup

He was out of his car before Brendan was out of his seatbelt. The big man didn't look in the least shaken. Just angry, very very angry.

Fight or flight? Brendan could choose. Either way, he fancied his chances. That bloated belly wouldn't enjoy walking as far as Hay, let alone running. As a jockey Brendan was accustomed to running several miles a day to keep fit, though he hadn't been in training since his fall. Equally, in a punch-up, Brendan's manoeuvrability would more than compensate for Kantor's bulk. He looked forward to sinking his fist into that fat belly. Until he saw the gun in Kantor's hand.

'Get down,' said Kantor. Brendan lay down.

From his waist, Kantor produced handcuffs. He was just the sort of man who would carry handcuffs about, Brendan thought.

'In the boot.'

Brendan did not want to die. Neither was he keen to be into the boot of Kantor's car. He lowered his head and charged at Kantor, ignoring the gun.

Kantor could have pulled the trigger. But he was not one for mess, at least not mess on roads where other people would pass by and awkward questions be asked.

He brought the gun down smartly on Brendan's head instead.

As a jockey you get used to falls, kickings and to seeing stars. It goes with the trade. But this was a whole bloody galaxy.

*****

David Lipsey

The moment at which he regained consciousness was one Brendan long remembered as the worst of his life. The darkness was total. He could hardly breathe. His head hurt like hell. Something was dripping onto his cheek and seeping into his mouth. It tasted like blood – his own, he guessed.

He seemed to be lying beside a sack of potatoes. Then the sack of potatoes moaned. He guessed that he was sharing a lift with Kantor's brother. They lay united in misery. It seemed like an age. In fact it was less than twenty minutes from the sheep to Felindre.

The car pulled up. The back opened and Brendan saw Kantor, gesturing him down the garden path.

He thought of risking all on a dash for it. Then he was violently sick for the second time in hours, the vomit mixing with the blood on his shirt. What a horrible way to go, he thought.

They lurched to the house. Kantor locked the door behind him. Then he went to get the sack from the car. Only as Brendan saw him walking down the path with Matt over the shoulders did he realise the animal strength of the man.

Brendan was reconciled to dying.

'Just get on with it,' he heard himself saying to Kantor.

'Get on with it? Oh no, certainly not,' Kantor grinned. 'It's not just that I enjoy seeing you sitting there waiting to die. There's that two-bit whore of yours, the one who pulled that trick on me in Cannes. She knows too much about this affair.'

'She's nothing to do with it.'

'Bollocks, son. I reckon she'll come looking for you quite

Counter Coup

soon. And I can assure you, she's going to enjoy a very warm welcome - along with her smart arse of a boyfriend.'

'Boyfriend?'

'What sort of bleeding amateur do you take me for, Donoughue?'

Kantor drew a box of matches from his pocket. He struck one, and contemplated the flame thoughtfully. Then, without removing the aim of the gun for a moment from Brendan's forehead, he walked into the little larder. He came back with a five-gallon tin, and quietly unscrewed the top.

'Paraffin, in case you can't smell too well through that broken nose of yours. It burns beautifully, especially if you spread it about a bit. Besides, there are all these books in the house. Take a bit of getting alight books, they tell me, but when they get going....'

Mike was into his boasting phase that Brendan remembered from Cannes, relishing the supposed cleverness of his violence. 'When Matt's lover-boy gets back,' he continued, 'he's going to find nothing but a smouldering ruin.'

'So will the police,' Brendan protested.

'What have they got to investigate?' Mike gave a derisive shrug.' A well-known local eccentric has his house burnt down, happens all the time. Pity he was in it, but that's life - or death of course,' he chuckled. 'As for you and your tart - I suppose you did actually get round to fucking her, didn't you?'

Brendan didn't give Kantor the pleasure of knowing the truth. Kantor carried on. 'Well, as they don't know you are here, I don't suppose the police or anybody else will know when you're gone. They probably won't even look for the teeth.'

He began to scatter paraffin around the floor, whistling as he did so.

Outside there was a crunch on the gravel and a knock on the door.

'Come in,' said Kantor, almost sweetly.

Becky and John came in and stopped in the doorway.

'What the fuck?' John shouted.

'I hate repeating myself,' said Kantor, the gun pointing at them menacingly. 'So I'll let your friend here tell you what I have planned for the afternoon. But just before he does, if you don't mind - or even if you do.'

For John, he found a pair of heavy manacles. For Becky, he used what looked like a silk rope. He fastened it around her wrists so tight that her hands immediately began to go grey.

'Brendan, are you OK?' Becky asked, even as she was being tied up.

'Not too bad,' he lied.

Kantor gestured to them to sit together on the sofa. Then he stood across the room from them and admired his handiwork before, gun in one hand, he continued drenching the room in paraffin: the carpet, the curtains, the books.

'What are you doing with that?' John demanded, 'You can't just...'

'You're the scientist. What do you sodding think I'm doing? And yes I can just...'

Dodgson and Simmonds did not bother to knock. They were, after all, ex-policemen, and they had not got where they

Counter Coup

were by waiting on ceremony in a crisis. They rushed in, Dodgson's little moustache bristling with excitement.

Unfortunately, they had another police characteristic. They were not good at thinking before acting. They saw the bound figures through the glass, they smelt the paraffin, and they didn't hesitate.

They did not see Kantor or the gun. Dodgson soon felt its barrel, a sharp disorienting blow to the back of his head. As soon as he was down, Simmonds got the same treatment. Soon they too were trussed chickens on the second sofa, with Matt in a sack at their feet.

'They say that burning human flesh smells a bit like pork,' Kantor mused. 'I'm looking forward to finding out if that's right.'

A gambler needs cool nerves. Where most people committing multiple murder would be sweating salt, he was enjoying himself. He turned on the radio so that any screams would be drowned out by the jabber of an inane disc jockey, and the strains of the music.

Kantor yawned and he stretched. A thin mean smile played across his lips. Then he started to lay a fuse. He rolled a newspaper into a tight bundle, then others, laying them end to end, sprinkling each with paraffin as he went.

The trail went through the kitchen, into the garden. There would be plenty of time for him to escape the flames.

'I must be off,' he said, poking his head round the door and gazing pleasantly at his victims. 'Sweet dreams.'

Kantor had not reckoned with Smith returning early but it would not have made much difference if he had. After all he had under captivity a fit jockey, a young couple, his fat brother and two ex-policemen. A weed like Smith was unlikely to be much of an obstacle. And one more in the blaze would matter neither here nor there, though the forensics might be starting to think it was an odd congregation for a small house in Felindre.

Smith looked feeble, true, but there was nothing wrong with his brain. He could see quite well what was going on. He could also see something that mattered more to him than the lives of innocent people, more even that the death of his lover. He could see a threat to the books.

People were disposable, replaceable. Old books were not. And one of the best eclectic collections of old books in the land looked as if it was about to go up in flames.

Smith did not consider himself a man who went about armed but, like all bibliophiles, he knew that you occasionally came across a volume with uncut pages. What you needed then was a sharp knife. Better to have it and not need it than need it and not have it, that was the old insurance adage, and it applied to bibliophiles and knives too. Smith kept one permanently in the pocket of his battered jacket.

Every man has a point beyond which he will not be pushed. This was Smith's. He ignored the revolver.

He drew the knife and steadily, purposefully, he advanced on Kantor.

Kantor could have fired. But he couldn't take a threat from Smith seriously. Besides, if he had to pull the trigger, there would be an explosion and if there was an explosion, it might

Counter Coup

ignite the paraffin and kill him. It was a risk he would rather not run.

'Put it down, you idiot,' he ordered quietly.

Smith did not speak. He just advanced. When he was two feet from Kantor, Smith drew back his arm, and slashed Kantor with unexpected ferocity across the cheek.

Kantor didn't drop the revolver, but neither did he fire it. His other hand went to his cheek, and disbelievingly he felt the wet blood dripping between his fingers. Then, with the agility of the maniac, Smith was on him. All the years of humiliation, all the bullying, all the submission that his partner had suffered at his brother's hands found its expression. Smith became a tiger.

The two grappled on the floor. Smith, for all his desperate courage, could not last long against a man of Kantor's weight and power.

He didn't have to.

For they had barely locked arms when a another figure let himself into the room - taller and better prepared.

Henry Brecon was the old-fashioned style of landlord. Not a thing moved in south Powys without one of Henry's tenants or employees seeing it. Not a thing happened that Henry could not, for the effort of a couple of phone calls, find out, just as he had found out where they had been staying the night before. The cottage was on his estate. It was the duty of his little army of retainers to report any strange comings and goings. The arrival of a second Kantor, even weirder in appearance than the first, was a strange coming indeed in Felindre.

David Lipsey

Put that together with the danger to his daughter and Henry was not going to shrug it off.

'Gentlemen,' Lord Brecon called out in the firm, calm voice a Master of Foxhounds customarily employs with the kennel hands. 'Might I have your assistance please?' Then he whistled, loudly. 'Come, dogs.'

Through the door burst a dozen foxhounds. Their blood was up. They looked as if they understood the order 'kill'. And it did not look likely to be long before Brecon gave it.

Behind them, in pink, came the Huntsman and several of his men, whips in hand.

'We were just onto a good strong scent in the meadow up the road when my mobile went,' Brecon remarked to his daughter affably as his men disarmed Kantor and Smith. 'Even organic farmers have mobiles these days, and this one had seen strange cars moving too fast and guessed we might be having a spot of bother. It's as well that he did, eh?'

Already, with the huntsmen's help, the prisoners were being freed from their shackles. Henry found the key to Brendan's handcuffs, and transferred them to Kantor.

'Time, I think, for the police,' he said loudly, punching numbers into his phone. 'It's a good thing the Lords can be relied on to throw out the anti-hunting bill, don't you think?'

Counter Coup

Chapter 21

Jockeys were a superstitious breed. Nearly all of them, like Brendan, had a pre-race ritual; an order in which they put on their boots, a lucky charm to put in their breeches, a particular trick with the whip. Brendan, betraying his ancestor's origins in the Emerald Isle, had added a twist of his own. For big races, really big races, he reversed his usual order - left boot first, not right and so on. Then he tucked behind his right ear a sprig of lucky white heather, bought from one of the gypsy women who always frequented the jockeys' car park.

The Cheltenham Gold Cup was possibly the biggest race in the jumping calendar. The Grand National might have been the best known steeplechase in Britain, but it was a silly business really. It was a handicap, so the good horses had to carry extra weight in their saddle cloths. The field comprised mostly second and third-raters. The horses ran over an absurdly long distance and terrifying fences in a huge field which ensured they kept crashing into each other. You could have stuck a pin into the list of runners and have a fair chance of picking the winner.

The jockeys went along with Grand National hype because they knew it made good television and (save when a horse or two was killed) good publicity for the sport. But the Gold Cup was always the one they really wanted to win.

Here the best horses competed, on level terms over a classic 3 miles, 2-and-a-bit furlongs. Cheltenham's fences were stiff, but fair. The course undulated in a way that tested a horse's stamina and conformation, but allowed it to gallop enough to let it really stretch. And then there was the final hill: the long lung-testing climb from the last fence to the finish. A horse that could get up that when the race was on and the whips cracking wasn't lacking in guts.

The Gold Cup had been run in all kinds of conditions, including, once, in a snowstorm.

But snow, that year, six months after Brendan's fight with Kantor across the Severn valley in Hereford, was no more than a bad memory. The winter had been mild, though there had been enough rain the morning before the race to keep the turf well watered. The wind that could howl off Coombe Hill had taken a break for the Festival week. The March sunshine was just taking on a hint of warmth. The ground, everyone agreed, was riding just about perfect. And the crowds were enormous, beyond capacity and spilling out onto the centre of the course.

The English were there of course, the old national hunt crowd in tweeds and felt hats, and the new in sharp suits.

Counter Coup

Most of the time, though, it was like being in Ireland. The Irish may not have made up a majority of the crowd but they certainly made most of the noise. The air was thick with the craic, all Jameson's breath and tales of betting derring-do.

There had been romance in the week already. The Champion Hurdle on the Tuesday had been won by a horse which, two years before, had broken down so badly that he was not expected to live. A seventeen-year-old girl who was the daughter of a paralysed ex-jockey had ridden out of her skin to take the Triumph.

On the Wednesday, the Queen Mother had won the Champion Chase, at last finding a top-class chaser after more than eighty years. The field in the National Hunt chase had all been brought down thanks to a loose greyhound at the 13th - all that is except a horse that had never won, having its hundredth race, that was so far behind that he could pick his way through the trouble. 200/1 was the price: nice if you got it.

Even in such a week as that, Brendan's story took some beating. A few months previously he had been the butt of every racing man's contempt. Now he was lionised as never before.

Naturally, Becky was brought into the story. The newspapers at first played up the romantic angle. Eventually, when Brendan threatened a writ, they abandoned that for the beautiful genius angle. A picture of her sunbathing topless in Goa was sold to one newspaper for £45,000. *Hello* bought the rights to her wedding to John Scadding for three times that figure. Brendan was still good copy, though, and the celebrity rags were soon queuing for the story of his reinvigorated relationship with Tanya Smyth-Robinson. It was announced the week before Cheltenham that she was five months pregnant, though marriage plans were said to be on hold until the end of the jumping season. Her parents carefully hid from the press any sign of their disappointment at the pedigree of their future son-in-law and grandchild.

Brendan must have lost a dozen rides as a result of the court case. Mike Kantor naturally pleaded not guilty. One jury had to be discharged after it emerged that an undiscovered source had offered a large bribe to the foreman. Another had to go after three members received violent threats. Kantor declined to go into the witness box. Instead he occupied himself sketching the jurors, perhaps hoping that they would think he would be able to use the pictures one day to find them.

The judge, however, had no intention of letting him get into a position to threaten anyone ever again. Attempted murder was found proven - together with half a dozen other offences.

'In your case,' the judge told Kantor, looking at his bloated figure, 'I suspect life really will mean until you die.'

Matt Kantor cut a sorry figure still limping from his Hereford kicking, and in mourning, after the shock of his mother's sudden demise. He pleaded guilty.

Knowing Mike as he had, Brendan did not thirst for revenge against Matt. And, fortunately, neither did the judge. Matt got two years, and those to be served in Ford Open Prison.

Counter Coup

'That's the prison library sorted,' thought Brendan.

Even after the trial, it was not all plain sailing for Brendan. There was Grey Finch for example, the apple of his eye. Officially, Brendan did not get the ride back because his successor and most despised rival, Sean Fitzpatrick, was doing well on the horse.

Unofficially, Brendan's agent was told that his trainer would never put Brendan up again. When Gressop asked him why he was told, 'no smoke without fire'.

Brendan had his suspicions about Fitzpatrick and they had been there from the beginning. For he had as good a motive as any for wanting Robber Earl to fall.

If Brendan was banned, Sean got the ride on Grey Finch. And he knew, too, from Richard Pott's identification in Bradburn, that Fitzpatrick's mucker had been with Matt Kantor at Bangor. Perhaps Mike had not been confident that Matt would go through with it. Perhaps he had agreed with Fitzpatrick that he should send his assistant along, just in case Matt lost his nerve. Perhaps, just perhaps, he had a spare blow-tube for back-up.

Fitzpatrick was unlikely to have been prepared to take any risk that Brendan would get away with it. He would have seen there was still the possibility that Brendan would somehow escape the Jockey Club's clutches. With Brendan's reputation for honesty and his gift of the blarney, perhaps he might have persuaded them that it was a genuine accident and that he was innocent.

So Brendan had found out, during the Kantor trial and

David Lipsey

once the mouths of the racing gossips had been opened, that Sean had taken precautions. To a man like Fitzpatrick, double-crossing Kantor was par for the course. So when he stumbled across the old picture of Brendan and Kantor together in the winners' enclosure, he had seen his chance of further smearing his rival. If the Jockey Club once knew that that Brendan was in with a crook like Kantor, his chances of getting off were surely nil.

Brendan was pretty sure he knew the source of the anonymous letter that had reached Dodgson and Simmonds. But Fitzpatrick was no fool - not fool enough to write the letter himself so that the handwriting could be traced. Brendan might have his suspicions, but there was no way could he prove them. Anyway, much though he loved Grey Finch, Brendan had every reason to hate the connections. Grey Finch was one danger in the Gold Cup he was determined to beat, especially with Fitzpatrick in the saddle.

If he could not ride Grey Finch, Robber Baron - Robber Earl's full brother - was the one Brendan wanted to be on. A promising novice hurdler, though just short of top class, he had blossomed since being put over the larger obstacles. A string of facile victories in novice chasers had persuaded Hattie Parsons, his trainer, to avoid the normal race for an inexperienced horse of his kind, the Sun Alliance, and to go straight for the Gold Cup.

Yet as Brendan had scanned the *Racing Post* that morning, he was reminded of a dozen reasons why Robber Baron could not win. He was only six - far too young for such a gruelling

Counter Coup

test (for an English horse at any rate: the French, who had less hang-ups about age, had already won with The Fellow as a five-year old in 1994). Bred as he was, he could not be guaranteed to stay the distance. His bold jumping would be too risky in such company. His greenness must find him out. And, one kind commentator suggested, 'not everyone agrees that Donoughue is the jockey he was before his warning off. Some think he has lost his bottle'.

The word bottle had not come out accidentally. The reference to Brendan's drinking habits would be spotted by everyone in the know – everyone, that is, who refused to believe the truth: that Brendan had taken no alcohol since that day in Felindre.

It was not a two horse race. It was the hottest, most open Gold Cup that most people could remember.

Of the fifteen runners, at least half a dozen could be given some sort of a chance. The French horse, More Trouble, for which a noted Irish owner had paid a million punts in the autumn, had scored four times around Auteuil.

The Irish Bogtrotter, trained by the inscrutable genius Pat Magee, had trotted up the previous year. The Northern hope, Fazakerley, had won the Hennessy easily, under twelve stone.

And then there was the king of Cropredy, Paul's Mum, who had yet to taste defeat, fresh from winning both Cheltenham's two-and-a-half milers in the run-up to Christmas.

Hattie Parsons told the radio commentators she thought Robber Baron was even better than Robber Earl had been as a young horse. Against that lot, he would have to be, Brendan thought. The bookmakers agreed. Grey Finch was the marginal favourite, over Bogtrotter and More Trouble. Robber Baron was put in as a 9/1 shot.

That was before the Irish opened their wallets. One pile of patriotic punts followed the home of the horse for Bogtrotter. Another followed the nationality of the owner for More Trouble. As they walked around the parade ring, a canny punter who could get round the crowds would find 10/1, 11/1, even 12/1 in a place against Robber Baron.

As a jockey, Brendan was not allowed a bet. Becky thought betting illogical. Hattie was so nervous for the horse that she found the race impossible to watch anyway. She planned to spend it hiding behind the grandstand with earplugs in, then ring on her mobile phone to find out the result. She was in it for the love, not the money.

Henry Brecon, who had just sold the estate cottage where Brendan had holed up to a couple from Streatham for 240 times what it cost to build, had staked £16,000 to win £200,000. At any other meeting, that would have freaked the market. At Cheltenham, it caused hardly a ripple.

The hours before the race had been almost unbearable for Brendan. But once he had swung into the saddle he relaxed. Hattie knew better than to burden him with detailed instructions. Brendan knew the horse, and he was paid to know what to do.

'Good luck,' was all she whispered as Brendan walked out of the parade ring, acknowledging the crowd with a wave of his

Counter Coup

whip.

The start was not far from the stand, so there was no long canter down. Brendan took a peep at his fellow jockeys and saw they were at least as nervous as he was. The thought of the jockey's share, 10% of the winner's prize of £160,000, was part of the reason. But the spotlight, the eye of the nation, the glory mattered more. And, of course, each of them knew that they were one bad jump and a bit of bad luck on the landing side away from a wheelchair for life.

'They're off,' the PA system barked.

The early stages were uneventful. A couple of the rags set out far faster than they could hope to keep going. The owners of outsiders often like to see them in front so they can dream the dream of victory for a moment, even if in their hearts they know they cannot stay there. Their jockeys play to their vanity. More Trouble was awkward at the first ditch, and Bogtrotter got a slap down the neck to concentrate after the next, but, so far as Brendan could see, all the rivals were going well.

So was his mount, Robber Baron. There was a zest to his stride, a smooth power that Brendan had never known bettered. His relative inexperience showed in a tendency to look around himself rather than keeping his head down and getting on with the business - nothing, thought Brendan, that a few seasons at the top wouldn't knock out of him. But where it really mattered, Robber Baron showed he was a quick learner.

When a rank outsider blundered in front of him, flinging the jockey off the side, and briefly staggering like a drunk across the course, Robber Baron sidestepped him as if he had been doing it all his life.

A circuit gone, one to go as they passed the stands for the second time, and already the Big Six had it between them. Then, at the cross fence, the end came for More Trouble.

Opinions differed afterwards as to whether Francois Fronteau was to blame. British journalists, prejudiced against foreign riders except when they were Irish thought that he was. So far as Brendan could he see he had done nothing wrong. But the horse stood off too far, clipped the top and was gone.

Half a mile on, Bogtrotter was showing signs of distress. The ground was much livelier than it had been in the year of his triumph and Bogtrotter clearly galloped best in a bog.

At the top of the hill, there were four in it. At the third last three, as Paul's Mum came under pressure.

Now they were running to the last. Robber Baron was in front but not by much. Grey Finch, on his outside, was going ominously well.

Brendan pushed and shoved and eventually gave the Baron a crack. Fitzpatrick held the reins tight. Glancing across, he gave Brendan a look that said 'gotya'. It was not a look of sympathy. It was a gloat.

Brendan did not want to lose. But above all he did not want to lose to Grey Finch, his slander-spreading trainer and a jockey whose role in his downfall was as culpable as Kantor's. Yet on the clear evidence before him, lose was what he was about to do.

Brendan almost wished a Kantor would materialise from the crowd and do for Fitzpatrick what he had done at Bangor.

Counter Coup

But one Kantor was in the prison library, and the other in maximum security.

Then if there was no Kantor to get Fitzpatrick, there was no Kantor to befuddle Brendan's brain either. This time, on this run to the last, his mind was as clear as a bell. And he had one more trick up his sleeve.

He was still a yard to the good. He remembered something he had been taught as a youngster. Just occasionally, if one horse is just ahead of another, and the first horse takes off, the second will take off too. And if the first is the right distance from the fence, the second horse may be too far away to get across.

It's a high risk operation – for emergencies only. For such tactics only need to be deployed if the horse in front is the more tired of the two. If his jockey asks him for a big jump, and the horse fails to answer the call, a fall is inevitable. A fall when going for a big one is the hardest fall of all.

This Gold Cup, Brendan knew, could mark the end of his career as sharply as the warning-off had seemed to. He could end up in a wheelchair. He could even die.

Brendan knew all that. But he also knew that the only alternative was to lose, and to Fitzpatrick. For him, the issue was not in doubt. Fully three strides before the fence, Brendan drew back his boots and kicked the Baron hard on the underbelly.

'Come on young fellow, let's go for it.'

As he kicked, Tanya, in the stand, felt the baby in her belly kick in sympathy.

David Lipsey

Robber Baron was dog tired. But Robber Baron was also brave. And he had been trained taut to the minute. Standing back from the fence, he took a mighty leap that had the crowd gasping for breath.

The one gasp had hardly been heard when it was followed by a second. For Fitzpatrick on Grey Finch had been comprehensively done. Pull the reins as he might, scream at the horse as he did, he knew Grey Finch was going to try for a big one too, with Robber Baron. And he knew that he could not possibly make it.

Grey Finch pitched down onto the fence, only his neck over it. Fitzpatrick flew over his head, shoulder first, then back, then legs hard into the turf. Grey Finch's back legs tumbled over his front legs, giving Fitzpatrick a fierce kick in the kidneys. Then a ton of horse landed full on top of Fitzpatrick's prone body, before Grey Finch stumbled away.

Fitzpatrick was a hard man but for years after, Brendan could hear his scream.

Robber Baron was clear.

Clear, yes, but the race was not yet won. Fazakerley had been outpaced down the hill. But he was a dour stayer, trained on moor and in mud in a school that left horses who could take it fit and strong.

As they landed, there was perhaps three lengths between the two. Up the hill, that kind of distance can evaporate in half a dozen strides.

In the stands, the Robber Baron's team looked first at the leader, then at the challenger, trying to calculate the yards to

Counter Coup

the line, the rate Fazakerley was gaining.

The roar of the crowd could be heard in Gloucester. Fifty yards out, and Fazakerley was at the Baron's tail. Twenty five yards, and the gap was down to a neck.

Ten yards, level.

For a long time after, some of the most knowledgeable racing aficionados in the world were stretched to describe what happened next. In the shadow of the post, using all his strength, Brendan seized everything together and seemed to lift Robber Baron past the post.

It was a desperately close thing. The judge called for a photo. The TV and Radio commentators, looking at the replay, said it was too close to call. Only one man knew who had won.

Brendan, at that moment, knew that day the angels were with him.

As he walked in with the shattered Robber Baron scarcely able to put one foot in front of another, he could barely hear the announcement over the roar.

'First, number 8, Robber Baron; second number 1, Fazakerley, third number 12, Paul's Mum. The distances; a short head and twenty lengths. A short head and twenty lengths.'

As he turned left from the path to make his way to the winning enclosure, an ambulance passed Brendan's right, siren full on. Sean Fitzpatrick would not be celebrating that night - or ever.